THE STELLAR TRILOGY

Book 1: Among Us

Envy McKee

ArkyM Books

ISBN-13: 978-0615821269
ISBN-10: 061582126X

★ DEDICATION ★

For... Aubrei and my family

For... Dupris, Joey V and Imani

For... Dr. B

For... Mr. Barto

For... ALL the Star Daughters on The Earth and their children.

L.O.V.E.

Truth 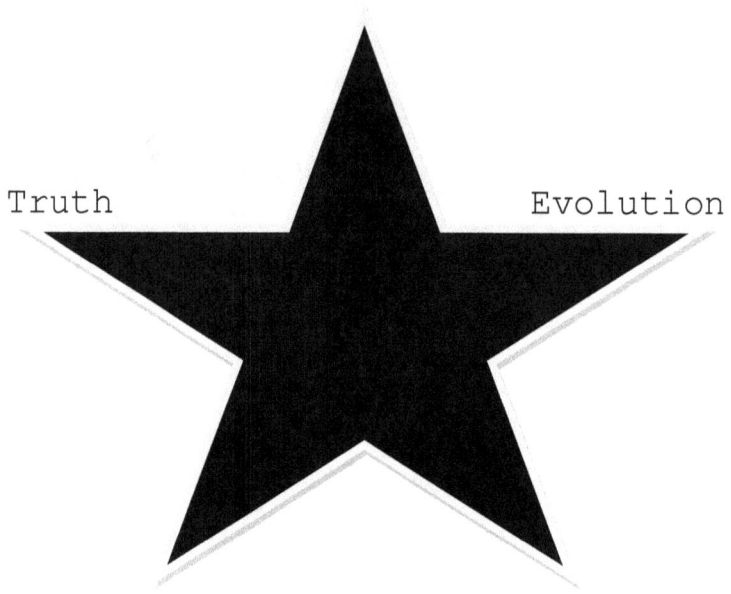 Evolution

"All endeavor calls for the ability to tramp the last mile, shape the last plan, endure the last hours toil. The fight to the finish spirit is the one... characteristic we must possess if we are to face the future as finishers." ~ Henry David Thoreau

 CONTENTS

DEAR READER:

"There are four questions of value in life... What is sacred? Of what is the spirit made? What is worth living for, and what is worth dying for? The answer to each is the same. Only love."

~Don Juan de Marco

K ai is you. We might as well get that tidbit out of the way now. Kai is you. Knowing this doesn't take anything from the story. It actually adds to it. It's all about self- discovery. From the very first page, see this story as your own biography, but through fresh eyes. Don't get caught up in gender or different languages. Just feel your way through it as Kai does. The life metaphors are all there.
I will say, this book has been a journey of self- discovery for me as well. It all started with a few paragraphs scribbled in one of my red journals yeeeeears ago. Then one random day in 2008, I read those paragraphs to a dear friend who told me, with every amount of emphasis, this book MUST be written. I laughed at him. At first. But then I kind of played with the idea of writing it, until finally, I sat down to write it.

Over the course of many months, I wrote chapters. After I finished one or two I would call him and read them to him. Before I knew it, it was finished. My very first book. But at the time, I was really new in my own personal journey of self-discovery and most of the metaphors and themes in this book didn't make much sense to me. It's fair to say, at the time, they scared the living crap out of me. I didn't feel like these ideas were mine, so I didn't have a lot of confidence that this book was any more than something to do because a dear friend suggested it.

I will say, I circulated the first draft around to a few friends and publishers, but after about a dozen rejections and "WTF"s, I had the good sense to tuck it away on my hard drive, until I was good and ready to revisit it again with a clearer understanding and passion for it. That didn't happen until 2010.

Another dear friend and I were talking and I told him I wrote a book. He asked me to read it to him and I did, editing the chapters as we went. Some things were added, some others were removed. By the time we got through it, I was like okay. This is pretty good. I can put this thing out. But no. I couldn't. The story was rounded out, but it still wasn't mine. I was still afraid of it. It still felt disingenuous in a lot of ways. So I tucked it away on my hard drive again until I was ready to fight the good fight. Until I was ready to own my own work and put my own name on it.

The thing is, this is *Book 1* of three. I promised myself that I wouldn't start writing *Book 2*, until I published *Book 1*. I had to make this promise to myself because I know me. I often have nine projects going at once, and if I don't set specific "finisher" boundaries, I'll be overwhelmed with piles of all sorts of things sitting somewhere half done.

So then, *Book 2* started marinating in my spirit. All these pictures were popping up in my head, but I refused to work through them, because the original story hadn't been "made square" to my satisfaction. So. Several months ago, without much warning, but armed with five years of personal adventure and life exploration from my *Eat, Pray, **L.O.V.E,** LIVE!* journey, I sat down with *Book 1* for a solid squaring session. My goal was just to read through it and make the story *feel* finished, so I could transcend out of my self-imposed writing purgatory and get to working on some other writing projects I have in my mental pipeline. It all began with an affirmative prayer. "My business is God's business. All of my affairs are adjusted in the right way, immediately." It continued with a question."What will you have me do?" The rest, as they say (cliché and all), is history.

That's the back story of *Book 1*. This brings us back to the "real" story of The Stellar Trilogy. Kai is you. You know how I know? Because Kai is me and WE are all connected. ALL of our lives and work and life's work are connected. There is one theme in particular that comes up a lot in *Book 1*. "Fear Lights a Man's Way to Darkness." It's something that Kai is reminded of throughout the story, but she doesn't quite grasp until the end. A lot of times we let our fear of something or someone determine how we live. We let our background or upbringings determine if we'll be successful or worthy and/or confirm for us that there is no way we can be successful or worthy.

Meanwhile, just as Kai discovers, L.O.V.E. really is the only thing we live for, because it's what we are. Fear only exists because we've forgotten who and what we truly are, back of our very human experiences. L.O.V.E. (Living Our Vision Everyday) is why we're here and what we came to re-discover about ourselves. The trickiest part of our collective journey of self-discovery is learning that if we don't do what we came here to do, someone else in the universe will miss something vital they need to do what *they* came to do. After a while, we discover, this is the whole point of self-discovery. If one of us drops the ball to fear, the ball drops for us ALL.

Osho Lovian Osho,

-e-

May 25, 2013, Aphroditia

PROLOGUE: BEFORE AND BEFORE AND BEFORE...

"Every man and woman is a star." ~Aleister Crowley

The wood panels of the old church floor creaked. With every step the priest took, his bones and the floor moaned in one accord. When he reached the end of the long corridor, instead of opening the door to his office, he let himself lean on his walking stick. The stick was shaped like a tree branch twisted into lean, painfully beautiful knots. It was much older than he. It had seen many more things than he had. The ornate carvings on it held secrets that he would never know. Mysteries of the universe not meant to be uncovered just yet. Not by him anyway. He knew that the time for revelation was coming. He felt it as he stood in the cold, quiet, long forgotten basilica.

As he stood, barely breathing, anticipation for his visitor to arrive began to overcome him. He felt old. He had been here a long time, waiting for the last portions of his purpose to be fulfilled. He felt his sense of peace shift with the unfamiliar sensation of nervousness. He knew what was happening around him was beyond his control. He knew that once the procession began, the world as he'd seen it for so many years would finally spiral beyond anyone's understanding. He knew all these things and yet, he hadn't fully grasped the magnitude of what was happening. His impending visitor was a universal marker of the kind of progress no one speaks of in polite company. Or any company. The wait was brutal. Eons long. His very bones exhaled when he felt Tanzin's presence.

"Osho Lovianhal friend." The Priest's voice was almost a whisper.

"Osho Lovian Osho."

Tanzin didn't bother with a bow. These two were long past formalities.

1

"The years you have been here are beginning to show Priest. Soon, you will be able to hang up those old bones and transition like the rest of us." Tanzin said.

Tanzin sounded matter-of-fact, but they both knew his statement was an attempt at humor. Neither of them laughed.

"Yes... old friend. I've been here a long time. And yet, I've always enjoyed my work. Just this one last thing to do. Of course, I don't have the easy job you have." The Priest chuckled awkwardly and then cleared his throat with a cough that sounded painful. "I'll assume things are on divine schedule."

"The child will arrive within days."

The Priest breathed out the loud sigh of relief that follows the weary before they speak. He refused to contain his inner celebration. He clapped clumsily, balancing his left elbow on his walking stick.

"That *is* good news! Her surrogates? The Third? They've all been chosen?"

"It is so. No detail has been left to chance. We have all waited too long to do things less than what has been written." Tanzin said.

The Priest sighed again. He realized in the moment just how tired he was. His voice crackled like embers in an ancient fire.

"Soon... soon." He said. "This old, forgotten church will bustle with activity again." His voice trailed off into his thoughts.

"Yes." Tanzin said. "It will. We must remember that there are some things that will manifest that we cannot know or prepare for. The child may not do all that she is capable. She may not—"

The Priest interrupted Tanzin with his raspy chuckle.

"--No child does as his parents expect. But they always do what

2

they came to. This child will do much more than that. She will change everything. Our only charge is to see that she is prepared and protected. The child, when ready, will do the rest. Isn't that what we've waited all this time for?"

Tanzin nodded.

"You were always wise, Priest. I can think of no other still on The Earth plane worthy of the job you face. I bid you blessings and look forward to having you with us soon. Osho Lovianhal."

"Yes, Tanzin. Osho Lovian Osho."

Before The Priest could re-adjust himself on his walking stick, his visitor was gone. The Priest was moved to tears of joy, sadness, frustration and knowing. **Soon,** he thought, **soon...**

1 BIRTH DAY

"The greatest work of art created first by God and then by man, is the creation of life. The whole process is an amazing art in itself. The fact that it takes two artists, man and woman, each bringing their own parts of a pallet to create a work of art that not only has a piece of both artists but is also a living, breathing, ever-changing piece of art with an identity of its own." ~Bethany Jane Andrews Hoey

It was bitterly cold that morning. Everything in that ordinary town was covered in ice, snow and the kind of opaque air that only happens during snow storms. Everything in town was in purgatory. Nothing outside was moving besides the wind, and no one indoors dared leave the warmth of their homes.

It didn't seem like the kind of day that a miracle would be born. It just seemed like any other regular day animated with Mother Nature's odd sense of humor. Because the roads were so awful, only four sets of parents-to-be made it to the hospital that night. It was part of the miracle that they made it at all.

The strangest part of the maternity arrivals was the young woman who arrived at midnight. At the time, it didn't seem odd to anyone that she arrived, precisely at midnight. There was a gush of wind that walked through the door with her. It emphasized the very mystery that surrounded her. She was breathtaking by all accounts. Her hair was a silky crown of raven curls that fell just past her shoulders. Her clothes looked almost other-worldly against the cold, bleakness of that night. It was hard to describe exactly what color she was wearing, but as she glided in the maternity ward with no bags and barely a cloak around her shoulders, it looked as if she brought the sun with her.

Though she was in labor when she arrived, she showed no signs of pain or distress. She was as calm and peaceful as a spring breeze. She had the strangest effect on everyone she came across. Prior to her arrival, everyone in the hospital was in a buzzed state of anxiety. It was the middle of a storm and supplies were low. The doctors were running around trying to keep patients calm, while they themselves were freaking out. But when this woman arrived, it felt like time stood for her specifically. The buzzing about the hospital transformed into an elegant waltz. The yellows, golds and pinky oranges in her gown seemed to reflect upon the walls a glowing warmth of love that no one in the building that night could or would resist.

The hospital itself and all of its inhabitants breathed more deeply around her, like she came with more oxygen. They gave her the best room they had. Everyone daunted over her, although she made no fuss. There was just something unexplainably vast about her. Like she was of some known, but unspoken royalty. The people in that old hospital in the middle of nowhere, acted accordingly.

In the room next to hers, a girl child was born. Unknown to the parents, the child, for seemingly no reason, died within the hour. None of the doctors or nurses told the parents of their loss. Instead, they waited. They didn't know why, they just did. The new parents waited too. They didn't know why, they just did.

At precisely 2:22 AM, the woman who brought the sun with her in the middle of a snow storm pushed out her own child. She made an "Ohmmmmmm" sound. It was the kind of sound that seemed to come from the depths of her womb, resonating through everything around it, making the walls fizz and the tiny hairs on people's arms stand up on end. When the "Ohm" finished ringing through the air, her child slid out into the doctor's hands, as though placed there and never pushed. The woman's skin began to glisten and glow as though her sweat were made of pure gold and light. The doctor handed the baby to her mother in a robotic way, like he was in a severe and reverent trance.

The woman looked upon her child lovingly, as though she were the only creature on the planet. The two began to glow together. Then, the baby opened her eyes, as her mother spoke words to her that no one else in the room could hear. A pinkish-gold wave of light swept around them. Then, the mother kissed her child on her forehead. After this was done, without warning, gasp or sigh, the woman lay back on the birthing table and died. There was no fanfare about it, she simply stopped living. Everyone in the room stood breathless in front of her and started to weep uncontrollably. A pinkish-gold light rose from her body like a heavy cloud and then dissipated into the harsh hospital lighting.

Then everyone turned their attention toward the child. She hadn't cried when she left her mother's body, but now she was wailing, as they looked on. All of the doctors and nurses stood staring at the newborn with their mouths fixed open. In the place of her mother's kiss, they saw a 5 point star that looked like it was drawn in blood. It was seeping and gurgling on the baby's tiny forehead, like it was about to erupt. Within moments, it did erupt. First it glowed and then exploded the room with light. The more the child wailed, the brighter the stream of light poured from her head. The light was so bright and encompassing, it filled the birthing room and then the hallways. Then it filled the hospital itself. Everyone was so blinded by it; they covered their faces to shield themselves from it.

Then, just as abruptly as the light happened, it stopped. The star on the baby's head was gone. The baby was quiet. There was no dead woman on the birthing table. Everything in the hospital went back to what it was before the woman who brought the sun with her arrived. Except, it seemed, for the package she came to deliver. But no one noticed. The doctors didn't remember a star on the child's forehead or the light taking over the hospital. The only thing the attending doctor seemed to know was that he had a newborn baby in his arms and she belonged somewhere. Without thinking, he handed the newborn to a young nurse who appeared in the doorway, literally from out of nowhere.

The nurse cleaned the baby meticulously and took her to the room next door. The new parents were elated to see their new daughter. Both looked at the baby and then up at the nurse with a hint of confusion. Although they had named their daughter not but an hour ago, looking at the baby they held, they simply couldn't remember that name. The nurse suggested a short, but powerful name that she said meant "love". The parents agreed. The nurse wrote "Kai" on the newborn's birth certificate. And it was done.

2 SLIDE, MUTE.

"Every abuse ought to be reformed, unless the reform is more dangerous than the abuse itself."

~ Voltaire

Kai was odd. Everything about her development was odd. She refused her mother's breast milk. She refused formula, and yet, she still grew plump and fat. When she ate table food, she only wanted fresh fruits and vegetables. She grew much too fast. She began walking at 6 months old. When she fell, she healed too quickly. She never used baby talk and she rarely cried. She was speaking in full sentences by 9 months. Neither her parents nor her doctors could understand how this was so. As she got older, they would find her sitting up in her crib, talking to someone in a language that was not English. She would have full out conversations with a corner of her room or a wall. Sometimes they would see a bright light coming from her room. When they opened Kai's door, no light would be on. Everything about her, especially the intense way she looked at them, made her parents secretly believe that their daughter was possessed.

They took Kai to a priest to have her looked at, but the priest could not find anything about her that would support her parent's claims. He told them it was simply a bit of new parent jitters.

As the years went by and the two added to their family, they paid less attention to Kai and more to their more "normal" children. Although Kai was sweet and helpful to her family in general, she grew very sad. Her parents were cruel to her and she didn't know why. At first. When they walked into a room she was in, they would frown at her. When her brother or sister would make too much noise, her parents yelled at her. When something was amuck in the house, she was to blame at all times. Even when the other children were caught in a naughty act, Kai would get the punishment for it.

Kai would see the way other kids in her school would interact with their parents. They were supportive, loving and actually talked to their kids and checked their homework and didn't pretend they didn't exist. To counteract her parents' cruelty toward her, Kai began to play up her strengths. It was the kind of rebellion that happens when someone who knows something rubs their knowledge in the faces of those who don't. It played out everywhere Kai was. She questioned everyone and everything. She knew more than they and she made sure they knew it. Kai's rebellion was a subtle, verbal one. It was about questioning people's fragile beliefs. To anyone with little but their faith to hold on to, questioning that faith was paramount to threatening their very lives. Kai knew this, instinctively. She didn't know how or why she knew, she just did.

Late at night, she heard her parents' whispers of their fears of her. They simply could not understand her, nor did they want to. They were a simple people. They didn't want much. Kai was extraordinary in a way that makes people who don't want much feel empty. She had this effect on most of the people she came across. It was the reason she didn't make many friends. It was the reason her very presence made her parents weary. It was the reason they sent her away.

3 HAPPY BIRTHDAY

"I remember when the candle shop burned down. Everyone stood around singing 'Happy Birthday.'"

~ Steven Wright

It was Kai's 11th birthday. It was a very cold winter day. The air was thick and opaque as though a storm was brewing. Kai's mother had a particularly smug expression on her face for most of the morning. She, ironically, looked possessed as she stuffed all of Kai's simple belongings in a big green trash bag. At exactly 2:22 PM that afternoon, they packed Kai and her trash bag in their car and headed off. They decidedly left their other children with relatives and hadn't bothered to tell Kai where they were going. Kai was visibly sad. Both of her parents were visibly anxious. After a few hours of driving in murky silence, Kai couldn't contain her words.

"Where am I going?" Kai asked. Her face was plain, but her words were not.

"You are going to stay with your Aunt Myra." Her mother said flatly.

"Who is Aunt Myra? I didn't know I had an Aunt named Myra. Whose sister is she? Yours mom?"

Her mother frowned. "She's neither of our sister. She's just a nice lady we know from when your father was growing up. She's great with children like you...with issues."

Kai coughed through her disbelief. Her head became hot instantly.

"You're sending me away to live with some stranger because you think I have issues?! That's rich." Her sarcasm lay in the air like a venom cloud.

"Who you talking to girl? That mouth is one of your biggest issues. The truth... is your father and I... aren't right to raise you. We've done the best we can... and you just don't seem to be..."

Her voice trailed off because she was angry and she hadn't noticed her anger until that moment. Even she knew there was something irrational about what she was feeling, but she couldn't help it. It was too late. She felt like a puppet whose strings were being strained to their fray. She knew that if she didn't get rid of Kai, something fundamental in her would snap. She had no reason for what she felt. So she made something up.

"...You have no respect, no discipline and at the rate you're going, you'll likely end up in jail, dead or pregnant at 16 if we don't get you some help. Aunt Myra will set you straight. We hope. And if she doesn't, well then that's just your cross to bear, isn't it?"

Kai's mom was practically out of her skin when she spoke. Her voice reeked with loathing and fear. It was as painful for her to speak as it was for Kai to hear. Kai was quiet. She was staring at the backs of her parent's heads with a ball of disgust stuck at the top of her throat, threatening to choke her. She was stewing, but also in a state of panic. She didn't want to be dumped at some stranger's doorstep. Her family was all she knew, even if she thought them cruel. In spite of herself, Kai was really just a child. She sobbed quietly in her hands for a few minutes until the sting of her pending reality softened some.

"What did I ever do to make you hate me so much? I'm just a kid."

Caught by surprise, her mother nearly choked on her laugh.

"Just a kid? Now *that's* rich. You've never, ever, in the entire time I've known you, since you were born-- been just a kid. You've always been weird. You've always made me feel like you got the devil in you.

Your father and I rightly thought that you were possessed by a demon or something when you were little. You just might be. But that don't even matter now girl. If you are possessed by something, Aunt Myra with exorcise it right out of you. Mark my words."

Kai sat back in her seat hard and folded her arms. She shook her head, trying with all her might to make this drive and her mother's words make the slightest bit of sense. It didn't. The things her mom said simply weren't true. Her mother interrupted her thoughts with another verbal jab.

"You know what else, Kai. You are a disruption to our family. You just don't belong. You're lucky Aunt Myra has agreed to care for you until you're old enough to care for yourself. That is a blessing because if not for her, I don't know where we'd have to send you."

Kai's head was so hot, it hurt. She just couldn't wrap her mind around anything that was happening. It was her birthday and instead of cake and singing happy birthday with the little ones, she was on a rickety road to nowhere with two people who couldn't know her any less.

"Why can't you just love me for who I am? Instead of expecting I should be something else! I came from you, shouldn't that mean something to you? Shouldn't you love me anyway?" Kai said, almost pleading.

A knot formed simultaneously in the throats of both parents. Kai's words affected them so powerfully; Kai's father had a hard time keeping the car in control. His knuckles turned pale, he was holding the steering wheel so hard. While he spent the car ride looking through the rearview at Kai or at his wife or at the road, he said nothing the entire trip. He didn't know what could be said. He sniffled in the tears, welling in his eyes. Kai's mother was not nearly as sentimental. She was more concerned with saving face. She had to let Kai know that she was being sent away because something is wrong with her. Not wrong with them. They were okay. She was the one who was possessed. This was an important distinction for Kai's mother, because her ego wouldn't stand for any noteworthy smears in her character. It was a tricky denial dance. But Kai's mother had rhythm. This dance was easy. A child always yearns for a mother's love. If the child isn't loveable, it's not the mother's fault, but the child's...

"You aren't capable of loving anyone but yourself." She said, half smirking. The words slinked out of her face like a silk snake.

When they reached Kai's ears, a burning began under her skin. It started at her toes and worked its way up her legs, her seat, her spine and then through to the top of her head. Her forehead began to itch and burn like a fire would spill out of it. The feeling was overwhelming. She rubbed her palms across her face and the glimmer in her eyes began to darken. She felt blunt and red. She was about to say something, but a glimmer of light in her peripheral caught her attention. She saw a face. It was entangled in light and little bubbles that sparkled and bobbed as they moved about in the seat next to her. An effervescent hand put its pointer finger to its mouth, telling Kai, in essence to be still. In that moment, the fire that was taking over her body and mind began to cool. She felt wrapped in a blanket of love, peace and contentment. Her mother's final words to her stopped mattering. The road became a blur until Kai's eyes closed and she was able to sleep for the rest of the hours long car ride.

It was dark once they arrived. There weren't many lights, so pulling up to that old plot of land in that non-descript part of that non-descript town, was like driving up on a horror film. Kai's eyes opened slowly. All she could see through the haze of the fogged up window next to her was garbled trees and dead grass. The somber sight made her heart sink under her stomach. A light came on in the distance. As they drove up the long driveway, a woman's silhouette appeared on the porch. Kai lifted her head and tried squinting to get a better look at what she was being dumped into. It wasn't until she relaxed her gaze that she saw it. It looked like black smoke, but it wasn't smoke. It was like a black wind wrapping around the woman on the porch. The wind came to rest on the woman's shoulders and then disappeared.

Kai didn't bother to say anything. Her parents didn't bother to do much but open Kai's door so she could get out and pull out the green trash bag with all of her belonging in it. She walked slowly in front of her parents toward the porch. The closer they got to it, the more intimidating the silhouette in front of them. Aunt Myra was clearly tall. But Kai still couldn't see her face. She started to walk faster, so she could see who or what she'd be living with. When she got close enough to the porch to make out the woman's face, she was surprised. Instead of some scary monster, she found a woman who looked exactly like an Aunt Myra.

Aunt Myra was "older", but wouldn't be considered elderly. She had thick, wavy salt and pepper hair that she wore in a very tight bun on the top of her head. Her eyes were so dark; they almost looked black against the backdrop of her very pale yellow skin. Her lips were pursed in some variation of a scowl.

"It took y'all long enough. I was expecting y'all hours ago." She said tapping her foot in such a way that the porch shook.

"Apologies Aunt Myra, we headed out late. Um... this is Kai. We don't have much time for pleasantries. We have to get back on the road so we can pick up the other kids before morning." This was the first time Kai's father spoke the whole trip.

Aunt Myra looked sternly at him with her lips pursed. She waved him off, as she looked down at Kai.

"So you the one possessed by the devil, is you?"

"It depends on who you ask, I suppose." Kai said. Her instincts were screaming that this line of questioning wasn't safe for her.

"I asking you, youngin'. You possessed by the devil girl?"

Kai couldn't help but look over at her parents cowering their way back to their car. Watching them try to sneak away from their mess made Kai angry. She didn't intend to be cheeky, but when she turned back to Aunt Myra, she said what made the most sense, not what would have saved her.

"I'm not sure my answer will satisfy you either way, ma'am. It sounds like a trick quest--"

Before the rest of Kai's sentence could make its way out into the air, a fist the size of a tennis racket swooped down and punched her in the face. This sent Kai crashing backwards into the dirt. Kai's mother let out a smug laugh as she and her husband tumbled into their car and drove off. The last thing Kai heard her mother say out the car window was "Happy Birthday."

4 THE THIRD

"One and God make a majority."

~ Frederick Douglass

A unt Myra was tall, stout and strong with a very heavy hand. She treated Kai exactly like gum on her shoe—an 'ingrate' she called her almost every day. Other days her adjective of choice was 'demon'. It was under these circumstances Kai was forced to go to church, sometimes twice a day, and learn the ways of being a solid, "God-fearing Christian".

Kai was stuck in a routine of unmanageable chores and daily regurgitation of biblical scripture. She wasn't even allowed to go to regular school. She was "home-schooled", so she was never around other kids her age. Aunt Myra was adamant that the influence of other people, especially other teenagers would only make Kai worse. As far as Aunt Myra was concerned, all a girl needed to get her life on track was Jesus and discipline—in that order. Kai knew she was smarter than Aunt Myra and Aunt Myra knew it too. The only difference was, Aunt Myra was bigger and stronger than Kai and made sure she knew it. In the beginning, because Kai healed quickly, she took her lumps to speak her truth. After a while though, she got tired. Rather than willingly go the route of the most pain on purpose, she played the game Aunt Myra wanted her to play.

It didn't take long for young Kai to become fully aware of how the game was played. Anytime she would question anything at all, she would be beaten to within an inch of her life with whatever was handy. She was surprised she lasted as long as she did. She was beaten almost daily for any number of things. Aunt Myra thought her own beans too salty? She got a beating. She said a bible verse too cheeky? She got a beating. Ask if going to a real school, much less college was a possibility? Beating. Want to know if her parents called or wrote her? Beating. She was beaten so much; she had bruises on every length of her body. Even though she healed quickly, there was no way she could have healed quickly enough to have no battle scars. Kai's entire body became a battle scar.

On the night of her 16th birthday, something miraculous happened. Kai was lying in her bed, looking at the ceiling. All she could think about that day was how she would ever escape Aunt Myra. She wanted to believe, more than anything, that her life was meant for something greater than suffering. She was the child who was so special that her parents dumped her on this woman's doorstep. Right? For all Aunt Myra's efforts, Kai still didn't feel normal. She ached everywhere, but she still had glimmers of her true self. Whenever her face started to burn in anger, the light bubbles would appear to her and she would get through whichever brutality she faced that day with a sense of peace and acceptance. Aunt Myra seemed oblivious to this light because she would beat Kai until she was tired. Kai didn't have to be conscious for this.

Kai felt cold. Even on her birthday, there was no kindness toward her. No cake, no present, no day off from chores or beatings. This day was the same as every other of her days. Cold, grueling and painful. The only thing she wanted for her birthday, and consequently, the fifth year anniversary of her arrival to Aunt Myra's doorstep; was a place to run far and away from this horrid existence. With the ceiling as her mind's palette, she daydreamed about what freedom would look like. What playing with kids her age would feel like. What having a boyfriend would be like. More than anything, in this moment, Kai wanted a normal life.

It was then, her room filled with a warm, pink-orange light. Her room had no windows or doors, so there wasn't any place for the light to come from or through, it was just there, making her infinitely more aware of where she was. Her eyes stung as she took inventory of where she had lived for the past five years. Besides being oppressively cold, her room was tiny enough to be a broom closet. Her bed was an old stained mattress that was pushed against the furthest wall, but was barely three paces from the door. Her sheets were so thread bare they had tiny holes in them and her blanket was just about as thin as her sheets.

Kai imagined that other girls at 16 had cute clothes and shoes to wear, but she owned practically nothing. Only the few things she came with, that just barely fit and some old, oversized dresses Aunt Myra gave her. Aunt Myra was adamant that Kai didn't need anything—just Jesus and discipline. Kai didn't bother to argue the point. She thought it not worth the beating she could save for something else. The only other furniture in her room was a half chewed up dresser and a small reading lamp that barely illuminated her feet at night. Her room was so small, not much else could fit in there besides her anyway.

Just as Kai's stinging eyes were about to form actual tears, a golden key the size of a very tall person appeared. It filled the room both with itself and with its pulsing, pink-orange light. Kai was so awed, she reached for it, but the key would not be touched. It stood directly in front of her bedroom door. Kai thought the key wanted to take her somewhere, so without the slightest bit of hesitation, she got out of her bed to put on some clothes. She was fully prepared to follow the key anywhere it wanted her to go. It didn't surprise her in the slightest that she wasn't afraid of a glowing key standing in her bedroom. She was bored. She hurt. She wanted to believe in something other than suffering. She wanted an adventure to relieve some of the numbness that had begun to take her over.

Her face throbbed when she pulled her sweatshirt over her head. She thought her jaw was broken from an earlier encounter with Aunt Myra, a metal spoon and a misspoken bible verse. She ignored the pain. She decided long ago that no beating Aunt Myra could give her would ever compare to the pain from her parents' rejection. She thought about it every single day. Some nights she cried herself to sleep.

18

When she was dressed, she stood looking at the key still standing at her bedroom door. She wondered how she was going to get out. She also wondered how the key even got in. Aunt Myra locked Kai's door from the outside with a padlock to "keep the devil in or out at night". Before she could finish her thought, her bedroom door swung open. A beautiful, bell-like voice filled her room. "Oshharu Mairahu Nura Osho", it said. Even though she didn't understand the language, she thought the voice was telling her to follow the key to her freedom. Kai didn't hesitate. She pulled on her flimsy jacket. Although she didn't know this, at exactly 2:22 AM, she walked out of her room. The key illuminated her way through the dark, old house and through the wide open front door.

It was winter. It had snowed the night before. But where Kai stood in the front of Aunt Myra's old house, was a glorious field of the greenest grass and the most beautiful trees she had ever seen. She knew it was the middle of the night, but where she was standing, the air was warm and full of light, like it was noon on a spring day. Everything she could see was breathing with her. The colors she saw were breathtaking. There was someone in front of her she couldn't see. She squinted to try to see them better, but she couldn't. The key kept moving and Kai kept following until finally the light was gone, and so was the key.

Kai strained to open her eyes. She was groggy. A wave of disappointment coursed through her when she realized she was awake and in bed. Grudgingly, she started to get up to wash, dress and get started with her chores. Then she heard the beeps. They were tinny and shrill, like a machine was making them. The room she was in was dim and her face was covered with something. She pulled her hands out from under several blankets and saw that one of her arms was covered in bandages and the other, had a cast to her shoulder. She let her fingertips explore the length of her face, which was also covered in bandages. When her eyes fully adjusted, she realized she was in a hospital bed. A nurse came in, not even a few seconds later, but Kai couldn't really see through the gauze.

"You awake, precious one?" the nurse asked with a sing songy voice.

Kai nodded with some effort.

"It seems we made a mistake doesn't it, putting you with them and then with her?"

Kai wasn't sure if she heard the nurse correctly. **Does she know me?** She felt tired. Her instinct was to nod in agreement and she did.

"I promise you young one, it was no mistake. You had to see for yourself what the world can be like, to understand your true role in it. Each of your experiences will show you other sides of *the* human experience. It is all for good reason... to get you ready for what you are here to do. Fear not. Be patient Kaiwon. Your time will come soon. Sleep now. Heal. You'll be good as new when you awake and you'll be ready for what comes next... Oshharu Mairahu Nura Osho. Never forget..."

The sing songy voice trailed away as Kai fell off to sleep. The nurse called her Kaiwon. She didn't remember this when she woke up several days later.

As Kai got older and became more comfortable about what was expected of her by the world, she began to blend in. She was eventually placed with a nice older woman, who just wanted some company and to help an underprivileged child get through college.

Kai, for her part, became like any other "normal" person—which is exactly what she wanted. She had friends. She wore fairly cute clothes and shoes. She had a decent bedroom. She had cake on her birthday. She finished High School. She graduated from college. She found a career she loved. Her foster mom died. She fell in love. She had a child and had her heart broken. It seemed that there never was anything extraordinary about Kai after all. She was just human. Just like everybody else. Sometimes she saw herself as more, as special. But most of her days, she was content with existing as simply as possible. To fitting in. All of the things that made Kai extraordinary at her birth and as a child had long been filed away and forgotten to her.

5 THE WEATHER

"Activity conquers cold, but stillness conquers heat."

-~Lao Tzu

The heat was overwhelming. Twelve days in a row of this scorching, choking heat. The only difference between day and night was darkness. The air was so thick and cloud like it was almost impossible to breathe. Kai could barely stand to walk the ten paces it took to go from the air conditioning in her car to the air conditioning in her house.

On this particular night, her dread of leaving her car and shuffling herself, her 6 month old daughter and all of their collective stuff into the house was met with the first reviving breeze in almost two weeks. The breeze was a relief, but Kai didn't dawdle. She never did. She always moved with a mission. Dawdling simply wasn't in her character. She kept to her plan of taking the baby in the house first and then coming back out for all their stuff afterward.

The breeze fluttered through the trees and flowers. Kai was surprised that she paid so much attention to it. It seemed to her like she could actually SEE the wind moving. Not just through the trees but in general. Like the wind had color and a form, as it does in cartoons. She walked slowly to her front door, the pending night threatening darkness on the mother and child watching the summer foliage dancing to the rhythm of the wind. *Something...*

Kai didn't know why, but she felt this night weird. Something was happening around her that she couldn't place. She was moving quickly, but the quicker she moved, the further away her front door seemed. *Something doesn't...*

At this time of day, Kai was in the last leg of her daily grind of waking up before the sun, getting ready for work, readying Taylor for daycare, actually getting to work, staying at work for 10 hours, picking Taylor up from extended hours in daycare and then driving the 30-45 minutes in traffic to their home in suburbia.

It only took a week after her break up with Henny to find the place she and Taylor called home. She was only a few months pregnant and had virtually nothing when she moved in. It wasn't her dream home or the circumstances of motherhood she had in mind, but it would more than do. Two floors, two bedrooms, two bathrooms, a big eat in kitchen, tiled floors, black marble countertops and cherry cabinets. The master bedroom had a huge bathroom with a beautifully tiled soaking tub. She bought first her dream mattress—the one that made her feel like she was sleeping on a cloud. And then she bought a beautiful white stained mahogany 'Rococo' bed, ornate with hand carved details that reminded her of a queen's throne. She outfitted the rest of the room with plush reading chairs and a chandelier, to make her feel queen-like when she came home fatter every night.

At the time, she was upset she didn't have anyone she cared about to rub her feet when they ached daily. She would go through days when she would cry uncontrollably. Eventually, her sadness gave way to elation about the prospects of being a mother, despite what the challenges of the circumstances presented for her. Every time she went to the doctor and heard her baby's heartbeat, she got more excited, so she worked on Taylor's nursery at night before bed and on weekends she was off. The purchase that finally made their little house a home was a beautiful mahogany stained wooden crib, fit for a princess.

Taylor's birth was odd because she practically gave birth to herself. When Kai's labor began, she didn't call anyone. She didn't think to. She didn't know why, she just sat down and waited. Within seconds of her first contraction, however, her Doula was knocking at the door. Kai remembered thinking it to be the strangest thing in the world that her Doula just knew to be there at the perfect moment. It struck her as strange too that for the life of her she could never remember the woman's name or even what she looked like.

Kai wanted a water birth and so her living room was set up with this special birthing pool. Her Doula was very specific about time. She put Kai in the pool at exactly midnight. She didn't do any of the breathing exercises they practiced together, the Doula spent most of her time in prayer and meditation. As her labor progressed, Kai found herself in a trance of some sort. She was so relaxed, she felt no pain. She remembered vaguely that her eyes were so heavy, it was impossible to open them. She swore she heard chanting of some sort in the background—it was like music. Om Namo—something. But it wasn't coming from her house, it sounded like it was coming from the sky. There were also voices. She swore she heard people around her, more than a few. She couldn't open her eyes to see, so she wasn't sure. She remembered vaguely feeling light on her face and hearing birds chirping, smelling grass and trees and flowers around her... the sound of water flowing. The next thing she remembered was being in her bed with Taylor in her arms. Her Doula suggested a name—it was weird. Whatever it was Kai said no.

From the moment she looked in her baby's face, Kai loved being a mother. Taylor's birth changed her life forever. She vowed to live each day as though she had something important to accomplish. That importance included making sure she did her best to contribute to the world her daughter would grow up in. At the time, she had no idea what that meant. So she simply worked harder at work. But Kai felt stifled by both her ambition and not having anyone she loved romantically to share all her new motherhood experiences with. She had a few friends, but they didn't have kids and she didn't want to burden them or bore them to death about things like breast feeding, cramping and how unrealistically fast she was recovering after childbirth.

In 7 hours and no more, Kai was completely back to her pre-baby body. No stretch marks. No pudgy middle. She didn't think it was weird until she read "new baby blogs" and the women were constantly complaining about all the pounds they couldn't seem to lose. For some of them, it took years to lose half the weight they gained during pregnancy. Kai regained her natural 6 pack like it was never covered over with a belly the size of Mount Rushmore. Everyone said Kai was lucky. She had no idea all of this was a testament of who she truly is.

The idea crossed her that Taylor was also extra special one day when she was rushing and didn't strap Taylor into the stroller properly. Taylor was 5 months old. Their townhouse was on an incline and Kai knew better than to take chances. Before she could get to the edge of the walkway, Taylor had slipped through the bottom of her stroller and flew through the air and flat on her face. Kai screamed like it was her own life sprawled face first on the pavement. Without thinking, she peeled Taylor from the asphalt, afraid to find the worst. She was crying, but it was more of a hunger cry than an "in pain" one. Kai was mortified by all the blood and the baby's mouth swelling before her eyes. Kai was certain she saw bruises everywhere she looked.

By the time the ambulance arrived though, Taylor was calm and feeding like nothing happened. While in the ambulance, she seemed to connect with one of the EMTs tending to her. Kai was barely calm, but Taylor was quiet and peaceful, staring into the technician's eyes intently. She never looked away from him.

He relayed to Kai that he and his wife were considering having kids, but he wasn't sure he was ready. Taylor giggled at him. The technician smiled lovingly into the baby's big, effervescent eyes. Kai remembered thinking the exchange between the two was weird, but she just chalked it up as psychosis on her part.

By the time they arrived at the emergency room, Taylor's mouth was no longer swollen and by the time she was seen by a doctor, there were absolutely no bruises of any kind anywhere on the baby's face or body. By the time the two arrived back home, Taylor was picture perfect. Kai was the only one still shaken and mortified by her own carelessness. It was like the accident never happened. It was like Taylor was trying to show her mother something about her truest nature—one they both shared.

Kai replayed the scene in her head daily and every single time she did, she grasped what happened less. Healing quickly is one thing, but healing within hours is something else entirely. Wasn't it? Maybe Taylor didn't fall as hard as Kai thought she did. But Kai was certain she heard that splat of her baby's face as it hit the asphalt. She was sure she saw the facial damage when she picked Taylor up. Maybe her mind was playing tricks on her, but there was something there, Kai couldn't see. Like the way Taylor looked at the EMT. Did Taylor fall out of her stroller on purpose? Is that even possible?

This night, not but a month after the stroller incident, Kai was being extra careful. She carried Taylor like she was made of glass, holding her close to her bosom, up the walkway incline. Kai noticed from the corner of her eye that the moon looked ominous. It was full and brighter than usual. It was hanging in the sky loosely like a burnt orange ball. Kai felt like if she stepped too hard, the moon might fall out of the sky and land on them. And the wind. She swore she could see the wind swirling around her. Kai tried not to rub her eyes, so she adjusted Taylor in her arms. All she wanted to do was be in her house already. Those 10 quick paces to her front door, felt like she had already walked a thousand. **Something doesn't feel right...**

There was something next to her she couldn't see. There was something changing, evolving in the breeze and laying on the trees like dew. There was something, she sensed, that was talking to her in a whisper. Something was calling her. Her forehead itched in such a way it was impossible to ignore. She thought she heard rustling in the bushes along the walkway. She looked around straining to see and hear what it could be, but chalked it up to a late roaming rabbit or cat. She wanted to place the weirdness that was all around her, begging her to notice more than the low moon and the thick, opaque breezes.

For some reason, her small garden along the side of her house caught her attention. Looking at the flowers made her feel better, less anxious. It wasn't yet sunset, so she allowed herself to linger a bit. In fact, she was no longer intent on getting to her front door. A wave of calm rushed over her and she took several very deep breaths and put Taylor on the grass in their little front yard.

Kai started reminiscing again as she watched Taylor crawl toward the splay of flowers in front of her. She remembered vividly being a child who was fascinated with watching things grow. Every spring, like clockwork, when her mother's efforts were ready to bloom, patches of unwanted plants would crop up causing her mother to bristle and then scold. Her mother liked order about her flowers. Kai was a seed thrower. Looking at her small garden now, flowers of every which kind spread about, these memories filled her mind and she breathed through them, smiling thoughtfully. She grabbed her watering can.

The air was abruptly sweet with the fragrance of those flowers, like her nose suddenly started working better. She looked around at the potted Lilly plant, the Sweat peas, sun flowers and these teeny white flowers she never found out the name of. There were also spiky red flowers and tall pink flowers, and short yellow flowers that looked like sun flowers but shorter. Kai's garden, to her, was great, for something she put next to no time into. She watered them regularly, and often times would throw seeds around that she found in the dollar store to see if they would actually grow. They always did.

She was in a kind of trance. She was calm. And then, Taylor began screaming at the top of her lungs. Kai thought maybe she was hungry, so she pulled Taylor up to her breast. Taylor screamed louder, as though something hurt her. Kai searched her little body for a bug bite, a nick, a bruise. There was nothing. She rocked her, sang to her, held her close, but Taylor was inconsolable. Frustrated, Kai took her in the house and no sooner than they walked through the doorjamb, she was sleep in her arms. Just like that. Kai sighed. She walked her upstairs, put her in her pajamas quickly and tucked her in bed.

Instead of fixing herself something to eat and making her way up to bed, Kai was drawn to go back outside and finish watering her plants. When she opened the door, she noticed that the moon looked like it was even lower than it was before. The sky went from almost light to completely dark within the 10 minutes she had been inside. The burnt orange color of the moon now looked deep red. Kai shivered. She felt antsy, as though she knew something was about to happen. She didn't know what it was, but she knew it couldn't be good. The moon meant something to her. It was a signifier of something she was supposed to do. **What is it?** She tried to place it, but she couldn't. She shrugged and let the last gulp of water hit her flowers and then walked toward her door to turn in for the night. No sooner than she put her hand on the doorknob, she stopped stick still in her tracks. Someone was behind her.

6 VISITOR

"Do not forget to entertain strangers, for by so doing some have unwittingly entertained angels." ~ (Hebrews 13:2)

Kai." The low voice was matter of fact and literally came out of thin air. Kai nearly jumped out of her skin. She whipped herself around so quickly, when she faced the voice behind her, she was dizzy. He was tallish, yet unassuming in stature. He had pleasant features, but she couldn't tell if he was black or white or of any ethnicity in particular. It crossed Kai as odd that he didn't seem to look like anyone she had ever seen, or anyone she would ever see again. Yet, he was familiar to her. It was also odd that the second she saw him, her forehead started itching.

"Kai." The stranger said again.

"Do I know you?"

Her neck rolled a little because she was being purposefully cheeky, but she wasn't confident about it. She was actually trying to posture to buy herself some time. She wasn't sure why it made sense for a stranger to sneak up on her at night like that. While she was trying not to overreact, it dawned on her that her pepper spray was in the car. Meanwhile, this guy didn't seem at all dangerous. She was trying to give him the benefit of the doubt. Something about him struck her. She hadn't decided if she cared enough to find out what it was.

"Yes. You know me." He said.

Kai inched toward her door. By this point, she pretty much decided being inside was safer. She was positive that the situation was creepy. She was fairly sure that she did NOT know the man standing in front of her. But his voice. There was something. His voice was low, but sing songy. Kai shook the thought from her head. She couldn't know him.

For whatever reason, despite what she was feeling about the stranger—that he would never harm her—she was thinking of an escape plan. She was thinking about how fast she could get in the door, lock it, get Taylor, call 911, get her keys, get the baby and herself in the car, and then somehow high tail it to a hotel because there was no way she was staying where she was. All of these things were rummaging through her head when the stranger interrupted.

"There is no worry for you or your child. I am here to protect The Vessel and She Who Has Been Chosen."

Kai's jaw dropped.   She just stood there, looking at the stranger with her mouth open until she felt wetness dribble down her chin. Embarrassed, she closed her mouth with some effort. Her forehead went from itching to burning. It wasn't painful, as much as it was disconcerting. It felt like hot water prickling out of her face. She wiped her head with her hand gently, hoping that rubbing it would make the burning go away, but it didn't. Her fingertips started to burn as an extension of whatever was burning on her face. She shook out her hand, trying to put out the fire, but there weren't any flames. This startled her. Without warning, a light shot out in front of her. She thought her visitor turned a flashlight on her. She looked over at him and saw he wasn't holding a flashlight, but he was lit up as she looked at him. Every which way she looked; the light was still in front of her. She turned back to face the stranger. The light was still there, glowing brighter and brighter and then just as abruptly as the light began, it stopped.

Kai continued looking at the stranger without speaking.   She was studying him. She was trying to place him and ignore the fact that she thought --and this was just a thought—that the light she saw was actually coming from her own head. The word "crazy" sat in the front of her mind like a boulder. All she could think about was getting out of "crazy's" way and in to her house. The stranger did not move from where he stood. He was still staring directly at her.   The deeper the stranger looked at her, the less comfortable she felt. She felt like her entire world was spinning and at the verge of coming to an abrupt end.

Kai liked her world. She didn't want anything to change. She just got to the point where she was comfortable. Whatever was happening, she didn't like nor want. **No more changes!** She was screaming in her head. **I've been through enough changes!** The feeling of frustration overwhelmed her. She couldn't stand there anymore. Without saying anything, she turned on her heel, ran into her house, locked the door and practically jumped the whole way up the steps to Taylor's room. Baby in arms, she went to her room to find her keys. She grabbed her cell phone from her dresser and then turned toward her bedroom door and screamed.

The stranger from outside was standing right in front of her, matter-of-factly, as though she invited him to stand there. How he got in she didn't know. He didn't move. He looked at Kai holding Taylor, expressionless, almost robotic. Taylor was awake now, but didn't cry. She giggled at the stranger toothlessly, and then raised her little arms like she was conducting a symphony. In one swift movement the stranger's entire body was flat on the floor, nose to the carpet. Kai could not believe her eyes. A teeny tiny voice in her head began to question what was really going on. She was trying to reason. She was trying to intellectualize the scene before her that she really didn't want to be a part of. She kept waiting for somebody to jump out of her closet and say "Smile! You're on Candid Camera!" Nobody did.

Deep inside, something was buzzing about, ringing in her ears and mind to look around. To see the signs begging her to be witnessed. The burning of her forehead and then, the unexplained light. This stranger, who could walk through a closed, locked door with no effort and who is now face down in some sort of reverence to her own daughter--just because the child raised her arms. Kai did not want this weirdness in her life. She did not understand this weirdness. She could not breathe. All of the air was being sucked out of her with every breath she took in. She swallowed hard, holding on to the wall closest to her. She had to get some air, but she couldn't move.

"You are not in danger while in my presence Vessel Kaiwon. It is my charge to protect you. You must see what you refuse to see. You must remember. You must do this quickly... time is a premium..." his voice trailed off. "We must get She Who Has Been Chosen from this place. They are coming for her on this night." His voice was muffled from his proximity to the floor.

Kai was stuck. She couldn't fathom any of what was going on. She was confused and becoming angry at herself for not being able to control the moment she was in. Finally a question popped in her head. She asked it without being fully prepared to know the answer.

"What... are you?"

The stranger lifted his entire body from the floor in one completely fluid and dancer-like movement. It was both startling and beautiful to watch. It was like he was floating. When his body was erect, he tilted his head toward Kai slightly and looked intently in her eyes. He took two paces toward her and she squinted to see him more closely. She thought there was something. She looked as hard as she could, but nothing clicked. She either couldn't or refused to grasp what the stranger was trying to show her. There was a glow around him that she could see if she relaxed her gaze. Kai's forehead continued to burn. She didn't bother to rub it. Finally, the panic she felt took over. Without thinking, she leaped over the stranger and flew down her apartment steps. She was out the front door and in her car within seconds. She fumbled with the keys a bit, looking through her rear view to make sure he wasn't out of the house yet.

Finally, she got the keys in the ignition and turned the car on. She backed out of her parking spot quickly and sped off, although she had nowhere to go. Taylor was in her lap, face down and Kai was trying to find her cell phone. She swore the phone was in her hand, but thought she had thrown it in the bag sitting in the passenger seat. In one jolting movement, her heart sank and she screamed. There he was. In the passenger seat of her car, while the bag she was rummaging through was sitting on his lap. Every molecule in her body could not comprehend how he got there. Her eyes couldn't help explain how she hadn't noticed him there merely seconds before. She could have died right there. She felt utterly helpless. Tears welled in her eyes. The car swerved, but miraculously, they didn't crash. The car found its bearings all by itself. Kai was so busy staring at the stranger; she had no real interest in steering or watching the road. She was still trying to make what was happening make sense.

"Why is this happening to me?" She caught herself saying out loud.

"*This* is not happening *to* you, Vessel Kaiwon. This is happening *for* you... for *The ALL*." Kai heard the words, but she wasn't really listening. She was stuck in a place between helplessness and anger.

Taylor lifted herself up on her tiny hands and stretched her little neck to look at the stranger in the passenger seat. It looked like she was doing yoga. Then she giggled. The passenger bowed his head.

At this point, Kai resolved that she was actually crazy. Her watery eyes evolved into full blown tears. Not long after, her tears morphed into uncontrollable sobs. After the worst of her sobbing was over, and some of the pounding in her head subsided, she was calm enough to talk.

"Who—I mean-- WHAT are you?" She squeaked this as she fought through her purse for some tissue to blow her nose with.

"I am Cinqo." He said.

Kai looked at him blankly and then blew her nose loudly to add emphasis to the situation.

"I am with you now to bring *you*--The Vessel, and *She* Who Has Been Chosen to safety."

"Forgive me." Kai paused to wipe her face and gain some composure. "You keep saying something about a vessel and a chosen and safety. I have no idea what any of that means."

"You do." He said.

Kai frowned.

"Are you some kind of an asshole? Do you think I would be asking you anything if I knew what any of this means? Either I'm bat shit crazy or I'm dreaming, but whatever is happening isn't making sense. All I'm asking from you is some clarity. You're here. You've performed some clever David Blaine tricks. What. In. THE Hell. Are you?!!"

"I am what is called an Angelic. I have been protecting you since your arrival." Cinqo's tone remained matter-of-fact, like Kai just offered him tea to go with his cake.

Kai rolled her eyes at him.

"Protect *me*? You?! Everything I ever needed protection from is over. I'm okay now. I'm free now. Why would I need protecting NOW? What in the world would WE need to be protected from, except for you? Our lives were just fine until YOU made your way to my front yard."

She looked at Cinqo bitterly and then turned to face the road. She still hadn't bothered to hold the steering wheel. The car was still driving itself. Cinqo was quiet. His silence made her even angrier. She wasn't sure if he was ignoring her or still being an asshole.

"Can you at least tell me where we're going?"

Cinqo shook his head. Kai was more than frustrated at this point. She slapped her hands on her face and sighed.

"Okay, can you tell me *what* I need to be protected from then?" She called herself circling back.

He chose his words carefully.

"Do you truly not remember who you are? Who I am? Who *she* is?"

He motioned toward Taylor, who was asleep in Kai's lap.

"No. I have no idea who you are or who you think I am. I have even less idea who you think this little baby is. I only know this car is steering itself right now and its creeping me out."

He placed his hand over Kai's head and without any fanfare; the three of them were sitting in different places. Cinqo was in the driver's seat. Kai was sitting in the passenger seat and Taylor was in her car seat in the back, still sound asleep. Kai sat staring into space, shaking her head in rebellion.

"You, Vessel Kaiwon, are very important to our cause. But it is not just our cause. It is your cause as well. Your biological mother was--" He stopped abruptly.

"My biological mother was what? A psycho crazy who dumped me on the front porch of that other psycho crazy's house when I was a kid? They all said I was possessed. I wasn't possessed. I'm not possessed. I was a child. Maybe I was a bit different, but I can't think of anything I did or said as a child that would warrant how I was treated. I've been over it a thousand times and can't think of one thing I did that was so bad. The only thing I ever wonder is how they justified their... who does that to their own kid?"

Kai didn't realize the depth of her wounds and how talking to Cinqo made a part of her heart feel like it was shriveling.

"When you were a baby, we would talk every day. Do you remember? You and I would laugh at how scared your surrogates were of you. You used to tell me Oshharu Mairahu Nura Osho-- Fear lights a man's way to darkness. When you were born you knew the secret language of Tuahstai. You've been through much since you arrived here, but your mother tongue is in your bones, so it is impossible to forget."

Kai felt like Cinqo was taunting her. Of course she didn't remember talking to him as a baby. Babies don't speak in secret languages. They sleep and eat and cry and gurgle. That's what Taylor does. Kai put her head in her hands. She was too tired for this. All she wanted to do was cry. She decided that it didn't matter what made sense or didn't. Parts of her were curious. Parts of her wanted the truth. But the biggest part of her was afraid that her parents' fears were justified. That they had every reason to be scared of her. Right now, she was scared of herself.

Cinqo hesitated. He knew Kai's fears. He'd been with her through all of her experiences on The Earth. It had always been his role to protect her from herself, but not necessarily to save her from others. She had to experience the anger and insanity for herself. She had to know what had become of the planet and people she had once committed to save. He's seen all she's seen. Everything she experienced was for her greatest good. It's what brought her to now. He didn't have the time to explain this to her. He wasn't sure if he should proceed with the discussion. He knew he couldn't say too much before he removed her and the child from the Earth plane safely. He knew ears were everywhere. He also knew his natural sensory fortifications could not safeguard them completely from what lingered about on this night. He continued with caution.

"Nothing is as it seems Vessel Kaiwon. Your unique birth circumstances required that you be matched with Earthbound souls who would guide you toward your ultimate purpose on The Earth plane. It is all by divine design." He said.

Cinqo looked saddened, although everything looked sadder through the threat of Kai's tears. Kai choked. Her face was flush with the swells of disgust and the stinging of unformed tears. At this point, she just let the tears fall.

"You're telling me that my parents—those monsters... are not actually my parents. They're some foster parents who couldn't hack me because they said I was a demon. So they handed me over to a real life demon that beat me mercilessly while quoting bible scripture. I didn't catch a break from abuse until my jaw was smashed to bits on my 16th

birthday. Consequently, my life has been a cake party since then --until about an hour ago. Fine. Who are my real parents?"

Cinqo looked at Kai and shook his head gently. He knew he was making no progress with her in this realm. When he spoke, he sounded a bit breathless himself.

"I am unworthy to make these things clear for you. What you need to know will be explained at another time. What is important is that I take you and She Who Has Been Chosen to safety."

"Her name is Taylor!"

Kai was exasperated. Everything that moved through her lips at this point was hostile. Cinqo was unmoved.

"Her name as it is written in Kaitu. Your name as it is written is Kaiwon".

Kai laughed out loud nervously.

"That's just classic. I'm Kai one and she's Kai two. This is a joke right?"

"I assure you, there is nothing funny about my presence tonight."

There was a twinge of something in Cinqo's voice that gave Kai a start. The way he said it was powerful enough, that it felt like a slap in the face. It was the kind of verbal slap meant to snap a hysterical person 'out of it'. Kai was quiet. She turned her head forward to watch the road and zoned out. She stared at the lines in the road unable to fathom what was supposed to happen next. Cinqo placed his hand over her head and she felt like she was floating out of her own body. As much as she wanted to keep her eyes on him, and on the road and piece together everything she saw and heard, she was happy with the quiet. As her eyes closed, she heard Taylor giggle before everything went blank.

7 THE WHITE ROOM

"Naked I came from my mother's womb, and naked I shall return there." ~The Book of Job

H er eyes opened slowly. She was standing, naked, in a bright, white room. The thought crossed her that she had been abducted by aliens and was about to be probed. It also dawned on her that she couldn't move her arms or legs. It was like being stuck standing in concrete. Her head bobbed a bit forward and then backward as she fought within for her bearings. She looked around the bare room and then down at her own nakedness. She was alone, but that didn't stop her from trying to cover up. The fact that she couldn't move revived her anger. Plus, she couldn't see Taylor anywhere.

"Taylor? Taylor!!?" She yelled at the room in general.

"She is safe."

Cinqo's voice was in her left ear, but she couldn't see him. Then he appeared from out of a quiet breeze. She was startled, but she rolled her eyes. She hated that she couldn't move, but *he* could appear from out of nowhere. This irked her terribly. She didn't ease into the conversation. She barked straight away.

"What do you mean, she's safe? Where is she? Bring her to me!"

"In due time." He said.

"Not in due time Cinqo. Right now! Do you hear me?! Right now! And while you're at it, tell me why I'm naked and stuck here. And while you're explaining that... Tell me please where I am and why in God's name I'm even here to begin with?"

A bit of spittle escaped Kai's mouth. She was screaming at the top of her lungs and it was ugly to watch. She looked like a gauge in her head had just blown. Even though Cinqo looked blurry to her now, Kai thought she picked up amusement on his face. He didn't laugh though.

"You are here, Vessel Kaiwon, *as* God's name." He said, matter-of-fact.

Because Kai couldn't move her hands, she couldn't act on her first instinct which was to reach out and strangle him. She instead put her energy toward calming herself down and taking a closer look at her surroundings. The room was not really a room. It was white, but it was translucent, like a cloud. It glowed all by itself, from within itself. She couldn't see how she would have come in or how she would get out because there were no windows or doors anywhere. Even weirder, the room seemed to breathe as she did. It was vast. It looked like it went on forever, although, there was no echo when either of them spoke. She was naked, but she wasn't cold. She was angry, but it didn't linger. There was peace around her, trying to find its way inside her. She knew she hadn't eaten, but she wasn't really hungry. She missed her daughter, but she knew she was safe. It was like whatever Kai was thinking was being absorbed by the room itself. Like the room was a living thing she was standing in.

Kai jumped a bit when another voice, a woman's voice, boomed toward her. It sounded like a million tiny speakers had been installed next to her ears. The voice floated around her in such a way, there was only one conclusion to come to. Although, this voice wasn't what she expected the voice of God to sound like.

"You, Vessel Kaiwon, have a mouth and mind that never ceases moving. It is wise of you to practice stillness here, so you can absorb what is being shared with you." The voice in her ear was pleasant and yet firm.

Kai squirmed. Her head felt hot and her forehead began to itch. She couldn't scratch it, so she was annoyed instead. She felt this overwhelming sense of herself to speak freely. Considering this was her wildest dream yet, she went for it.

"Forgive me, um... Lord? I'll assume I can be honest with you... now that I finally, actually have your, um... ear. Look, this, uh... 'Vessel', 'She Who Has Been Chosen' and *the* least protecting protector I could ever even imagine in my grandest fairy tale... all of this... even though I'm standing someplace that makes less sense than everything I've experienced thus far... never once in all of my adult life has any of this come up before. So I'm going to assume I'm dreaming. And I'm going to tell myself in this dream to wake up. And when I wake up, I'm going to be in my own bed sleeping. With pajamas on. Thank you. Amen." Kai exhaled.

Out from thin air, appeared a youngish, oldish, tallish, shortish completely hard to place with regard to ethnicity—woman. She walked right up to Kai and plucked her on the mouth gently. It stung so much Kai's tongue hurt. Then the woman smiled. She was blurry. It was weird. Kai really thought she was dead because where else would she come face to face with God, and then find out God is a woman with the softest, hardest pluck ever.

"Forgive me, Lord, I--"

"Silence. Please refrain from calling me Lord. I am Meoshe. I am the Keeper of The Great Book."

Kai blinked at her. She felt stupid, so she didn't say anything else. Meoshe spoke like she was praying.

"I know you would like to know why you are here. I will tell you in due time. You are tired. Your soul force has been tested by your travels and your work on The Earth. We need you to be in your full power for what you have been called to do. Presently, you will rest. No thoughts or burdens will reach your mind. You will find peace. Your body will slumber. When you awake, you will be given what you need to continue your purpose. Osho Namoru Yasuru Yasuru Yahmehrah Yahmehrai. So it is."

Before Kai knew what was happening, the room disappeared. The last thing she heard Meoshe say was,

"Oshharu Mairahu Nura Osho. Fear not Vessel Kaiwon, your destiny is foretold. She Who Has Been Chosen is safe. You must rest. You will see her when you wake."

Meoshe's words rang through Kai like the tingling of a gentle bell. When the last syllable reached her ears, something deep within stirred then settled. Then there was nothingness.

8 WILL... POWER

"Do you want to know who you are? Don't ask. Act! Action will delineate and define you." ~Thomas Jefferson

K ai didn't feel like she was sleeping. Nor did she feel that she was awake. She just felt this amazing wash of peacefulness over her. Her eyes opened abruptly, mostly because her breasts were swollen and leaking milk. She knew Taylor was hungry. Not even a moment later, Cinqo appeared with Taylor in his arms. She seemed happy. Kai relaxed a little, but she really, really wanted to give her daughter a big hug and kiss.

"Taylor! Hi mom baby! Mommy missed you. Were you a good girl? You were? Come give your mommy kisses." Kai's instinct was to run to Taylor with her arms open, but she was still stuck in the invisible cement.

"Can't you do anything about this?" She was rolling her eyes at Cinqo when she asked.

"Sadly, no. Your soul force is still rejuvenating itself. The power in this room is still too great for you to maneuver through. Your motherly instinct is strong, which caused you to wake and Kaitu requires feeding, so I am here with her."

Everything that Cinqo said and the way he said it made Kai want to hurt him.

"Do I look like a cow? I can't nurse my baby without using my arms." Kai shook her head.

Cinqo didn't respond. Meoshe did.

"You will be able to move when you are ready and not one moment before. There are universal laws around you that will not be manipulated, Vessel Kaiwon. When you are rested and have accepted your truth, you will be made free, with ease and grace. Your rebellion, your refusal to make peace with your truest self is binding you to where you stand. Where you stand is a place of truth. Truth is one of the greatest powers here. Only those beings willing to let go of their lie can roam freely here. Find your stillness. Find your peace. Find your truth. Let go of your fear. Oshharu Mairahu Nura Osho. Fear lights a man's way to darkness. Those are your words Vessel Kaiwon. You must remember. Until you can accept who you truly are, we cannot proceed."

Kai couldn't help her impatience. She tried flimsily to play along with this crazy dream that had spiraled so far out of her scope, she was over it. All she could do with any amount of emphasis at this point was sigh.

"I appreciate all that Meoshe. It sounds really great. It also sounds easier said than done. All of this is a lot to digest in one sitting. I'm not trying to be smart. I really just want to be with my daughter. I know she's hungry because I'm hungry and my boobs are leaking. Can you bring her to me, please...and do you have any food?"

Meoshe looked Kai up and down. She wasn't sure what to make of her. Maybe her short time with her surrogates had actually tangled her true nature. Maybe the darkness sweeping over The Earth was powerful enough to sully a female Sialovehal and in shorter cycles. If this is true, the inhabitants of The Earth stood little chance against it. Meoshe knew time was a premium. Kai didn't understand this and was quite resolute in fighting everyone around her. Meoshe turned her face as though someone had stopped to talk to her. She was listening and nodding, although there was no one next to her that Kai could see. Meoshe bowed and said, "As you wish." Cinqo glided toward Kai.

Oddly, Kai's arms and legs felt like the cement crumbled away. Somehow she was able to meet Cinqo several paces before he reached her. Kai scooped her baby in her arms with hugs and kisses. She was so focused on Taylor; she missed the exchange that happened between Cinqo and Meoshe. Cinqo's matter-of-fact demeanor, melted in that moment. It was actually more like shock. He turned to Meoshe for explanation. She could offer none. She looked even more surprised than he did. A bowl of brightly colored fruit and vegetables presented itself next to Kai. As soon as she saw it, she began chewing and feeding Taylor at the same time. She ate every morsel lain in front of her without actually tasting what she was eating.

Meoshe bowed quickly in the direction of Kai, Taylor and Cinqo, and then disappeared. Moments later, she was gliding through another white hall. She stopped when she found who she came to see. She bowed.

"Osho Lovianhal", she said.

"Osho Lovian Osho". Tanzin said and bowed back.

"Tanzin, I am wondering if I might council with you." she said.

"How may I support you Meoshe? How are our guests?"

Tanzin was a tallish, shortish, stoutish and slenderish Elder who showed no identifiable age. He was wearing similar white robes as Meoshe. She wasn't sure how to begin.

"I am acutely aware that there is no precedence with The Vessel. She is Sialovehal. That is understood. I will say, neither The SHE, nor The Passion refers at all to the level of power she is bestowed here."

"We are not to be privy of such knowledge. Nor should it be your concern while she is in our care." Tanzin was matter-of-fact.

"Of course." Meoshe said.

"What is your concern then?" Tanzin asked.

"I witnessed... I am not sure if there are words. I can only describe

44

it as seeing her will is stronger than this place."

"No will is stronger than this place, Sialovehal are not exempt from the law." Tanzin's words were solid. He was sure.

"That, Wise One, is why I am here. When she woke she was bound, as was expected. She does not remember anything. Not even Oshharu Mairahu Nura Osho. Sialovehal always remember their own words. Life on The Earth has made her defiant. It is not that she cannot remember, she does not want to. Maybe we showed her too much. She feels lost. Betrayed. It has become a part of her. She carries great fear. Like he did. Nothing that is happening now is as it was written." Meoshe was visibly shaken.

"It is not yet time Meoshe. We cannot judge her. She will find her way. We must trust her unique process."

Tanzin was trying to be comforting. He felt the changes since The Vessel's arrival. Meoshe was overreacting. He was sure of it.

"Of course. And yet. With only her intention to hold her child, she was no longer immobile. She was able to walk to her." Meoshe said.

Tanzin was quiet. He turned from Meoshe to find something in his understanding that he hadn't seen before.

"Ah", he said. "The child is chosen; maybe it was the child who beckoned."

Meoshe moved closer to him. Her gesture gave the words she was to speak a dramatic inflection that her tone could not.

"It was not the child. It was she who moved. " She said.

Tanzin moved forward a few paces and then turned gently back to face Meoshe. Again, he had that bright "eureka!" feeling tone about him.

"A mother's love has great power", he reasoned, "This is a place constructed by love. I am sure there is no call for alarm. We must assume that many unusual things will happen while The Vessel is here."

Meoshe nodded.

"Of course..." Graveness washed over her matter-of-fact feeling tone. "...my concern is not so much for Kaiwon, as it is for what this... power may mean if she becomes aware of it. There is only one other Sialovehal who passed through this place with such power. We have no need to discuss what became of him", she said.

Her graveness dispersed as she finished her statement. Tanzin turned away. He spoke with his back to her.

"I am sure there is no call for alarm." He said.

He didn't need to look back at Meoshe for her to see and hear the cold trickle of uncertainty ripple through his words as he spoke them. She felt the same. Meoshe bowed.

"Osho Lovianhal", she said.

Tanzin turned to face her.

"Osho Lovian Osho". He said grimly as he bowed back.

9 EARTH CHANGES

"Everyone thinks of changing the world, but no one thinks of changing himself." ~Leo Nikolayevich Tolstoy

The Earth was going through its own changes. Chaos doomed normally quiet blocks in normally quiet towns. It was as though anger had formed a time bomb and was beginning to blow up in the minds and hearts of normally docile people. Fights raged in every state, in every town, in every community in almost every person. The news from early morning until late at night was filled with what it looks like when the world has simply gone mad.

NNN reports:

"There are record numbers of murders being reported this morning in cities across the country. There has been more than a 25% increase of violent crimes across every state line. Urban areas, where violent crimes have been increasing steadily throughout the last few years, have seen record numbers of homicides. The big news however, comes from reports that many docile suburban and rural areas are also reporting record increases of violent incidents among neighbors, friends, and relatives. The police departments in all areas have been on high alert since last week. Some cities have called for support from the National Guard, fearing an uprising from frustrated citizens. Some experts are speculating that the 50% average climate increase around the globe as a source of this phenomenon. Other experts speculate this perceived "heat" frustration to actually be a symptom of astronomical gas and food prices and the apparent high demand and short supply of everyday necessities. Experts note that the supply shortage can be attributed to the unseasonable weather this year. The President is set to hold a press conference later on today to

address these concerns..."

Every TV station was relaying the same kinds of reports. Rising food and gas prices, high cost of living, frustrated citizens, higher incidences of road rage, and more people than ever checking themselves into mental hospitals for treatment. Constant fighting and bickering amongst friends and relatives leading to violence and often times, death. Jails were beyond capacity. The world seemed on the verge of anarchy. The experts on talk shows seemed a bit more on edge to argue their points. A well-known spiritual talk show host did a two week series on anger management and a fight broke out in the studio. Even the Evangelicals on TV seemed more "frustrated for the Lord" than usual. Their members fought next to each other in the pews. Routinely, police were called to break up fights that happened during church services. The news started calling the Sunday break outs, "Sunday, Bloody Sundays". The world as seen on TV was an angry mess.

Everyone waited with baited breath in front of the TV to find out what The President would say about the actual state of the union...

"My fellow Americans...I feel your unrest during these trying times. We are working diligently to find a solution to these...that is, all of our growing concerns. We all are feeling the pinch of the high prices of our everyday necessities. While we work these problems out administratively, there are a few measures we all can take to help ease some of the strain on our wallets, as well as on our spirits. We've talked about climate change and its effects for some time. This is the greatest time of any to start taking a more proactive approach to this concern. The heat has been hostile across the country and around the world, causing crops to die in record numbers. This, in part, is pushing up prices in our local supermarkets. The oil companies have refused all of our proposed measures for gas relief, but we have been working with car companies to provide a tangible solution for the gas crisis. In the meantime, as much as we all can, we must try some new things. Try to carpool to work or take public transportation..."

The President's words seemed to go in tiny openings posing as ears, ring around a bit and come back out without moving anybody to do anything. He brought on an agriculture expert to field questions and give advice about planting trees and home gardens, utilizing in-home greenhouses. He talked a lot about urban gardening resources and conserving water—but nobody was listening. Everybody was just too angry.

The anger began to fester and the festering began to spread. It started long before him. No one could really pinpoint where their anger came from, they just knew they were angry. They were so angry that whomever they stood next to caught the brunt of it. With regard to their respective countries, the after effects of constant war, government greed and the isolation people felt from the world outside of their respective neighborhoods, these effects were coming to a head. To the people of The Earth, it was too late for redemption. Too late for solution finding. To the people who watched their worlds crumbling around them daily, it was just too late.

10 YOUNG ELDER

"The atrocious crime of being a young man . . . I shall neither attempt to palliate nor deny." ~William Pitt

66 **I**t is almost time for her to do what she is here to do." The Young Elder said as he glided toward Tanzin.

Tanzin didn't answer. The Young Elder was hoping for some sort of acknowledgement, but when he realized it was not forthcoming, he continued.

"The unrest is more than apparent now. His plan is fulfilling itself. Guardians are reporting Purveyors everywhere and the anger plague has taken over most of the Slides and Mutes. We must bring the Stellar, Kindred and Comforters here to prepare them for the war."

Tanzin stopped mid-movement and turned to face The Young Elder.

"Osho Lovianhai." Tanzin said as he bowed.

Caught off guard and recognizing his mistake, The Young Elder bowed as well

"Osho Lovian Osho", he said.

"The SHE is aware of what is happening on The Earth presently. And yet... we must not react. Time does not determine this war. She does."

He was one of the more eager Elders. Most of them evolve to a state of emotionless matter-of-factness. This Elder was recently transitioned and was prone to 'remembering' some of his more vivid human tendencies. His zeal came off as overzealous; however it was all for the love of humanity.

"I am aware of our orders Elder Tanzin; it is my hope that we would move more quickly to counteract the loss of life." He said.

"Your love for life has always been your strength. However, do not allow your fervor to fool you into believing that you know better than SHE." Tanzin said.

"Forgive my inexperience, Wise One. That was not my intention. I was simply relaying what has been reported to me from The Earth, as was requested. It is my sincerest wish to be utilized toward my greatest purpose here. Osho Lovianhai." He said with a bow.

"Osho Lovian Osho" Tanzin bowed and went about his purpose.

At first he was going to continue his studies. He was obviously of no use to Tanzin and the higher Elders—since they knew everything. He knew that The Vessel and the Chosen Child were being kept close to where he was, so he moved to nourish his curiosity. Surely, 'The Vessel', written in The Passion as the template of The Stellar on The Earth, would help him make sense of the coming war. And more, he felt like she would help him understand how he fit in the balance of everything. He thought she could help bring clarity to the unrest he was feeling in his own spirit. He didn't know why he thought this, he just did.

As he moved about the vast white halls, it was not long before he found who he was looking for. A woman was sitting naked with her baby, laughing and playing like the two had no cares. He watched her until he found his words. He was sizing her up in a way, because she was not at all what he expected. He thought her pretty, which was irrelevant, and he wondered why this thought crossed him. It was the physical nature of The Stellar to be tall and warrior-like. She was not. She was petite, almost dainty. Her form was athletic like a runner or a dancer, but not at all substantial enough to be Stellar. From the way she was playing with her daughter, she seemed also very free, like a wild horse. Stellar are reserved and calculating. Her energy was fearless enough, which was a signature Stellar trait, but her fearlessness, he sensed, was more reckless than anything else. He thought it strange that he spent so much energy looking at her. He was engrossed with the way her raven colored curls crowned her head. He hadn't seen actual hair in some time. She reminded him of someone. He started to feel a twinge of something he didn't dare to place. He chalked it up as anxiousness to meet the mother and child who would help balance The Entwine.

"You are The Vessel, Kaiwon." He bowed. "Osho Lovianhai" he said. "And you are She Who Has Been Chosen, Kaitu. "Osho Lovianhai. It is an honor to be in your presence."

Kai looked up, but she wasn't impressed. He looked blurry to her, like Meoshe, so she wasn't expecting much from him. She looked back to Taylor and continued making funny faces. Taylor went back to giggling. Kai addressed him without stopping what she was doing.

"I don't know too much about all this Vessel Kaiwon, Chosen Kaitu stuff. My name is Kai and this is Taylor. You don't have to bow to us. But what does Osha Lov-i-in-hi-ee mean? That's a new one for today."

He was taken aback by Kai's abruptness. Her energy felt like she was above the natural order of things. If that was possible. This intrigued him.

"Apologies. It is not appropriate to truncate our written names. Osh-oh Low-vy-an-hi-ee... Osho Lovianhai is how we greet each other here. It means Light the Love in All. When I bow and say Osho Lovianhai to you, you bow and say Osho Lovian Osho to me in return. It means Light Brings Love to Light."

"What language is that?" Kai asked the question, but she wasn't sure she cared that much.

"The original language. Our mother tongue, Tuahstai. You don't remember? It is the language we all know before we learn any other."

He was confused by Kaiwon's question because if she didn't remember their language, there was no way for her to remember how to balance The Entwine.

Kai shrugged.

Impossible, he thought. "You don't know where you are?"

Kai looked up at him when she shrugged this time. Although she was annoyed by the interruption, she obliged the question, in hopes he would go away after she answered it.

"No. I don't know where I am. No. I don't know *your* language. I can't even pronounce what you just said. So far, I've met a book keeper and an Angelic, rather, *my* Angelic who is useless in general. Meanwhile, nobody told me a thing except that I need to rest so that I can move. Which turned out not to be the case. Because here I am moving." She giggled at herself, and continued. "I've resolved that either this is the most involved dream of my crazy life or I've been abducted by aliens. So far, my money is on an alien abduction scenario... either way, Taylor seems happy enough, so this place can't be but so bad." Kai noticed the Elder's robes and felt uncomfortable. "Hey, why is it that you guys have on clothes and Taylor and I are naked? Not that I'm cold or anything. It'd just be nice to have clothes on front of strangers, you know?"

"Of course." he said, somewhat breathless.

She talked so fast. In an instant two golden robes appeared in his arms. He leaned forward to hand them to her. As they hit her hands, she and Taylor were wearing them like they had been on the whole time. Kai was pleased. She let her hands run over the fabric and she couldn't place what it was. It felt like she was wearing air and at the same time, she felt comforted, like lying by a fire with a warm blanket and a good book. She looked up at him and smiled. She was trying to see him through all the fuzziness, but her efforts were unsuccessful.

"Thank you." She said. Her tone had softened considerably. "I mean, Osho Lovianhal", she said as she bowed.

He found himself both charmed and mystified by The Vessel Kaiwon. Her accent was perfect. It wasn't lost on him that she added an 'l' to the end of Lovianhai. He taught her the 'new' way. The way Kaiwon pronounced it was the original way, the way the elder Elders addressed each other. She said she didn't remember, but he knew she did, in spite of herself. He couldn't stop looking at her. There was something so familiar about her. She reminded him of his last life on The Earth as a young man. His physical body was killed protecting a family from certain death. As he stood there watching her, his mind began to race. It started in jumbles, like someone threw out a box of puzzle pieces in front of him. Then all the pieces began to move toward their proper place on their own. By the time all the pieces found their mark, his mind followed.

...It was around 2:00 in the afternoon when he heard the gun shots ringing from outside of the Community Center. He was expecting Dr. and Mrs. Abdullah and their young twin sons to come by to talk about plans to expand The Center. They wanted to create a math-based after school program. Dr. Abdullah was a University Economics professor and Mrs. Abdullah was an elementary school teacher. They got the idea while visiting friends abroad and wanted to try them out in their new community home.

When the shots rang, all he could think about were the Abdullahs being caught in the cross fire.

The gun violence had been escalating in this part of the city since the police murdered Shawn Bennis. Shawn was unarmed in a truck full of his buddies, when 5 plain clothed officers shot up their truck, killed Shawn and wounded all but one of his friends. The trial was a travesty because the officers were acquitted of all charges. There was a terrible riot. Businesses were burned to the ground and young boys in the community transformed themselves into soldiers of the worst kind. They felt terrorized by even the idea of justice, so they became the terrorists. They called themselves 'Bangers'.

The gun shots rang like vile church bells. Instead of ducking, The Young Elder ran to the front doors of The Center and peered out of its large grilled windows. He just barely saw the Abdullah's squatting in front of their car and behind another. A young Banger was approaching. The Abdulluah's twin boys were whimpering loudly. Mrs. Abdullah was trying everything she could to quiet them. It wasn't working because he could hear them through the thick metal doors.

The Banger couldn't have been older than 9 or 10. He was tiny in stature and had an automatic rifle, almost as big as he was, postured in his small arms. He had a possessed look in his eyes like he thirsted for blood. The Young Elder knew this little kid didn't care whose blood he shed.

Without thinking, He pulled open The Center's heavy doors. He had no weapon, but he stepped in the path of the kid before he could reach the Abdullah's. The kid startled, but didn't shoot. He just pointed the gun at The Young Elder indignantly. Meanwhile, The Young Elder motioned with his eyes to a terrified Dr. Abdullah to move his family to the other side of the car they were squatting behind. When they did this, they were completely out of sight.

"What's with you kid?" The power in The Young Elder's voice was not something anyone ignored on purpose.

"I ain't no kid, Nigga. You want some of this? You look like you want some."

The Bangers in this area were notorious for shooting first and not caring later. This kid looked scared and hungry. The Young Elder tried not to think about why he was still alive and talking. He shook his head.

"It'd be better if you put that gun away."

"Nigga, you must be bulletproof. I ain't scared of you. But you need to be scared of me! I'm the one holding the gun."

The kid pointed his weapon to the sky and shot a few rounds into the air. Then he clicked his teeth. Keeping his eyes focused on the kid, The Young Elder took a step back.

"Look. Ain't nothing going on around here but a broke down community center. You can come in if you want. We can talk if you want. If you hungry, I got food."

The kid looked like there was a fight going between what his body needed, his stolen childhood and the fragile power he held in his hands. His hunger won.

"What you got?" He asked, trying to sound hard.

"I got all kinds of stuff. A refrigerator full of food. There's a kitchen in there too. I can make you some spaghetti. You like spaghetti lil' man? Why don't you come in and I'll fix you a meal?"

You could see his inner fight play out on his face. A part of him was tired of fighting. He was tired of death and being angry. He wanted to be a kid again. Yes. He wanted to eat spaghetti. He wanted to care about life. He wanted this man in front of him to have the answers. The kid started to move. He started to put his gun down and leave it right on the pavement. He started to leave his anger and being a 'Banger' right there too. Something in him knew he would die if he didn't. But his anger returned. He was possessed with it. It ran his life and his thoughts. He couldn't stop it now. It was too late.

"This a set up. I ain't going nowhere whichoo. Step aside, fore I shoot holes in yo' Nigga ass."

"I'm sorry, brother, I can't do that." The Young Elder knew that if the kid saw the Abdullah's, he would lose it.

There was a redness, a sadness in the kid's eyes as he cocked back his head and further brandished his gun. The Young Elder swore he saxw the black wind swirl just above the kid's head. This saddened him because he knew he couldn't help that kid no matter what. He was possessed. The anger had him. One of the Abdullah boys whimpered loudly, which caused The Banger's paranoia to quicken. In slow motion, The Young Elder jumped the kid, which broke the gun, but not before a few rounds discharged into his chest. He landed flat on the kid full force with all 200 of his muscled pounds. The kid was trapped until the militarized police arrived. They only came because of the international importance of Dr. Abdullah and his family.

He recalled his last journey was about sacrifice. He passed his final check point and found himself as a 'new' Elder with a 'new' name. As hard as he tried, he could not remember what his last Earthbound name was.

"Was there something specific you wanted...uh...?"

The Young Elder tried to shake out the wrinkles in his head, although, it took him a minute to figure out Kai was speaking to him.

"Apologies. I am called Yamin."

"Great. Was there something you wanted, Yamin?"

Yamin had forgotten himself for a moment. He never had memories of his Earthbound life before. They were so vivid, like he was there. He wondered if this happened to every new Elder. Kai was growing impatient. She thought Yamin was ignoring her.

"Hello? Are you there?"

Yamin shook out the wrinkles in his mind again.

"Forgive me. I...I came to greet you. That is all." He hesitated as he looked at her, somehow linking his memories to being in her presence. "I was anticipating I could find answers to growing questions I have."

"About me?" She asked, this time looking at him with her full attention.

Yamin froze. He felt exposed. She was looking through him. He didn't like the way he felt, so he doubled back.

"About you in part. My concern is mostly about all that is happening on The Earth."

"Why would I be able to help you with any questions you have about anything? As far as I know, Earth is fine. But what do I know? I just learned Osho Lovianhal. I do have a question though. Are you a book keeper like Meoshe or a pointless Angelic like Cinqo?"

Yamin was amused, but didn't let on.

"There is only one book keeper, as you call her, and Cinqo is the only Angelic here because you are here—you are his charge and he must stay with you."

"Lucky me. So what does that make you?" She was gesturing for Yamin to get to the point.

"I am an Elder."

Kai nearly spit out her laugh. *Of all the things*, she thought. This guy was *the* very last being she expected an Elder to be.

"I don't know if this will come off as offensive. I can't tell for sure how old you are, but you seem more young than old. I'd like to assume an Elder to be older and wiser *and* not prone to asking questions they should be able to answer. I mean. This is *your* turf isn't it? Shouldn't *I* be asking *you* questions about all the strange things happening to *me*? Shouldn't *you* know everything? Isn't that the perk of being called an

Elder?"

Yamin was feeling increasingly more vulnerable the longer he was in her presence. Something in him was beginning to understand the nature of Sialovehal and why she was here. She had a way of cutting through every triviality and seeing things as they are, not as one would have them be. It was either that, or being with her was making him lose his sense of self. Either way, Yamin felt off. She was the kind of being who could unknowingly face the devil and get even him to question his own existence. He thought this a tremendous gift. It was all there, he could see it in her. She was like a rock star of The Stellar. She was written in The Passion as Spiritual Royalty. He didn't know all of the details, of course. There were some things that were meant to unfold, or so he was told.

"I am a 'newer' Elder, what is called a Neo. We are not privy to all the information that the higher Elders are. So in that way, yes, I am young. I have transitioned from being an Earth bound soul, so in that way, I am… old."

"That's got to suck."

Kai was deadpan, Yamin laughed.

"I suppose it does." He was careful not to let on that he wasn't sure what she meant by 'suck', but the way she said it, was exactly how he felt about being a Neo. He relaxed considerably and felt good enough to move closer to her and sit. Kai seemed relaxed also.

"So where are we anyway?" Kai was looking around.

"The Heaven." Yamin said, like she should know.

"Don't you have to be dead to be in heaven? So I am dead then? I don't remember dying. I certainly don't feel dead." She looked down at her giggling baby. "Taylor, do you feel dead?" She looked back up at Yamin. "Taylor says she doesn't feel dead." Kai sighed, because she was making light of a situation that was frustrating.

"There is no need for alarm Vessel Kaiwon. You are not dead. You are here because there is no place on The Earth where you will be safe."

"That doesn't even make any sense. How is this even possible?"

Kai hugged Taylor tightly and started to cry. The more she learned, the less she understood. It was like a whole chunk of her was trying to show her something and a whole other chunk couldn't see it if it had neon blinkers around it. She wanted to scream. Yamin wasn't used to the physicality of human emotion. He didn't know how to comfort her.

"Why are you sad Vessel Kaiwon? Everything you are experiencing presently is your design, in part. Your only present charge is to remember your purpose, so we can proceed. There is a war coming."

"A war? I'm here for a war? What kind of war? None of this makes any sense." It took a few beats, but finally Kai asked the question she really wanted answered. "I'm not just a person am I?"

Yamin paused to reflect.

"No." He said. He wasn't sure what else should be said. It was clear to him that he should not force her memory or her understanding. She would have to find her truth on her own terms. "Apologies Vessel Kaiwon, I've said too much. I should not have come. Certainly, I am not the one to reveal these things to you."

Kai lifted her head and wiped her tears.

"Don't apologize Yamin. It's not your fault. Everyone I've met so far keeps saying the same thing. You're here for a grand purpose! But you can't know what it is! Is it that big of a secret? It's obvious that everybody around here thinks they know something about me I don't, but it's also obvious nobody wants to just tell me. If what you say is true and I really just have an odd form of amnesia... if I can't remember, I can't remember. Just tell me what you think I'm supposed to know already! This is what I do know. Heaven is the place people go when they die. You say I'm not dead, but I'm in heaven. Does that make any sense? No. It doesn't make any sense. Can you tell me something that makes sense?"

"Memory isn't static. It's fluid. We cannot just tell you who you are and you will remember everything. We hope that something said will help you, and yet you are demonstrating that there is a process for you that we will not know until you do. For what you are here to do, you have to know. Your knowing is what powers your purpose."

"But if my knowing is so important, why did I ever forget?"

"You can answer that better than anyone, Vessel Kaiwon. There's a reason for everything. It may be better to accept that you're here and don't remember why, than to rebel against it. Maybe your fight is keeping your memories from you."

Yamin hoped his words were kind enough. The fact that The Vessel didn't know her own truth in the place of all truth didn't make much sense to him either. But he chose not to question divine intention, or Kai's intentions for that matter. He figured maybe it would help to start at the beginning and try to explain things to her as close to "human" terms as he could.

"Most Earth bound souls believe as you do with regard to The Heaven. It is a common misrepresentation. The Heaven is actually the place where the Elder's dwell and The Passion is kept. When souls have transitioned, they travel beyond here to a realm called Enlightenment. It is the source of all life force."

Kai was quiet.

"You do not understand?"

"You can't read my thoughts like Meoshe and Cinqo?"

"I am a Neo. My Elder abilities have some limitations. While I can sense certain things, I cannot as yet read thought energy, particularly of the highest realms, like the higher Elders and those who have been here far longer than I."

"How long have you been here?"

"I do not know. Time is different here than it is on The Earth plane. You may live an entire lifetime there and no time will pass here and vice versa. That is what I have been told. I have much to learn before evolving into my full potential."

"Interesting. You seem like you'd be the cool Elder of the group."

"Yes? I am trying to remember if I know what cool means. Is it like being cold?"

"Probably not in the way you're thinking of cold. It means fun, relaxed. It means you're down to Earth."

"Certainly, I am not down on Earth, I am presently with you."

"Noooo. Not literally down on Earth. It's like... never mind. It's a good thing."

"I shall take you at your word." He said smiling.

The two locked eyes for a few moments. They looked at each other like they noticed something very unusual.

"I was once like you. A Stellar." Yamin said.

"A what?"

He hesitated. He looked above him like he was searching for an answer in the air. He wasn't sure if he was helping or hurting the process by continuing to introduce Kai to things she wasn't prepared for. He was torn.

"Apologies. I was certain Cinqo would have told you."

"You know what? He may have. Cinqo and I got off to a rough start. I'm pretty sure I ignored everything he was telling me because there was too much other stuff going on at the time."

Yamin shifted.

"Of course. I imagine your mind has much to consider."

Kai looked down at Taylor, who was sound asleep in her lap. She put her head in her hands and tried desperately to remember what Cinqo said to her that night in the car. There were glimmers. She tried to make the words take form in her head space like typed sentences. She sat up, straightened her back and even closed her eyes. She breathed in deeply and tried to allow what she wanted to know to come to her. She did all of this instinctively, but she didn't actually know what she was doing. After a few moments, she threw up her hands in defeat.

"I don't know Yamin." She sighed loudly. "I remember him saying that my psycho parents weren't my actual parents—somebody picked them for me. He started to tell me who my biological mother is, but then I ended up here. He said when I was a baby; I had all kinds of fun. I spoke secret languages and everything. I don't remember most of what he said. It all sounds silly if you ask me."

Yamin just looked at her. He knew that anything he said at this point was either going to confuse her further or create further turmoil in general. But every ounce of his being wanted to buy more time with her.

"I am not privy to know when Meoshe or The Elders had planned to tell you about the Entwine of Mirth."

Kai's forehead began to itch. She rubbed it intently with the whole of her left palm trying to squash the sensation. She looked annoyed. Yamin watched her in astonishment. He didn't know exactly what he was looking at, but he sensed it was important. He decided he would tell Kai what he knew. At least some of it.

"Souls are designed to interlink, or to entwine into an intricate weave of consciousness. The goal, we are told, is to master our place in the weave. It takes many lifetimes to fulfill our purpose in the universe."

Yamin waited for a reaction from Kai, but got none.

"I'm listening", she said.

"Souls, as you may have learned of them are born. Soul forces as I've been taught are moved around in different life experiences in order to be made complete. The way it works is that until all life force is made whole, The ALL cannot be whole. We are not taught what is to come next, because our experiences are fluid. We are only taught that each of us has a purpose to unfold and until we all unfold completely, none of us can experience what comes next for existence. So each soul force of a being must acquire a series of capabilities while they experience a body. In theory, they accomplish these capabilities through a succession of human form lifetimes and then one higher form lifetime."

"In theory?"

"It is so. This is the way The Entwine was designed; it does not mean everything has gone to plan."

"Oh..." Kai said.

She looked at him expectantly because she had a feeling there was more weight to what was being said than he was willing to share with her. Meanwhile, Yamin looked flush. He knew he was treading on delicate territory. He knew much more about Kaiwon than he said, but he knew it wouldn't be right to tell her more than she was designed to discover herself. Kai determined it was probably better to keep it light for the moment.

"Okay then. The Entwine doesn't seem all *that* complicated. It's a little like school, except our lives are our classrooms. And in this school, we all have to graduate or none of us do. No soul left

64

behind." She said laughing.

"It is so." He said, bowing his head to emphasize his agreement.

Yamin couldn't help but feel encouraged. Kaiwon was a natural translator of the word. Although he didn't know all of the subtext of her slang, he understood that she understood, and that at some point her gift for translation would be a benefit to the Earthbound souls who would require it. Kai interrupted his thoughts.

"I gather, you're on your one higher form lifetime."

"It is so."

"Wow. What's that like for you? Is it hard to be away from people, knowing you once were a person? Do you ever get to visit? Do you remember anything from any of your former lives?"

"I cannot say what it is like. Being here is always about being in the moment. There is no past or present. There is only now. There is no need to remember a past life because all of my necessary experiences have been integrated into the experience I am having now. I am designed to be here now and there is nowhere else I am designed to be."

Yamin wanted to tell her about his earlier vision, but he didn't understand what it was. Kai could tell he didn't like answering that line of questioning.

"I'm sorry for being nosey. I'm not sure yet what's considered offensive to your people." She said.

"No apologies required. They are your people as well Vessel Kaiwon."

Kai cringed.

"So... what is a Stellar again?"

"Certainly. To be Stellar is considered a final path for an Earthbound soul before being granted a more intimate service with The Creator. One must complete many earthbound life cycles to accomplish this."

"So I'm a senior in college and you're in grad school. Got it."

Yamin looked at Kai blankly. Kai looked impatient.

"All souls begin at Mute. Mutes are neither good nor evil. Because The Entwine is designed as a succession, it takes many lifetimes to learn the lessons necessary to reach the consciousness of The Stellar. Understand, the path of The Stellar is only one path of many."

"I get that. We all have our path right? Essentially, if I'm understanding you correctly, at first I was neutral-- what you call a Mute. Then I moved along to whatever the other things are in this Entwine, until I became what you say I am—which is Stellar. But I could have been something else. Fine. Meanwhile, all of that still doesn't explain what a Stellar is."

Yamin was still conflicted about whether it was his place to tell Kaiwon the truths in The Great Book, and yet he was at ease in his desire to do so. He paused longer than was comfortable for either of them and then continued.

"Stellar are human form of what The Earthbound souls call Angels."

"Wait. The Stellar are angels?! I'm supposed to be an angel?" She laughed out loud. "Wow man, I must have missed my wings. But then again, if I were born with wings, that would explain my fake parents dumping me, wouldn't it? You're kidding right? I thought Cinqo was the angel in this arrangement. I'm going to turn out like Cinqo?"

"Cinqo is Angelic. He's the highest form of Guardian. Guardians are called to protect our people through their final stages of their service to the Entwine on The Earth. There are Guardians and also Messengers.

Angelic are Guardians, but they have a separate charge. They stay by the side of very specific souls while they are evolving or when Sialovehal arrive on The Earth plane. Like a Royal Guard."

Kai's forehead was itching so viciously, it hurt. Tears began to swell in her eyes again. She looked at Yamin. She couldn't help the sadness she felt. She was certain she heard the words Royal and Guard. This meant there was much more to what was happening to her than even Yamin could tell her.

"Sialovehal? What the heck is that?" Her question barely squeaked out. She let the tears that had welled up roll down her cheeks.

"You, Vessel Kaiwon, are something altogether different. I told you about The Stellar—which you are. In a way. But, you aren't the kind of Stellar I was. And yes, you are an Angel. But it's not the type of angel you may have read about in books on The Earth. You are one of few, who came back to serve a great many. You are an original Stai, or Star People. You are Sialovehal. A Seed."

"A Seed of what?" She shook her head. "Yamin, there isn't anything in the world I want more than to understand what's going on here. Please don't think I don't appreciate your kindness, because I do. But you have to admit that everything you're saying is supposed to sound ridiculous to me because it would sound ridiculous to anyone. I still haven't worked out yet if this is some nutty dream I can't wake up from. I have to admit though, I've been playing along. I'm here right? I might as well. Here's the thing. In my dreams, I can make you make sense because it's my dream. For whatever reason, no matter what I seem to do and think, I can't seem to make this dream make sense. The more you claim to be explaining to me, the less I actually know. One minute I'm a Vessel and the next I'm an angel... then I'm Star People and now I'm Sah-ail-o... A Seed. If for just a second you would put yourself in my position, you would understand how ridiculous all of this sounds out loud. I'm so tired Yamin. I just want to be done with this already. But I have a feeling I won't be done with this any time soon because I also happen to be Dorothy and Taylor here is Toto and we're apparently on our way to Oz to find the Wizard. Please Yamin. I am begging you. Just tell me the truth."

Yamin looked down at his robes. He said too much. He wanted to answer her, but was moved not to speak. Instead, another voice rang through the room.

"You would not believe Yamin even if he told you what you want to know, would you Kaiwon?"

Yamin stood. He performed his quick bow to Kai and Taylor and then in the direction of the invisible voice.

"Osho Lovianhal", He said and then was gone.

11 THE ENTWINE

"The thinkers of the world should by rights be guardians of the world's mirth." ~Agnes Repplier

J ust like a breeze, Tanzin appeared in the room. Kai just sat there looking up at him. She missed Yamin already. She sighed because she was tired and all of it was too much. By now she was good and frustrated. As much as she thought she was beginning to understand, that last bit sealed her fate. Her reality at this point was surreal. She thought, **This can't really be happening. Any moment I'm going to wake up…**

Tanzin shook his head.

"You are not dreaming, I assure you. Everything you have experienced is quite real."

Kai looked at him blankly. It was a little annoying at the moment to not have private thoughts. She needed the alone time. She needed to process.

"Who are you?"

"I am called Tanzin." He said.

"What do you do here?" Kai was being thorny. On purpose.

"My role is an Elder." He said.

"Yamin is an Elder. You two are quite different. What does your version of an Elder do?"

"We are not that different. Elders are called to close service with The Creator. I am Yamin's elder, Elder."

"Ha. You don't know, do you?"

Tanzin was blurry to her like they all were, plus she had long since lost patience with everything.

"That is not what you really want to know is it Kaiwon? You want to remember and you cannot. You know me. You want to remember me, do you not? You know my role here. You know why you came to be here with me now. You even know who you are. Stop being afraid and remember. You may be a relative child in form, but you are not a child. Oshharu Mairahu Nura Osho. Al Heim Rom Ah. You must remember." He said.

Kai rolled her eyes. When she stood up, Taylor was no longer in her arms. She just vanished. Kai looked at Tanzin bitterly.

"Where does she go when she leaves me?"

"That is of no consequence. She is safe."

She clicked her teeth.

"Do you wish for me to pretend with you like the boy Elder? Do you wish for me to protect your human feelings, as though you actually have *human* emotions? You have lived among the Earthbound souls, but you are not of them. While we help you wake up from your eons long sleep, The Entwine is so very off balance. If we do not proceed, every individual still left on The Earth will have to transition and we will have failed. The Earth will be destroyed, and of course, you shall simply go back to where you have come. But WE cannot fail Kaiwon. Too many of us have sacrificed and toiled on The Earth and in The Heavens to make it possible for you to be here now. Al Heim Rom Ah." He said.

Tanzin turned away from Kai. Being in the same space with her made him feel off balance himself. Kai sniffled.

"I don't remember anything but abuse and brutality. Maybe it's just as well. Did it ever occur to any of you that I'm not who you think I am? Maybe you want me to be important to your cause and I'm really just not. I'm just a person. That's it. There's nothing special about me. I have skin and hair and eyes. I have human emotions because I'm human. Doesn't that make more sense than I just forgot? I can only be what I am, even if you think I'm something else."

Tanzin kept his back to Kai.

"Many, many, many lifetimes ago, The Stai arrived. They came to live amongst the humans on The Earth, to help them in their evolution. Some of what was tried has failed and some has shown benefits. At first, The Stai lived among them, but did not integrate with them. Humans are prone to an anger gene, that if left unrestrained... they forget themselves in superstition and fear. Essentially, after a time, genocide arises. Over many cycles, it was learned that if The Stai integrated with them slowly and in a calculated way, their anger gene could be transmuted. We discovered the only way to fully integrate was to create a system of evolution that would effectively blend the essence of The Stai with the essence of humans. The Entwine of Mirth was born from this understanding. It was a way to create a balance in the blending of our essences. The Entwine works through concurrent lifetimes. As Yamin revealed, a soul force transcends from Mute to Slide and then from Slide to Comforter, Kindred or Stellar. Of the latter three, a soul force may transcend to Guardian, Watcher or Elder. Guardians do not become Elders or Watchers; as Watchers do not become Elders or Guardians. Nor do Elders become Guardians or Watchers. The Entwine entitles equality between The Stai and Humans. They can evolve in the same ways we do, and also pollute our intentions. The Entwine is powered by choice, genes and soul. We hoped the anger gene would be eradicated, but after The Fall, we lost control."

Kai blinked hard when Tanzin turned to face her.

"You're still saying I'm not human." Her tone was indignant.

"You have integrated a good bit of human emotion after your

71

arrival. Most humans who transition here, including I, have experienced full integration of our roots as Stai and our intention as evolved Humans. Essentially, through The Entwine, WE have created an entirely new essence of Star People. The ALL of us here on the plane of The Heaven are the success stories of The Earth mission. Any soul force that evolves to Stellar, Kindred or Comforter is a part of this success, because our path here is clear. However, there are far too many Earthbound souls who bind themselves to Mute, Slide or him. Our people are greatly outnumbered on The Earth plane presently. There were only a few original Star People who came to The Earth first to initiate the original evolution and then later, The Entwine of Mirth. All of the original Star People transitioned beyond here eons ago, including you. A few through the last several thousands of Earth years have come back to push our intentions forward when humans lose control. As Yamin mentioned, WE call the original Stai 'Sialovehal' or 'The Seeds'. You are Sialovehal." He said.

She shook her head.

"I cannot convince you of your truth. This is something you must discover on your own. I have been made aware that your journey here will be one of discovery. I will not hinder your journey Kaiwon. I will answer any question you may have about the Entwine of Mirth, but I cannot tell you any more about yourself than you can." He said.

Kai was starting to grasp that whether she believed what Tanzin said or not was irrelevant. These people honestly believed the stuff they were telling her. It was very much like having a brick wall on top of her head that everyone around her could see, but her. She could only imagine that Tanzin was as frustrated with her as she was with him. Maybe more. In his mind, she was supposed to be the one with all the answers. Or something. She wasn't sure what a Sialovehal was supposed to be able to do. If what he said is true, her existence helped make his existence possible. Meanwhile, that didn't change the fact that she didn't remember anything more than what she came with, which made things pretty cut and dry from her perspective. Either they've got the wrong woman or everybody counting on her was in for a rude awakening, she thought.

"Okay. Fine. Let's talk more about this Entwine of Mirth then." She sighed loudly. "So people evolve from Slide, and then become Comforter, Kindred *or* Stellar?"

"It is so. A soul force may choose to evolve to Slide, from Mute. Slide is still considered a 'new' soul, but has some life experience. He or she should have learned about what is most important through many lifetimes as Mute. A Slide, however, is still considered a weak soul. This is still a relatively easy soul to turn. I'm sure we'll get to that at another time. Once a soul force has reached a level of understanding necessary to evolve closest to The Creator in an Earthbound form, these soul forces are repurposed onto the Earth as either a Comforter, Kindred, or a Stellar." He said.

Tanzin enjoyed talking about The Entwine. It gave him a sense of accomplishment. He knew what his choices could have led to and he felt joy in knowing he chose as he was designed to. Kai interrupted his thoughts.

"As Yamin was leaving, he said we were both Stellar, but he was a different kind. What does that mean?"

"The Stai are a highly evolved people and have equal traits of the Comforter, Kindred and Stellar spirit tones. But pure humans in the Entwine had a hard time with a full integration. As the Entwine evolved, we learned that by using groupings by dominant traits and individual spirit tones, the integration was most successful. Thereby, The Stellar are Warriors, Comforters are healers and Kindred are disseminators of information. The spirit tone of the Stai and most specifically, Sialovehal, are the template for each of the spirit tones in the current Entwine. Star People are the creators of the Entwine, but not of it. The Stai are still known throughout the omniverse as The Stellar, but there is a vital distinction. The Stellar of The Entwine are much different in essence than the template of its existence. Sialovehal always wear their birthright on their person. The Stellar of the Entwine must earn their birthright through evolution."

"What is it? What is this birthright?"

Tanzin turned away.

"This is not a subject to elaborate upon before you are ready. Certainly, you are not ready."

His tone was tense; she assumed it was about Yamin.

"Yamin meant no harm. He was trying to ease my anxiety about this whole thing. If you ask me, Yamin has been quite the Comforter and Kindred, for somebody who's only supposed to be Stellar." She said laughing.

"I am glad you and Yamin found common understanding. We felt that he would be a proper accompaniment for you while you are with us. Would you like to know more about The Entwine or would you like to rest presently?"

"Are you like me? Are you Sialovehal too? You've said 'our people' a lot."

"No, dear one. I am not Sialovehal. But I am a testimony that The Entwine serves a great purpose for the many of Earthbound souls it was designed for."

"Did you know what you were when you were on Earth? If I had to guess, I'd say you were Kindred."

He smiled.

"I was Kindred. I did not know my spirit tone when I was on The Earth. We do not know until we transition to this realm. What I find most interesting about The Entwine is that most in the same spirit tone groupings do not even know the others exist, nor are they in the slightest way attracted to one another. If you were to look upon The Earth right now you would see it as we see it. Full of colorful spirits meandering about searching for their way back to where they originated. Making up stories for each other to make sense of their experiences."

Kai bristled.

"You find all of this funny don't you?"

"Of course it is not at all funny. It is interesting how complicated Earthbound souls make their lives. It is all very easy when one stays on path."

"I guess it's easy to you because you aren't down there living the lives we have to live. We walk through crap to get to a shower, only to be covered in crap again. It's not as easy as you're trying to make it sound."

"Ah. And so you learned what you were put on The Earth plane to understand. It was all for divine reason."

Kai was washed over with every sordid experience of her childhood all at once. She rolled her eyes. Her bitterness was so fluid; it nearly dripped out of her mouth with her words.

"And what might that be?" She asked.

"We are all connected. Your fate, no matter how different from your fellow man is neither unique nor intangible. We are all designed to fulfill an individual purpose. And yet, if any of us fail to do so, our whole is not complete and we must all stay until the entirety of our work is done. Each individual purpose is linked to each other. It is our choices that differentiate our experience. The Sialovehal had already reached a level of evolution far surpassing humans. As they have done countless times, they reached back to help a newer race reach its fullest potential.

While others in the omniverse just sought to take advantage of them. Some have. Sialovehal gave up some of their wealth, so both peoples could have more, together. That was their intention for being here. By this example, they demonstrated the truth. Every soul force on The Earth is designed to help each individual fulfill their purpose for the good of the ALL. That is the truest nature of The Entwine, no matter how it may look to Earthbound eyes."

"I have no idea how you got all that from the life I lived for all those years. I can't even say I learned much at all except how to survive abandonment, abuse and church fanatics."

"You say this as though your one Earthbound experience determines the results of them all. Kaiwon. Do you think it was any mistake the circumstances of your birth? The nurse who handed you to parents seemingly unequipped to handle your specialness? The woman with the black wind swirling about her? You saw it. Do you know why you could see it, when most cannot? Was it an accident your surrogates left you with her? The way you escaped her... do you remember the golden key?"

Tears were forming in Kai's eyes again, but she refused to cry. She just nodded.

"Yes."

"Do you think your escape was an accident? Do you think your being there in the first place was just a cruel joke the fates play on unsuspecting children? It was all written before your current physical body ever took shape in your biological mother's womb to be born again on The Earth plane. You are the co-creator of your own destiny. You and your mother worked tirelessly together for you to be here now. You chose the specific nature of your 'birth' because you needed the people who would raise you and the person they would send you to live with and to learn what you learned from her. You learned something from every one of your life experiences up to this very moment. All of it is paramount to this part of your journey. You learned about the Human experience and the human condition. You needed to know what they face. You needed to know the nature of their fear. You needed to live what so many live. In order to experience the fullness of your purpose, you had to forget… in order to remember who you truly are. In this moment you are denying yourself your awakening. Because you are afraid. Where you are from, fear does not exist. I can only imagine that once one tastes fear in its most potent state, it is a difficult flavor to forget. And yet, you had to taste it for yourself, in order to know the power of what you came here to transmute. If it is not easy for you, a Sialovehal, imagine what is happening on The Earth plane as we speak. Vessel Kaiwon, who was it that guided you out of that house and to the hospital that night?"

"I don't know. I mean, I don't remember anything except the light, the key and the pain. I barely remember leaving that house. I remember the hospital a little. I remember the nurse. I remember her voice. Was it Cinqo that led me out of the house that day? Is Cinqo the key?"

"No. Cinqo is not the key. Cinqo was indeed the nurse in the hospital, telling you all was well. With regard to the key, you must figure that part out on your own."

"Who was my mother? Is she somewhere here?"

"I cannot answer at this time. I told you, your time here is about discovery. I am being led to tell you that you will discover much about your family tree while you are here."

Kai was back to painful territory. She didn't like asking questions and getting 'figure it out' answers.

"What does Meoshe do? I know she's a book keeper. Are there a lot of those here?"

"There is only one *Keeper* at any point in The Evolution. The Keeper, you should know is always what is considered a female soul and protects the translations of The Great Book until called to transition."

"Who takes her place when she transitions?"

"It is written that *you* will."

"Me?" Kai laughed out loud. "Me? That isn't possible. How'd you come up with that? I thought I'm supposed to help people transmute fear." She said.

"I can only relay to you what is written." He said.

"Okay so we'll move along. You said something earlier about soul forces evolving or devolving from Mute. How does that happen?"

Tanzin's voice went sour.

"Soul forces make the individual choice to not follow the divine path set out for he or she. To understand this, you must also understand that The Entwine as we know it now has become a mess of duality. There must be opposites, even though duality was not the original intention. Currently there is light and dark, day and night, good and evil—or so it has been called. It is the same with Earthbound souls. For every Angel, there is a Demon. For every Mute there is a Draw, for every Slide there is a Slider for every Comforter there is a Compound, for every Kindred there is a Kaw, for every Call there is a Quest, for every Guardian there is a Purveyor for every Stellar, there is a Moyo."

"I thought Yamin said the whole point of this is for souls to be made complete."

"Not every soul answers its Divine Call. Some soul forces choose the path of Firewah."

"Hell.", she said.

"Not exactly the concept of hell that has been fashioned on The Earth, but yes, it is so."

"But why? I've lived a version of hell. I'm sure of it. I know you said I chose it, but I wouldn't have chosen it if I thought I had the choice at the time. Why would somebody create hell for themselves if they knew they had a choice in the matter?"

"That is a good question to ask of you is it not? I will say, humans have turned out to be creatures of habit. They allow their life experiences to determine their beliefs. I will also say, far too many are victims of ignorance. They simply do not know. They do not trust their truest nature to guide them and there are many in place who feed the superstition. The superstition in turn feeds the anger. The anger feeds the violence. It is a magnanimous cipher he has put in place on The Earth. I will also say, in the beginning, when the Sialovehal first arrived, there was no Entwine. The Entwine evolved from necessity of The Fall."

"Dare I ask what 'The Fall' is?"

"Of course, you may dare. Earthbound souls created a legend about whom you refer to as the Devil or the father of all things 'Evil'. He was called Lucifer when he was an Elder."

"Lucifer was an Elder? I thought he was an Archangel like Gabriel or something."

"Gabriel is a Messenger presently transitioned to higher realms. Lucifer was not only an Elder, he was a Keeper."

"Oh. But, I thought only women were Keepers."

"That evolution manifested after The Fall. I should also mention that Lucifer is also Sialovehal. He is the greatest reason why our original people transitioned to higher realms after The Entwine was established."

"Okay... he's what I am? That's something, isn't it?"

"It is. A monumental something."

"Did I know him?"

"You did. He is a part of the reason you are here now."

"Ha! Because he screwed everything up right? First he screwed up the book he was supposed to keep and then he screwed up the Earth project. Apparently he's a screw up. What did God ever see in him? God didn't know he hired a fool?"

Tanzin treaded carefully.

"God, as you have been made aware, is not what you believe it to be. There is much you will learn about this while you are here. The Passion is not merely a book like you would read on The Earth. It is The Greatest Book. It is written in the stars. Some on The Earth plane call it The Akasha. But even what is said of The Akasha cannot be fully realized with the limitation of The Earth languages and forms of communication. The Passion is the blueprint of every soul force and every experience before and within The Entwine. It holds the greatest plan for every life on The Earth. To keep such a book is no easy mastery. Only one writes in this book and SHE is The Creator. Only one can interpret this book and she is the Keeper. The Keeper is in literal terms the translator of The Creator's plan."

"Wait. God really is woman?"

Tanzin smiled.

"I told you. There is much you will learn about the true nature of what you believe God to be."

"Alright. But based on what you just said, that still means Lucifer was a Keeper. Which also means he was closest to The Creator of the Entwine right?"

"It is so."

"Huh. But I guess that's not news. Even the bible says Lucifer was closest to God and then lost his mind and was tossed down to Earth as punishment. Is that how The Fall happened?"

"In essence, yes."

"So the bible got something right then."

"Right is a rather strong word for this conversation, Vessel Kaiwon. Lucifer was brought here to fulfill a specific purpose. He was here like all Sialovehal, to help humans reach an evolutionary state closest to The Stai. His time on The Earth changed him. He lost his sense of that purpose when he gained insight into his own power. When he came to full realization of his capabilities, he became arrogant in a way Sialovehal had long abandoned. He wanted to be The Creator, but of course, that was not his charge for The Earth mission. So he began his own plan to take over The Creator's work and beyond. Foolishly, he sought counsel with other Elders and convinced them that they could overthrow The Seat of Light. The Seat of Light will not be moved and so Lucifer was fallen from this place onto The Earth. He, however, had read from The Passion, had seen the map of the souls and used this knowledge to convert souls in The Entwine from their divine path of evolution, to his own path for them. He constructed Firewah as a reflection of The Heaven, but in opposite. Because that which is not created, cannot be destroyed, he can only influence souls at their place in the Entwine to its opposite. Thus, as I have already revealed, for every soul on path to their divine purpose, there is a soul on path to Firewah. With The Fall came the birth of duality."

"Wow."

That was all Kai could think to say. All of her thoughts and questions and fears started swirling around in her head and then stopped in one spot in the front of her skull. It was the part of her head that wouldn't stop itching. The more she heard, the more painfully obvious it became that she wasn't much closer to 'remembering' anything at all. Her thoughts rested on her mother and her surrogates and so many people she knew or saw or read about in her life. A question flashed in the forefront of her thoughts like a neon sign.

"If what you just told me is truth, how can so many people be so wrong?" It was a throw away question, more rhetorical than anything.

"Indeed." He said.

Kai took a step toward Tanzin, to get a closer look at him, as another less intense question crossed her.

"Is there a reason why my forehead keeps itching?" Kai was rubbing her forehead uncomfortably with the ball of her left hand.

"I have revealed all that can be revealed to you at this time, Vessel Kaiwon. It is important that you rest now."

Before Kai could protest, Tanzin intercepted her question.

"Kaitu is safe. She is in her divine element here. She will return to you when your rest is complete. Osho Lovianhal Sialovehal." He said as he bowed.

12 LIGHT, SAVER

"May the force be with you." ~ Yoda

Powerfully, abruptly, the room went dark. Even though she couldn't see with her eyes, her mind filled with light. At first, there was a massive field of bright green grass and flowers of all colors. Then through her mind's eye she saw a golden key hanging prominently in the sky. Her eyes drifted again to the field. There, walking toward her, she saw a beautiful woman. The woman had long flowing robes made of pure light. The light coming from the woman's skin was almost blinding. It was hard to describe her features. As clearly as Kai could see the woman's face, she could not describe anything about her, except love and beauty. What also puzzled Kai is that instinctively she knew her name. Kwa-yin. She found herself calling out Kwa-yin's name. She ran toward her, but every time she got close, Kwa-yin was suddenly not there. Kai felt Kwa-yin's presence behind her and there she was, but when Kai ran to her, she was no longer there. Eventually Kai got tired of running and decided to lay down to rest. It was then that Kwa-yin was floating above her and spoke. Her voice was like a bell. It was clean and crisp and as bright as the light that came from her skin.

"My child, you are here for a divine purpose. Your purpose here is so great, even one as wise as Tanzin may not articulate it for you. It is you and you alone who can perform the task before for you. Use your gifts. Use your birthright. It is always with you. Do not fear it. You need it for your work. Your spirit is bold, my daughter. Embrace it. Many will try to stop you from your path. They will try to protect you from yourself—that was their role before, but now is not before. Only you will protect you now because you are the key. Always remember this. The one you have born is the doorway. She is the answer to a divine question. Another will be born to you, a son. He is the light to replace the light we lost. He will overcome the darkness. The time is nearing for you to do what you are called to do, Love. Your rest is complete. Be bold. Be YOU. Have no fear. Follow your heart. The answers to all of your questions will be made clear."

Suddenly, the field was gone. The light was gone. So was the darkness in her eyes and mind. Kai opened her eyes slowly. She was in her apartment, in her bed. The light was on and it took her a few minutes to fully get her bearings about where she was. Her house was eerily quiet. She looked around trying to make out if she was really waking up from an intricate dream or if she was still in it. She was by herself. Her room was exactly as she left it. She was equal parts relieved and confused, but she was also infinitely relaxed. She felt refreshed like she had spent a year in a spa. Through the window she saw it was night. She looked over at the clock and it said 2:22am. She also felt like something was missing. Taylor.

Instinctively, she knew Taylor was not in the next room, although she felt this strange desire to confirm her suspicions. She rose from her bed and walked slowly across the narrow hall from her room to Taylor's room. It looked exactly as she left it. Strangely, she heard a rustling in the crib. It was subtle, but it was there. She crept toward the bed hoping that the rustling she heard was just a figment of her imagination. When she leaned over the top of the bed, she thought she saw the face of a baby. It was only for a split second she saw him. His skin glowed from within. His eyes were bright like two lamps. His hair was thick and set on his head like a crown of sunlight. He smiled at her as she reached for him, but he was gone before her hands could touch him. She allowed herself to revel a bit at the possibility that she may have just seen her unborn son. Then she laughed at herself, thinking-- **The son I haven't even conceived yet.** At least she didn't think so. She didn't feel pregnant. She put her hands on her belly to feel for any changes, and then resolved that she was still bat shit crazy. The bed was empty, and that was all she needed to know.

Kai cried so hard her stomach hurt. Her daughter was gone, so that meant she wasn't actually bat shit crazy. Just plain crazy. It also meant that her experience wasn't the dream she'd hoped it was. It also dawned on her that she had no idea why she was home and what she was supposed to do there. Was she supposed to wait around for somebody to knock her up? Maybe Henny was supposed to come back and impregnate her with the next chosen kid. She felt so full and frustrated, she kept crying. At this point, she didn't know what else to do. She missed her daughter. If all of this was real, she knew Taylor was safe. But if all she experienced was just some mind fuck she was playing on herself—she had no idea where her daughter was. She resolved if she actually had a choice of the two evils, she liked the first one better, although, not by much.

She walked back to her room. As she lay upon the thick white comforter that made her bed look like a cloud—she found herself screaming out and up to her ceiling—"Now What?!" At the exact moment her words left her throat, something-- a presence-- a wind of darkness swept toward her. It knocked her clean out of her bed and into the wall behind her. Her head hit the wall hard. Although she didn't lose consciousness, her body lay crumbled on her hardwood floor. She wanted to just lay there. She hoped that whatever got her would go away. After a few minutes of nothing, she found the courage to open her eyes. She saw nothing, so she sat up.

The dark wind swept through the room again. It was taunting her. When it came at her this time, from inside the dark wind appeared a starch white arm with bony fingers attached at the end. Kai swatted at it, but the fingers made its way to her throat and picked her up. Kai was struggling and kicking, but it pulled her all the way up to where the wall met her 9' ceiling. Then it dropped her. She hit the ground on her hip with a loud thud. The pain was excruciating. Kai screamed and then wept softly. The throbbing in her legs made it almost impossible for her to think clearly. She had no idea what was going on and most importantly, she had no idea how she was supposed to get out of this alive.

She stayed on the ground for a long while, sobbing quietly to herself. She felt defeated. She didn't want to get up and face whatever it was that was swirling around her room. She heard the thing laughing at her. Under normal circumstances, this would have made her at least try to posture, but this time, she just didn't care. She thought if she stayed where she was; it would leave her alone and go about some other business. It didn't. It swirled past her again. This time it lifted her by her legs. In one swift gesture on its part, Kai was upside down and on her way toward the ceiling again. She knew what it was trying to do and she wasn't sure she would survive being dropped on her head. Panic rushed her. She was squirming now trying to break her legs free from the bony fingers that held them. With some amount of effort, about halfway up, she freed one leg and used it to kick at the dark swirl. She must have hit something because it let her go. Kai was a few feet from the ground, but somehow she landed in a full handstand.

Like a gymnast, she flipped herself up to standing position. She had no idea she could do that, although she didn't have much time to think about it. The dark thing came at her again. It swirled around her like a cyclone. Kai was swatting at it, hoping to hit it again, but didn't. The more the thing came at her, the more she tried punching or kicking at it. She was growing frustrated and angry. Her panic morphed quickly into helplessness, but she knew she couldn't give up. This thing was trying to kill her and she wasn't at all ready to go to heaven for real. The only thing she could think to do was run. She ran toward her bedroom door, but was rebuffed by the dark swirl when it sent her again flying through the length of her room and crashing into the wall. Kai slid slowly to the floor. It came at her again. Without her knowing or trying, before it got to her, a light began to flicker in the room. This made the dark swirl retreat. When the light went out, the room was quiet.

Kai's head was itching hysterically now, but she continued to ignore it. She was barely able to breathe and she was tired of getting thrown around her room like a rag doll. She was slumped over, head down with the wall literally holding her up. She was standing, albeit barely. Everything that was happening in her head—her fear, panic, sadness—everything was whizzing through her, making her feel dizzy. She heard the wind coming toward her again. This time it was moving slowly. It was being cautious. Kai was too overwhelmed to care. She thought that if it really wanted her this badly, it could have her. And then she thought about Taylor. She could hear her baby's laugh in her ears and then her heart became flush with love. She remembered Taylor's smile and then her body stood up straight, in a power stance. She had stopped thinking completely. The love she was feeling for her daughter began to fill her, exactly like she was a bottle and her love was fluid. It started at her toes and kept pouring into her until she was full, right up to the top of her head.

The dark wind gained momentum and was headed straight at her. Within milliseconds, Kai's head went from itch to burn and from that burn, the contents of Kai's head were about to explode. No sooner than the swirl reached Kai's face, she raised her head and just like a light switch had been turned on in a baseball stadium, a thick rush of pink-orange light poured from a space between her eyebrows and filled the room with a light brighter and more clear than if the sun had landed there.

The dark wind screamed this horrid sound and crumpled into a man at Kai's feet. He had skin the color of office paper, blood red eyes and broken wings the color of ink. He looked up at her, using his arms to shield his eyes from the light. Despite his efforts, the light that had overcome the room was slowly dissolving his skin. He was turning to dust by the light coming from her face. First the man smirked, and then he looked afraid. He spoke as though he were trying to talk over a loud fan.

"I came for the child." He said.

Kai was no longer Kai in that moment. She was in some sort of a trance. She was conscious of what was happening around her, but she could no longer control her movements or her words. She felt possessed, like she was in her body somewhere, but someone else was calling all the shots. She never lowered her head to face the crumpled man. Her head stayed erect as the light poured from her forehead. When she spoke, her voice had an echo to it, like an amplifier had been attached to her vocal chords.

"You will leave without her.", she said.

The winged man cackled loudly, painfully.

"I cannot.", he said.

"You and I know it is not your destiny to leave here at all. At least, not in the same way you came."

Her words rang through the air, bouncing off all of the walls until the whole house shook from them. The winged man continued to cry from the pain the light was causing him. His cry offended the Kai stuck inside of the 'Super Kai'. She wanted it to stop. She wanted this whole surreal ordeal to stop. She didn't sign up for this. She caught herself thinking that she obviously missed the memo that Sialovehal was Tuahstai for Superhero. 'Super Kai' had her own ideas, apparently. She reached down and grabbed the dark man by the throat until whatever weight he may have had, was none at all to her. She raised his limp, cackling body over her head and cocked him back with one arm. She was about to throw him through the wall in front of her. At that moment, Cinqo appeared abruptly and intervened. At the sight of Cinqo, the winged man laughed loudly, tauntingly. Cinqo put his hand over the man's red eyes and they turned black and hollow. He collapsed onto the floor, lifeless. At the same moment he hit the floor, Kai's light went out. When she finally looked down at him, he was nothing more than a pile of fine, gray dust at her feet.

Kai started to regain herself. Whatever had possessed her was gone. She secretly hoped it was on standby in case another of those red eyed winged things was on its way. She looked at Cinqo, not sure if she

88

should be pissed or relieved. Then, without warning, she felt angry. Betrayed. Left to die by the one being that was supposed to be protecting her. Kai looked around her room at all the places she had been thrown or dropped. Her anger swelled. When her eyes finally met Cinqo where he was standing in front of her, she snapped.

"What the FUCK was that about?"

The power in Kai's voice and expression made Cinqo take a few paces back. His tone, however, remained steady.

"That was a Purveyor. Fighting them is futile", he said.

"What the fuck do you mean fighting them is futile? I got my ass kicked, Cinqo. I was thrown around this fucking room like a rag doll and almost dropped on my fucking head. That **THING** tried to fucking kill me! If it weren't for whatever that was that possessed me, there at the end, I'd be the one"—she kicked the dust pile in front of her for emphasis—"laying here on the floor like this."

Cinqo didn't say anything.

"You were here the whole time weren't you?"

She knew the answer already, but she wanted to hear Cinqo say it out loud.

"I am wherever you are Kaiwon."

"You picked the end of it to turn up?! What the fuck are you people thinking about? I CAN'T FUCKING FIGHT! I ALMOST DIED! And then nobody could have warned me before hand—you know, 'Hey Vessel Kaiwon, is it so that you're going to go 'rest', but when you wake up, you'll be in your house and your daughter will be gone, but no worries, a black wind thing is going to try to fucking kill you!"

She lost it. She wanted to lunge forward and strangle Cinqo, but she realized she was too tired to bother. Her attention focused on how she became that person that actually did fight that black wind thing. Cinqo interrupted her thoughts.

"I knew you would handle yourself", he said.

Kai gave Cinqo another seething look, but she was calmer.

"And what if I didn't? What if my light never switched on and he got to me? Then what?"

"You did exactly what you were designed to do and saw everything you were designed to see."

Kai laughed sarcastically.

"What? Was that some sort of test? To see if I could actually handle myself? Like to check if my headlight was defective?"

Kai was puffed up, but she was also a little proud of herself. She never had to defend herself before. Before, she just had to take whatever beating was handed her. Fighting back felt good. She did feel like a superhero. Cinqo interrupted her thoughts again.

"You had to figure out what power you have. He was not that hard to defeat, as you experienced. Purveyors are not fighters really. They are--"

"--Then why didn't you let me defeat him?" As she spoke, her chest deflated a bit.

"Purveyors are simply soul herders. They are like what you would call look outs. You were not equally yoked for battle. Battle is not what you are here to do."

"Does that mean you actually know what I'm here to do?"

Kai was so agitated by the whole thing. Plus, Cinqo's nonchalance to the whole ordeal made her feel worse. She couldn't tell if she wanted to laugh, scream, cry or feel relieved she was still alive.

"It is not my place to tell you what you must find within yourself Kaiwon. I am here as your protector. That has been my charge since you arrived. And yet, protection does not always look as we expect it should. You have much to experience while you are here."

Kai dry heaved. She was so beyond disgusted, she needed to throw up, but her stomach was empty so she couldn't. She felt betrayed and a bit used.

"Why didn't you tell me you were the nurse in the hospital? I never would have figured *that* out on my own, mostly because I thought the nurse was a woman."

"I can take any form I wish in front of Earthbound souls. Remember the dog that came to you when you ran away from your second foster home? The one that led you to the library?"

"That was you too?"

"It was. I handed you to your parents when your mother transitioned..."

Her mouth dropped. She felt like she had just been stabbed with an ice pick. Tears enveloped her eyes and her face felt hot as a crock pot about to boil over. She wanted to scream, but she couldn't even speak. It was a long while before she had any inclination to. She had never felt so betrayed in her life. Finally she mustered,

"YOU!"

"No, Vessel Kaiwon. You.", he said.

His voice was so quiet, it was barely a whisper. The last bit of breath squeezed out of Kai's chest. She remembered Tanzin's words to her. **She co-wrote her journey. She chose all the people in her life to help her learn what she needed for this journey.**

"You were just following orders? You couldn't have warned me about 'my' 'Aunt Myra'?"

Kai's sobs were loud and painful. She remembered that day her parents literally dropped her at Aunt Myra's doorstep and stayed not more than 10 minutes before they hightailed it back to whatever rock they crawled out of. Then they never, ever called or wrote. They just dumped her like a load of laundry. Cinqo tilted his head. He wanted to empathize with Kai's pain, but he also knew what he was revealing to her was what she needed to know and deal with if she was to move on to the next phase of her becoming.

"It is not my place to interfere with what is written Kaiwon. Deep in your heart and mind, you know this to be true. My role in your journey thus far has been to keep you safe as I can, give you encouragement when I can, but most importantly, keep you from the plague that has befallen the Earth and claimed your father. "

"What? No one has ever mentioned my father in any of this. I don't even know the truth about my mother. What about my father?"

"All I can say is that your father was once a great man. Your entire line are great people. They sacrificed much to help so many. Your family has been a blessing to us all. I know that Tanzin told you the parts of your story that he can. It has been made very clear to me that when it comes to your story, I cannot tell it to you. You must unfold it. It must be that way Kaiwon."

"But you said a plague claimed him. What does that mean? What plague?"

"You were told about the anger gene that humans carry."

"I think so. Maybe."

"This gene is actually more like a virus. When the Stai integrated with the humans, it meant that they too could catch it. Your people took every preventative measure they could, but your father was so passionate in his purpose, stubborn really, he thought the only way to truly transmute the anger was to live through it and overcome. He was wrong. Star People are pure, so every integration is a powerful undertaking. The anger took him over completely and changed everything. Not only for The Earth, but for The Stai. You were called here, Vessel Kaiwon, to save him. To take him home to his people. You and your mother cannot return until you do."

"Where is my mother?"

"That I cannot say. Everywhere. Nowhere. I can say, your mother is very much a part of this plan. Until your father is returned to his true home, The Entwine will never have balance. Until The Entwine is balanced, your mother cannot return."

"If I don't even know who my father is or where I'm 'from', how can I return him anywhere? I don't know my mother either, why should I care? Wasn't it she who dumped me with those people to raise me?"

"Your mother has never left your side. Neither have I. We all make sacrifices for those we love. Your family has sacrificed a great deal for a very long time. Longer than any have expected. The Stai leave no one behind. Many have stepped forward to help in this charge of saving your father, but every attempt has been unsuccessful. You've been here many times yourself. But this is the last time, Kaiwon. The damage is... if we cannot return him, everything that The Stai have worked for, will be destroyed. It was a tremendous risk to bring you back again, but you are the last hope for this cause. Everything has been planned immaculately. You are, in part, the architect of this plan. It is only because you do not remember that you say such things. Your unfoldment will clarify everything for you. But it is not my place to force it. Nor yours. It will come with acceptance, but not before. Oshharu Mairahu Nura Osho." He said.

"And Henny? Attempt to make sense out of Henny's point in my life."

"You chose the man who could help you bear your child. That is all.

93

Remember that everything you've experienced has been about balancing The Entwine, nothing more or less. You have one last cycle to do it. I am not privy to the intricacies of what you mean to do; I just know what is written. You must forget the sensory aspects of what you have experienced while here and try to expand your awareness as one who has a great deal to do in a very short amount of time. How would you accomplish what no one could, over eons, within the course of a standard human lifetime? How would you balance a world gravely off balance?"

She didn't know. She didn't know what to think. Now that she was told what all the fuss was about, all she had left was acceptance. But she wasn't ready to accept that she chose a fate she couldn't remember. How could she face what she couldn't remember? Save her father? It sounded preposterous, but at least it was a straight answer. Kai sensed that Cinqo risked a lot to tell her what he did. She was grateful and sad at the same time. She let the last of her sobs take over her shaking body. Cinqo didn't rise to put his arm around her, although Kai secretly believed he wanted to. He simply sat by her until finally, out of sheer exhaustion, she curled up in her beloved Rococo bed, put her cloud-like comforter around her whimpering body and fell into a deep sleep.

13 FIREWAH

"We are each our own devil, and we make this world our hell."~ Oscar Wilde

K ai heard screams in her head. The screams were so loud and so many it sounded like a choir singing a horrible song. She tried to make out individuals in the choir. She tried to make out faint distinctions of voices. She tried to make out what was being sung, but she couldn't. The choir just kept singing and she could not make it stop. The screams got louder and louder in her head until she could take no more and opened her eyes abruptly.

"Cinqo? Cinqo!"

"I am here."

"Did you hear that?"

"I did not."

"You didn't hear those screams? They were so loud, they could have been right here in this room..." Kai looked around frantically, still trying to adjust from sleep to being jolted awake. Her eyes stopped at Cinqo. "It sounded like they were saying something, telling me something, but I couldn't make out what they were saying."

Cinqo turned his head and looked out the nearest window.

"I am not privy to know what is being communicated to you from highest realms. We all have our own message."

"No Cinqo. This was something else. This was... damn. I don't know. It was hot. I could feel the heat on my skin. I could smell the sulfur. I can still smell it. Can't you smell it?" Kai pulled her hair to her face. "See, the smell is still in my hair. Here, smell."

Cinqo raised his arm as if to say "no thanks".

"I will take you at your word. Do you have an idea about what was being communicated through you?" Cinqo was clearly uneasy about this conversation.

"I don't know. There were the screams and this eerie song", she said.

"Think Kaiwon. What does it mean to you? What are your instincts saying of your experience?" He was pulling at something, but Kai didn't know what.

She thought for a moment and then shook her head.

"That's impossible."

"Nothing... is impossible." He said with some effort.

"It was like I could hear into hell. Like... I was *in* hell. I could hear every last soul in hell and they were talking to me like they knew I was there."

Cinqo walked to Kai and looked into her eyes as closely as he could. The non-descript, matter-of-fact everything about him, gave way to genuine unease.

"There are reasons for this, of course. Are you sure of what you are saying?" Cinqo was almost pleading.

"I'm not sure about anything, but you asked me what I think and that's the only thing coming to mind at the moment." Kai said, dreading the words as they left her mouth.

Cinqo turned from Kai so she could not see that his unease was forming into panic, which he was not used to experiencing. Once he gained his equanimity, he turned to face Kai.

"I will counsel with the Elders. For the moment, you will remain here."

"What do you mean, I will remain here? I thought you had to stay wherever I was?"

Cinqo was quiet for longer than a beat. He was torn about something he was not at liberty to say out loud. He looked at Kai and frowned. His sing-songy voice sounded strained.

"Under the circumstances, I am not sure that is best. You are more than equipped to handle yourself in this realm while I am gone."

Kai was confused. And then hurt. She too was quiet for more than a beat.

"You can't leave me here alone Cinqo. You just can't. I feel like something is happening to me..."

Cinqo thought for a moment in silence. He decided to let himself trust, instead of panic. He knew, more than Kai, what she was capable of becoming. It was why she was watched so closely as a child. It was why she was never allowed her light before now. Sialovehal are powerful. Her parents were the ultimate testament of this, perfect duality. Cinqo knew who she was, but instead doubting her, he decided to accept fate exactly as it was to happen. With this intention in mind, he walked over to Kai and placed his hands over her eyes. When her eyes opened, she was in the familiar vastness that she knew now to be The Heaven. She was pleased, hoping someone would bring her daughter to her. Cinqo appeared with Taylor and Kai ran to her. The baby put her arms out and giggled saying "Mai Ma! Osho Lovianhal. Mai Ma!"

Kai had never heard Taylor say anything but Ma. She was barely 6 months old, and yet, she just said a whole sentence in Tuahstai. A part of Kai really wanted to lose it. But after what she had just gone through, she resolved that EVERYTHING is possible. She kissed Taylor and praised her. Taylor giggled loudly and hugged her in her sweet way. A few moments later another familiar voice took over the room. It was Meoshe. She wasted no time.

"Cinqo tells us that you experienced something that has caused you..." Meoshe hesitated, "...alarm. Will you describe this?"

Kai was annoyed because what she was feeling now with Taylor in her arms was far from what she felt and smelled in her bedroom. She didn't want to relive the awfulness. Things began to crystallize when she looked down at Taylor's face and a slight remembrance of what she had experienced with the Purveyor, what she heard in her dream-- that eerie song, and everything Cinqo revealed to her began to haunt her happiness. Her hesitance was replaced with only a touch of purpose that she wasn't compelled to fight. She raised her head and spoke as plainly as she could. She explained everything she remembered about the screams, the song, the heat and the sulfur she smelled and how the smell lingered in her hair.

Meoshe said nothing. She looked less blurry to Kai now, which she thought odd. She made a motion which looked like the hand motion Dr. Spock used in Star Trek. Tanzin appeared in the room and walked toward Kai. There were other Elders with him. She wasn't introduced, but they all greeted her in the way she had become accustomed. Kai didn't have to repeat anything, nor did Meoshe update them on what was just said. Kai just stood in the middle of this large group of strangers until Tanzin stepped forward and looked into her eyes very deeply.

"Were you given an idea of what the things you saw *mean* to you, Kaiwon?"

His emphasis on the word "mean", made Kai cower her stance a bit.

"Yes." She said, straightening her stance. "I was there to see a man about freedom." And then it hit her. "Oh my God", she said. "Before that... right before I woke up at my house and the thing with the Purveyor...I had a dream...it was right after I spoke with you, Tanzin. I saw Kwa-yin."

"You know the name Kwa-yin? She came to you in a dream? He asked interest piqued, dread all but gone from his face.

"I think so. I mean, she didn't tell me her name, I just knew that was her name when she spoke to me."

For the first time, Tanzin looked at Kai with awe. He lowered himself into a full body bow instantly. Meoshe, Cinqo and all of the Elders in the room followed the action.

"What are you doing?" Kai asked, feeling awkward.

"It is time." Tanzin said.

"Wait. Don't you want to hear about the key?"

"You are the key, Vessel Kaiwon." He said as he raised his head.

Tanzin looked squarely at Kai, so she could get a good look at him. She could see him clearly now. He looked almost solid, as he would if he was still alive in human form, but he didn't look human. Not entirely. He looked other-worldly, and yet Kai couldn't really place what about him was different than what she saw when she looked in the mirror. Her inspection of him was interrupted when she noticed she was suddenly surrounded by people of every complexion, in an awesome assembly of bodies. There were hundreds of winged beings alongside hundreds of robed men and women. There were hundreds more of what looked like every day human beings, just like Kai. All of the robed and winged beings were bowing in Kai's direction. All of the humans looked confused. Kai was so impressed with the magnitude of the display, she bowed.

"Osho Lovianhal" she said.

"Osho Lovian Osho". They all said in one accord. And it was done.

14 THE ANGER AMONG US

"Anger dwells only in the bosom of fools." ~Albert Einstein

On Earth, the chaos was mounting. Seemingly normal tasks, like going to the grocery store were exacerbated by daily robberies, fights, and foolishness. Driving to work, for some, ended in death by road rage. Being at work, for some, ended in death for asking to borrow a pencil.

There was an incident that made world news about a young woman and her friend who was killed by her sister's boyfriend. No one knew why when the beautiful 28 year old woman answered her door, she was greeted with a Tec-9 and shot 53 times at point blank range. Her killer then walked through her home and shot anything he came in contact with repeatedly. Her couch. Her dog. Every stretch of her home's walls. When he got to the upstairs bathroom, he shot her 30 year old friend, into Swiss cheese. When he was out of rounds, he dropped his gun and lazily walked out of her home. He then got in his car and drove to his own home. There, he took a Molotov cocktail of pills and lit himself on fire. When firemen put out the fire that consumed his house, they found his remains. The man was laid on his burnt kitchen floor spread eagle, his middle finger outstretched to the ceiling as if to give God 'the bird'. A fireman, angry at the display, broke the finger off and stomped it to dust, which caused a violent fight among investigators at the scene. Weirdly enough, they all fought as though their lives depended on it. It turned out, it did. Out of the fifteen or so beings present at the scene, there were only two survivors. One of them was the home owner's teacup Yorkie, Maximillion.

It was as if anger was the only emotion left in the repertoire of most of the people on The Earth. It was anger so uncontrollable, the news couldn't cover all of the murders, and the broadcasters too began fighting. The people at home watching the news began fighting about what was being shown and anything else that came up.

No one was immune to the anger. All the while, there was a faint sound of laughter in the wind. It was an evil, sinister laugh so loud and yet so quiet in comparison to the out of control rumblings going on in people; they all were unknowingly dancing to the rhythm of it. And he was glad, for his plans were coming to fruition. He had undone all that The Creator had sought to build. He had herded every weak soul on The Earth to toil out of control. To submit to the anger. They danced and danced and he was laughing at them. His laughter taunted them in their peace-less sleep at night and then he laughed some more.

Lucifer did his work within concurrent lifetimes to fulfill his purpose as they all did. He was Stai. They set the standard for the omniverse. When The human race was created, he remembered thinking that it was a beautiful opportunity to do something different. He watched over time as humans suffered by their own fear and ignorance. Tried as they did, it seemed they just liked to be at odds with each other. This intrigued him for some reason. He was one of the first to volunteer for The Integration. He had the blessing from The Seat of Light. It was a many cycles long process. Of course, Lucifer didn't remember any of this. He certainly didn't remember any of his past before he became Lucifer, 'The Elder', 'The Fallen' from 'The Heaven'. The anger makes one forget.

In his first cycle of the integration, he was a simple fisherman. He had a small family that consisted of a wife and a son called Joseph. Lucifer followed his course without incident. His next cycle, he was a king of a small village, called Kuut. At this time, he was called Kutafama. He was both feared and admired. He had immense power and had a knack for acquiring knowledge from all over the world. He was also a great trader who prided himself on the wealth and knowledge his people amassed.

Some say it was Kutafama who was responsible for seeding the first great empire. He was awesome and God-like in the minds of his people and many empires around the world. He had compassion for his people in a way that a father has compassion for his smartest son. The greatest of his people, he elevated in the ranks of his small kingdom and the lesser of his people, he helped develop to their true potential. Kutafama had little patience for mediocrity of any kind.

The Creator was most impressed with the quick elevation of consciousness Lucifer was able to instill in the humans present with him. While he still had much work to do, Lucifer viewed his success as a template for how the integration would work best. Essentially he was instrumental in the earliest Entwine.

Lucifer's third and final Earthbound cycle was that of a slave for a rival kingdom of Kuut—the kingdom was called Kuman. His name was Namorun and while slight in stature; his mind was agile beyond anyone in his village or his masters. He was so clever, he quickly made his way out of bondage and was able to work his way to becoming the right hand to the king of Kuman. He helped that king find his heart of compassion and to release the slaves he had acquired from Kingdoms around the globe. Namorun furthered his cause by helping the king utilize each person's unique gifts to the benefit of both the Kumans and each individual. Namorun had in this life become the master of what is now called the laws of the universe. He had a divine gift for this and was able to translate his instinctive knowledge in ways that benefitted all in his presence.

When his work in this cycle was complete, Kwa-yin asked him to assist her in The Heaven with a group of Stai who acted as the original Elders, but who were not a part of the physical integration. She needed him, most specifically to work on The Passion with her. She counseled with Lucifer often and entrusted him with many secrets. She taught him how to read the stars as she wrote the stories of the souls there. Lucifer was not blind to his power, but he was blind to the anger that he somehow integrated during his third cycle on The Earth. Over time, he mistakenly thought himself as powerful as Kwa-yin, although, that wasn't his charge in The Earth mission. Of course, his purpose stopped mattering and the anger ate away at his more evolved memory. He forgot who he was and created a new self.

Most interestingly, the plague only spread to the male Stai. Exactly eleven of male Elders. Only one female Elder volunteered, although she was not infected, which made twelve. These twelve became known as the Legion of Lucifer. Shortly after The Legion was formed, a battle began in the Heaven between those who sided with him and those who sided with their original purpose. The battle lasted 7 days. Although the Legion of Lucifer was greatly outnumbered, Lucifer was a grand strategist and the Legion caused much damage to The Heaven, The Eden and the Stai who resided in The Heaven. On the seventh day, Kwa-yin cast Lucifer and his Legion to The Earth to heal from the plague. Instead, the plague spread with Stellar force.

Kwa-yin then used the acquired knowledge of the original Earth mission to create the Entwine of Mirth—the Joining of Joy-- knowing Lucifer would do exactly his purpose in The Heaven, but in opposite for The Earth. In time, Lucifer allowed what he learned of Kwa-yin's plan and his anger of defeat to consume him. Kwa-yin and everything she represented became his enemy. He worked tirelessly to destroy any trace of what she represented. He became blinded by what was originally heralded in him as vision. His self-importance led him to become a herder of soul force. He collected and then used these souls to create exact opposites of original intention. He never once imagined that *his* great plan would be a part of an even *greater* great plan. In time, throughout countless ages and lifetimes, the anger that consumed him, consumed The Earth as well.

15 EDEN

Then God said, "Let the land produce vegetation:
seed-bearing plants and trees on the land that bear fruit
with seed in it, according to their various kinds." And it was
so. ~ (Genesis 1: 11 – 12)

Kai was in awe of all the beings in the room with her. Holding Taylor in her arms, she was astounded with all the different emotions that coursed through her. Love, power, elation, sadness, joy, trepidation and "wow!" were all in there.

Kai scanned the room looking to see if anyone was familiar to her. Had she run into any of these people in her life? She recognized only the usual suspects: Tanzin, Meoshe, Cinqo and Yamin. In the moment, she felt particularly alone. She hugged Taylor more tightly and wept quietly. Taylor hugged her back, and said quite clearly, "Mai Ma, Ah Lovian Kai-tu". Kai choked. She was relieved when Tanzin interrupted.

"You are all wondering where you are and how you came to be here. This is not nearly as important as why you are here. While time to explain is of no consequence where you stand now, it is of grave importance for the place you have been called from. Instinctively, in your own individual times, you will know who you truly are when you are returned. Instinctively, you will know what you have been called to do. Each of you has been encoded with knowledge, a fundamental piece of a divine puzzle needed to do your work. This knowledge will lead you not only to each other on The Earth, but through the great battle you have been called to engage. At your core, it is important to recognize that you are Love. It is this Love that will guide your every step. Do not question it. Follow it. Your individual paths will be shown to you like a beacon of light. And as you follow that light, all questions yet unanswered will be made clear. Go now in peace."

Not more than a blink later, the masses of people were gone. Kaiwon, Kaitu, Yamin, Tanzin, Meoshe, and Cinqo were all who remained. Kai wondered why she hadn't left with the others. She was Stellar too, wasn't she? Tanzin intercepted her thoughts.

"You were brought here for a different reason than battle Kaiwon. You have work here left to do."

Kai looked at the vast blankness around her and was confused. Since this was all she'd seen, she thought it was all there was. Tanzin raised his arm and formed his hand in a similar mudra Meoshe used earlier. The blank slate of The Heaven opened into an immense field, like the one Kai had seen in her dream with Kwa-yin. It was awesome. Every color was more vivid than any color she had ever experienced. It wasn't just a field-- there were plants and trees of every variety she had never known existed. They were green and red and gold and purple and yellow and blue and every color she'd never seen before in between. All the colors and varieties reminded her of the garden in that famous movie about the chocolate factory. She wondered at once what the fruits of such trees and plants would taste like. She followed the Elders as they lead her, and took in the richness of what she saw. Above her, she noticed there were "stars" in the sky of every size, shape, and pattern as well as shooting ones. A sun and moon were present at the same time, so it was both night and day at the same time. As they walked, Kai noticed that it was quiet. It was so quiet you could hear the grass and the trees breathing. As she breathed, the foliage around her did too, on one accord with her.

Finally, they came to a massive river that was so clear you could see to the bottom. Through the crystalline water, Kai could see gold flecked sand laying still, glistening in the perfect light all around them. The Elders and Cinqo glided themselves across the water to the other side. Kai and Taylor were to follow. Kai thought to raise the golden robes she was wearing, as not to wet them. She found that she too glided across without a single drop wetting the fabric that touched the surface.

They continued walking until they came to a waterfall like none Kai had ever seen. It was fierce and tame, beautiful and overwhelming. The water flowed like it was sprinkling actual diamonds. It was clear as glass and at the same time, it muted what was behind it.

"This is the place I have been led to show you Vessel Kaiwon." Tanzin said.

"A waterfall?" Kai rubbed her eyes with her free hand.

"It is not just a waterfall. It is now your home while you are here with us." He said.

Kai rubbed her eyes again. She was hoping that the gushing water would transform into something else, but the waterfall remained.

"My daughter and I are supposed to live in a waterfall?"

"Go through it and see." He said.

Kai gave Tanzin a sassy look and then walked through the crystal clear water, fully expecting to be drenched before running into some rocky cave. Instead, she met the other side, perfectly dry. As her eyes adjusted, she saw the room she stood in was made out of pure crystal. It glittered like everything in it was also made of diamonds. The floor was golden sand that felt like silk between her toes. There was a table and two chairs also made of crystal, fresh fruits and vegetables in crystal bowls set on the table. There were rugs of moss that looked like the plushest carpets. As she focused further, she realized that everything she was seeing was from nature somehow. It was her apartment, only greener and far more 'blingy'. It was all so breathtaking. It was peculiar to take in, but very comfortable to her. Of course, there weren't any appliances. There were no books that she noticed, or that she recognized. The room also breathed on its own and had its own source of light that she couldn't see. The dwelling was both massive and cozy at the same time.

Holding Taylor, she walked beyond the main room and there was a bedroom of sorts. Both she and Taylor's beds were made of crystal and the detail was indescribable. There were no sheets, but the mattresses looked like floating clouds, though she did not know what it was exactly she would be laying on. She turned to call out to Tanzin and the others, but they were already next to her.

"This pleases you." Tanzin said.

"This is amazing!" She put Taylor down in her crystal crib. "What is this place?"

"I will assume you do not mean this room."

"You assume correctly, Tanzin." Kai said laughing. "I mean, I thought Heaven was all white walls and no doors. Where have you been hiding all of this?" She used her arms to round out the bigness of what she was experiencing.

Tanzin smiled broadly. It was the first time Kai had seen him smile so big.

"I will say that your presence is most amusing to me at times, Vessel Kaiwon. *This place* is called The Eden." He said.

"Eden? Like in Adam and Eve, Eden?"

"Ahhhh. The famed story of Adam and Eve. Where it was written in the also famed Old Testament that Adam gave up a rib to make his Eve." This time, Tanzin laughed. "The Scribes of old were quite clever weren't they?" He was unusually jovial.

Kai was used to seeing very little emotion, particularly from this Elder. Now Tanzin looked relaxed, like a corporate stiff who had loosened his tie and had a few too many drinks at the company Christmas party. She wasn't sure how she felt about it, but she just went with it.

"I'm not sure I know what a Scribe is. I don't remember you

mentioning them before. Are they a part of the Entwine?" She asked.

"They are not. But they are a part of the grand design, none the less. Scribes are an unusual life force. They write stories that seem to have slivers of truth, but since Scribes are not connected divinely, their writings actually become a perversion of what is actually so."

"I don't understand. I thought all souls start at Mute and evolve or devolve according to whatever choices they make."

"As with all things in the universe, not everything is quite as simple as that Vessel Kaiwon. There are souls who do not choose either. With these souls, they continue to be reborn, and by design, a soul will bring information they gained from past life experience with them to their new lives. Yet, these souls choose not to evolve or devolve. Some of these souls become Scribes. Many are transplants from lesser worlds. To the unevolved Earthbound being, their knowledge will appear to be prophetic. Most is closer to simple prose. There are many books on The Earth written by Scribes. Books that have led masses of people down very... interesting paths."

"Hmm." Kai said. "Are there any on Earth who have written the truth, truth?"

"There is only one Passion. All others have only pieces of, as you say, the "truth, truth". However, the creator uses connected writers called Tellers to disseminate bigger pieces of universal truth through their works. It is easy to tell the difference." Meoshe said.

Kai looked around at her new home as it breathed with her. She took a moment to breathe herself. She felt peaceful. Open.

"I have to ask. If you're all Elders-- and I'm going to assume this is your place of business-- where do you do your work or whatever it is you do...no offense. Don't you have offices or something? Are *your* houses like this?"

"Osho Nai!" Meoshe said with a laugh. "We do not need what The Earth bound souls need to survive. Our offices, as you call them, are the all of The Eden. Under each tree or by each river is a place we perform our purpose for The Creator. How better connected can we be but under all that is here? We can see all that goes on in the universe from any place we choose to look. This dwelling was created for you and Kaitu to feel at home. I am led to add that you may eat of every tree here that you find pleasing. Even..." she laughed, "...the tree of 'wisdom'. You will find no wrath-full God or serpent to dissuade you from your choices of nourishment. Osho Lovianhal." She said.

Meoshe, Tanzin and Cinqo all bowed and then were gone. This left Kai and Yamin looking at each other with equal parts "what in the..." and "now what?" in their faces.

"I was told to stay with you in case you needed anything." Yamin said.

"I thought that was Cinqo's job."

"This is so. However, Cinqo is more of your protector than your confidante. As you probably experienced, it is not in his nature to be good at conversation." He said.

"You'd be surprised about Cinqo. He takes some warming up to, but he has his ways. He's actually growing on me. My question is with you. Are you supposed to be my confidante or my personal spy? You know, to make sure I don't get into any trouble. Are you here to report back to the Matrix when I do?" Kai laughed.

Yamin hesitated.

"I do not believe there is any trouble even *you* can find your way into here. The Heaven is a bit transparent, as I hope you've noticed. There are no secrets, because everything is revealed when it is designed to be revealed. I also do not know what the Matrix is."

"No, I haven't noticed, because everything I ask is answered like it *is* a secret. The Matrix is a movie. So Cinqo goes where if he's not being my protector?"

"I will be honest; I do not know where Cinqo goes. What is a Movie?"

"Make this make sense. *You—an Elder.* Are going to keep *me*—a whatever I am—company—in Eden of all places. Meanwhile, you have no Earthbound needs or desires...you're just here to make conversation? Yeah, right. Come on Yamin. You don't remember movies?! Really? Never mind then." She said.

"I guess so." Yamin said. He didn't know what to respond to.

"You guess so what? About the movie or what you're doing here? Waaaait a minute. You guess so? Not, "it is so?" Are you kidding? You're starting to sound a little more human and a little less Elder, Yamin." Kai laughed, but Yamin did not.

"The truth is, Kai, I've been feeling a little more human and a little less Elder myself. I've been remembering my last life like I'm in it now. I even remember my old name. I mean, my Earthbound name, before I was Yamin."

"What was it?"

"Lani."

"Lani huh? I like that. I knew a guy named Lani once. He was super cute. Great body. I mean... He ran this community center in the really, really bad part of the city. I always thought he was too cute to be that crazy. We crossed paths every now and again, I have no idea why. We ran in totally different circles. He died though. It was so sad. He was shot saving this family from one of those Banger kids. It was such a shame. Last I heard, The Community Center is being run now by some idio-- oh my God. It's you... You're Lani Jones. Oh my God. Oh my God..."

Yamin didn't say or move a thing. Kai had that déjà vu feeling. What was odd about it is there was no way she stood where she was before. She'd never met Elders before. This whole experience happened in her life like a lightning strike. It was all so new to her and yet, so eerily familiar. In a way, she was comforted. But in other ways, she was even more confused. Every question that had been answered had been replaced with new, more complicated questions that needed to be addressed. She looked at Yamin, trying to find traces of Lani in him. He wasn't blurry to her anymore, but she couldn't see the Lani in him either. She was quiet, trance-like, trying to dissect the coincidence she was facing. Though she knew, instinctively, it was no coincidence at all.

16 APPLES

"The revolution is not an apple that falls when it is ripe. You have to make it fall."—Che Guevara

K ai didn't remember going to sleep. She certainly didn't ever in her life expect to wake up on a cloud, but she did. Taylor was sleeping next her, but gurgling and stretching like she was about to wake up as well. Kai's stomach growled. For the first time since this ordeal began, she was ravenously hungry. She remembered the bowl of fresh fruit and vegetables in the outer room, so she got up to get some. Yamin was 'sitting' in one of the two crystal chairs at the crystal table reading what looked like a glass tablet of some sort. Kai was a little surprised to see him, but didn't say so.

"Good Morning, I guess. Do you say good morning or good evening when the moon and sun are always up at the same time?" She asked.

Yamin's face beamed when he saw Kai walking toward him. He tried quickly to finagle some poise. He felt clumsy.

"You now understand the power of Osho Lovianhal, Vessel Kaiwon; It is not limited by circumstance." He said, bowing awkwardly.

"Yes, Elder Yamin. I understand." Kai rolled her eyes as she returned his bow. "Osho Lovian Osho Although, I was hoping we were over these formalities by now."

Yamin stood and gave Kai a deeper bow for his previous awkward one. When he returned to upright position, his eyes locked on hers. He couldn't help himself from staring. She was suddenly more breathtaking to him than any soul he had ever seen. His heart started racing and he couldn't control it. **Wait. My heart is beating?**

Kai noticed that Yamin was being weird, staring at her funny. She couldn't help feeling a little weird herself, so she tried again to make conversation about whatever seemed to be handy. "Have you tasted Eden fruit since you've been here?"

Yamin coughed, breaking his trance.

"I have not. I don't need to eat remember?"

"You haven't even been a little curious about what it tastes like?"

"I have not." He said.

For some reason, it did strike Yamin as odd that he had never wondered what the food in Eden tasted like. He was now curious. He didn't say so aloud, but he watched Kai with even more focus and intention. Without any further hesitation, and glad for the excuse to shut up and look away from Yamin, Kai let her palms roll over the tops of the neatly stacked fruit. As she suspected, the fruit buzzed under her palm, full of electricity. For whatever reason, she closed her eyes and let her hands make her choice for her. They did not disappoint. They picked from the bunch, a large, utterly gorgeous golden colored apple.

She pulled the fruit to her nose to smell it. The smell was more wonderful than she could have imagined. It was sweet and fragrant like an apple blossom. And the electricity coming from it was indescribable. She was magnet, it was metal. Kai bit into the apple and juice poured from the first bite. The apple juice was sweet and felt like rivers of clean, clear water hitting her tongue after she had spent years of her life in the desert with none. As she chewed the meat of the fruit, she was overcome by the texture. It was unlike anything she had ever put in her mouth. There really was no way to describe it. All she knew was that after a few bites, she was both satiated and full, feeling utterly beautiful and contented. Her breasts felt ripe and ready for Taylor to nurse. Kai sat in the crystal chair staring into the sky above her. Everything she saw was beautiful. Her vision was so clear; she thought she could see through things to their truest form. Even her heart was full. She felt so much love, she thought she might cry.

Yamin had watched Kai's entire Eden apple experience with his mouth open and practically watering. It was like he just experienced everything she had. The flavors, the textures, the satiation and the fullness. As Kai sat looking at the beauty above her, Yamin sat looking at the beauty in front of him. He shook himself out of it, when he heard Kai speak to him.

"Soooo." Kai was hazy and giddy like she was high. "Are we like roommates or something?"

Yamin choked.

"You are wondering why I am still here?"

Kai almost sounded drunk.

"You're a genius. You said you would be my confidante earlier, but I didn't hear that roommate was a part of the package. Will you be moving stuff in?"

"Stuff?" He asked, not sure of the context she was using.

"Never mind. What are you reading?"

"This is a lesson tablet. I am reading some of the wisdom passed down to me from my Elder."

"Is that right? Do you have to take a test after each one? Do you get graded? Do you have to write papers on your Elder's lectures?" Kai was laughing. She was also flirting. It didn't go unnoticed.

Yamin looked uncomfortable. His spirit face was flush; at least it felt that way to him.

"I am not sure what you mean. I am a Neo; my only task is to learn what is taught and to do what is asked of me."

Kai laughed and stood up. She was now full of a new emotion she hadn't felt in a long time. She wanted to be close to Yamin. To touch him. To see what an Elder felt like on the tips of her fingers. She wondered if he was as electric as the apple. She moved slowly toward Yamin as she spoke.

"I'm beginning to understand why everyone speaks so matter-of-factly around here. Your life is boring as I don't know what."

Yamin had an idea of what Kai was doing and he too moved from his seat, but in the opposite direction. He didn't want to seem obvious, so he attempted to give the impression whatever he had to say was of grave importance and required his walking as emphasis.

"What may seem boring to you Kaiwon is actually a great responsibility. You will come to this understanding in due time when you are called to Keeper." He said.

Kai sobered instantly and rolled her eyes. Yamin looked relieved.

"Yes, a greatly boring responsibility of sitting under trees and counting stars. I truly cannot see myself up here in whatever 'afterlife' you all think you've mapped out for me, doing any of what you do. One thing I do know for sure. I am not built for it." She said.

"You are speaking as a being that has been entrenched in the human experience. Once you remember your truest nature, you will do what is designed for you."

Kai laughed so loudly the trees outside their dwelling shook.

"I'm sorry. Have we been properly introduced? I highly doubt it, but we'll go with it for now if it makes you feel better. I think I'll go check on the Taylor." Kai giggled some more and strode off to the other room.

Yamin found his place again at the table. He was trembling. He was also intrigued by Kai's words and her confidence in using them, considering where they were. He was feeling something course through him that he did not recognize. His heart, which he did not have in his current spirit body—was in fact, racing. His face felt flush, his palms felt sweaty and he felt sick to his spirit stomach. **What is happening to me?** He felt the need to leave the waterfall dwelling and seek counsel with his elder, Elder.

17 AWAKENING

"A Poet knows himself only on the condition that things resound in him, and that in him, at a single awakening, they and he come forth together out of sleep." ~Jacques Maritain

Tanzin knew why Yamin was before him, but waited for him to speak. Yamin was barely composed.

"I must admit, Wise One, I do not feel myself. But rather, I feel a bit like a former self and I am wondering if being in the presence of the Sialovehal is causing this... to happen to me."

"It is." Tanzin said, matter-of fact.

"May I counsel with you... about... why this is happening?" Yamin let his final bit of poise wane, like the last bit of air leaving a deflated balloon.

"Yamin, there are many things that are to be revealed to you when it is time. It is not yet time." Tanzin said, as gently as he could.

"Must I then continue to stay at the side of The Vessel Kaiwon, even in the event that my duties as an Elder may be compromised?"

Tanzin was not at all alarmed by Yamin's words. In fact, he was even more amused with Yamin than he was earlier with Kai. He spoke carefully.

"There is nothing in your chest to fear, son."

"It is what is in my chest that I fear. I can feel my heart beating— racing. I am not still human. I have no heart to speak of in this form." Yamin's voice was just a hair below the yelling mark.

Tanzin raised his arm and opened his own 'palm' in the direction of Yamin's chest. He didn't need to touch him to feel there was a heartbeat. He pondered how to explain to the Neo Elder what was happening to him.

"I am lead to tell you that what you are experiencing is a part of divine design. Whatever you feel, you must feel and whatever you do not, you must not. Go to her and allow divine will to manifest." He said.

Yamin was more confused than outraged. His face was hot and throbbing, like it might explode. Still, he did not break ranks of his Elder's counsel. He was too upset to think straight, so he gave Tanzin a quick bow and left. Soon, he was outside of the waterfall dwelling. He stared at the crystal water of the waterfall for some time. He doubted his desire to go through it so powerfully that he stayed outside for as long as his own will would allow. He was afraid. None of what was happening to him was in league with anything he had been taught. The words **Oshharu Mairahu Nura Osho** swept across his mind. They were her words, but she didn't remember. A part of him wanted to find out what his role was. Another part of him was too afraid to ask the question. **Fear Lights a Man's Way to Darkness,** He thought. He shook his head. It took more energy than he hoped, but he found the courage to walk through the waterfall and do as his Elder counseled him to.

18 AS ABOVE, SO BELOW

"That which is Below corresponds to that which is Above, and that which is Above corresponds to that which is Below, to accomplish the miracle of the One Thing..."

~Hermes Trismegistus

On Earth, at the precise moment Yamin was dealing with a mounting inner conflict, the Stellar began to convene in a place called Cathedral. No one was able to say exactly where Cathedral was, or in which town they found themselves. It was a mystery to them how they found themselves there at the exact same time and place. Yet, there they all were. Hundreds, maybe thousands of them piled into this little church, and to their surprise, they all fit comfortably. Side by side they filed in and took their seats on the ornate, red velvet cushioned pews. The individual lights that guided them there, were like tiny spotlights in an audience of an enormous theatre. They did not speak to each other. The only sound heard in the room was the sound of the rustling of bodies taking their seats. Once they were settled, they waited. The smell of old church stone walls and recently burned sage filled their nostrils. Their hearts were beating in intense rhythms. Their ears were ringing with anticipation. They were waiting for what would come next for them. After a long while, a young Stellar with broad shoulders and chiseled features, stood up.

"We are here!" He said. His voice echoed through the church.

No one answered.

"We are here!" He said again, but louder.

No one in the audience made a sound.

"We are—"an old voice cut the young man off.

"--I know you're here son, now sit down and pipe down, if you don't mind."

The room gasped. They wondered as a group who would come out of the shadows to address them. They heard the slow, disjointed sound in the distance. **Slide, pop. Slide, pop.** The sound grew closer, until the pop, sounded most like a squeak. Finally a small, frail man in colorful and other-worldly ceremonial robes entered the sanctuary from behind the alter. His hair was pure white. His skin was pale and wrinkled. His features were gentle and wise. His eyes were bright and he walked with a short wooden stick that was intricately detailed with carvings that looked ancient. The little, slightly hunched over figure, hobbled across the alter to the front of his audience. Like a seasoned conductor, he raised his walking stick to the stained glass covered dome above them. The stick glowed from within until a single stream of bright light shot from the tip and took off on its own. It bounced from corner to corner of Cathedral, over the tops of their heads and under the pews. When it had touched every crevice of the room, it rose to the center of the dome and spread out like an omnipresent blanket. It filled the room with a clean, bright light. The cold Cathedral was at once, filled not only with a warm glow, but also a glowing warmth. When this was done, the little man lowered his walking stick back to the floor and he leaned on it like it was the only thing holding him up. He looked around the room at all the faces and soaked them in. He had waited his whole life for this one moment in time. He breathed that moment in before he spoke.

"You can never be too careful." The old man's voice crackled like a fire on its final embers. He voice was raspy and yet clear in a way that nothing he said could be misunderstood. He continued. "I should mention that contrary to popular belief, there is no safe place for you on The Earth. A church might actually be the least safe place for you... maybe even a touch cliché, if you were to think about it hard enough." He chuckled. No one in his audience laughed. He cleared his throat. "This place you sit is the oldest of all the old churches in the entire world. No masses are held here, I'll tell you. It just sits here, unassuming. A backdrop of this town, forgotten by most, hidden in the shadows of modern life. It bustles this night. It's bosom embracing this very moment in time. It's waiting over, I in it, for the day when you all would come to convene. It is truly amazing how things come to be. I know you are wondering who I am." The old man stopped to clear his throat again. It sounded like a series of wheezing hacks. "I have been called many names in my lifetime. Or should I say, in this lifetime. Lately, I have been called Devascus. I am a priest in theory, which is why I wear the robes. However, I am not a mere priest. I have studied under many great thinkers throughout the ages. Some of these thinkers have been charged with insights into the universe, its meanings-- and where you ALL fit into the scheme of that understanding. As it is above, so it is below". He paused to catch his breath. He chuckled this time at his body's frail nature, and then continued. "You are not who you seem to be. You were created to fight an evil that is consuming the Earth. Right now. Around us. As we speak in this place. For this moment in time, you may rest here. We are protected for a time by a power the evil we're dealing with can't yet see--"

"--What does the evil want?" a woman's voice rang through the air.

Devascus laughed and repositioned himself on his walking stick. He answered with a slow head shake.

"To be God, child... it wants to be God. I know you all have questions and it isn't my nature to be vague. I must say, however, that because there are so many of you with so many different purposes here, I can't even begin to help you decipher it all individually. I am told that as you rest here, your individual talents will be developed and your dreams will begin to unravel what it is you need to know. The fact that you all made it here is a miracle unto itself. You should use it as your first realization that divine design is working. A few of you will stand out as leaders of the lot. It may not be made clear right away, but it will be made clear." The old priest raised his walking stick again. "--Oh, if you don't mind, would you all stand up a moment please?"

The rustling began again in the quiet church as the Stellar—each tall and ageless with strong bodies-- rose and stood in one accord.

"Thank you so kindly." Devascus said.

He lifted his walking stick above his head, although it looked less like a walking stick and more like a wand of some sort. He circled it over his head in slow rings. The rings got wider as he rounded out the shape of an 'O' with the stick. Light circles formed from his movements until there were rings the size of the room over their heads and then those circles formed a kind of cyclone of light that rushed to the ground and spread out around them. The Stellar followed the light as it dropped, but when the rings of light hit the floor and then dispersed; the church sanctuary had been transformed into an even bigger room with comfortably made beds throughout. Each bed was different and there was one next to each person.

"You may take the bed closest to you, for ease and grace purposes." Devascus said.

Everyone looked amazed at how effortlessly the church had evolved before their eyes and the whispers among them echoed against the cathedral walls.

"Okay, okay young ones." The whispers and rustling stopped. I know you all must be quite hungry.

A young woman in an unusual nun's habit appeared. She had the stature of all the others in the room, but her demeanor was a bit shy. Her head was not held as high as those she looked upon from the alter-- which was the only thing of the old church that remained the same.

"Ahhhh. There you are child. This is Yoko. You are welcome to follow her to the hall downstairs and have yourselves a bit to eat before retiring for the evening. I cannot promise after this night what will be revealed, so..." he chuckled, "I would partake in any and everything offered you." He said with a bow. Then he and his walking stick hobbled

122

out of the room. All that was left of his presence was the **Slide, squeak**; and then the **Slide, pop** that faded slowly down a long hallway.

"You may follow me." Yoko said, meekly.

She gave a quick bow and stepped off the alter. She walked through the room of beds and the people standing next to them toward the front of the church. She made a quick left and disappeared. The Stellar, in succession, made their way to catch up with the shy, but quick nun. They walked a long, warmly lit hallway. No sight of the nun. They came to an open door and a set of steps. The steps started out plain, but as they traveled down, they were red and had unique carvings that grew more intricate as they continued. At the bottom of the stairs, which was also warmly lit, was another door, which was closed. The Stellar in front, Micah, opened the door. There was a warmer and even brighter light that washed over him and those directly behind him. He walked in slowly, with his mouth gaped open. There were about a hundred or so nuns scurrying around immaculate tables-- hundreds of them, enough to seat every Stellar present. The food smelled fantastic. The room was bright and massive. A subtle music was playing. It didn't take long for them to figure out it was the nuns singing. It sounded like a Buddhist chant: **Om Namo Rah Om. Om Namo Rah Om.** The nuns kept singing as though they were possessed by the tune. They greeted each Stellar with a smile, but never stopped singing. **Om Namo Rah Om.**

Each Stellar took a place at the tables and were not inspired to speak to each other. They were served and they ate until they were full. Yoko guided them back upstairs and the Stellar retired for the evening. The song of the nuns filled their heads as they slept. No one could remember the faces of the nuns, or even what they ate. All they remembered was the song. **Om Namo Rah Om.**

Micah roused from his sleep to see a bright figure floating above his bed. He did not startle. The being looked familiar to him. As his eyes adjusted to her light, he could see her more clearly. She spoke to him in her crisp bell-like voice.

"There are seven of you in all who will lead the ALL into battle. The battle is brewing around this place. They know you are here and you will invite them in." And then she vanished, her light with her.

Micah sat up in his bed and looked around the room. He saw all the Stellar in beds around him, deep in sleep. Walking toward him from out of thin air a man in white robes neared his bed. He could not place his face and he could not tell if he was young or old or describe his facial features. There were others like him in similar garb. Each one had a Stellar walking behind him or her. The man in robes motioned for Micah to rise and follow him. Micah did as he was beckoned and took his ranks behind the man.

They walked toward the front of Cathedral. The old, elaborate church doors caught Micah's eye. His heart sank, thinking he would have to open those doors now and begin fighting some unknown evil that lurked outside. He was relieved when the man in front of him turned left as they had earlier, for dinner. They walked down the same warmly lit hallway and through the same door, which was still open. They walked down the intricately carved red stairs and through the same closed door he had opened earlier. The room was now dark and much smaller than it had been when they were eating. There were no nuns singing and it appeared to be just a regular room. They literally could only see a foot or so in front of them as they walked to what Micah assumed to be the center of the room. The man Micah had been following lifted his arm and twisted his hands into a gesture of some kind. Warm light filled the room. They realized they were no longer in a church, but in a field.

Where they stood, the grass was the greenest that any of them had ever seen. The sky was so clear you could see the trees and foliage breathing in and out in one accord. Micah heard a faint singing in the background which sounded like the nuns from earlier. As the singing got closer, they could see legions of winged spirits floating above them. They were singing **Om Namo Rah Om** over and again until the sky was filled with their song. The winged spirits circled the standing 14. When this was done, the robed spirits stepped out of their weave between the Stellar, and formed a tight cluster of 7. This left the Stellar also in a cluster of 7. They faced each other in silence until the robed man who had brought Micah with him spoke.

"Osho Lovianhai. I am Nafi." he said as he bowed.

When Nafi nodded, the others introduced themselves one by one like robots on cue. They all looked similar and their features indescribable. The only thing that distinguished them was the obvious male and female sound of their voices. They each bowed when they spoke.

"Osho Lovian Osho. I am Rala", a female said.

"Osho Lovianhai. I am Kalan", a male said.

"Osho Lovian Osho. I am Reeir", said another male.

"Osho Lovianhai. I am Ceefi", said another female.

"Osho Lovian Osho. I am Kiru", another male said.

"Osho Lovianhai. I am Meeuu", said the last male in the cluster.

After all of their names were spoken, the winged spirits bowed, but never stopped singing. ***Om Namo Rah Om***.

Nafi nodded at each of the Stellar when he spoke their names aloud. He did this as if introducing them to themselves.

"You are Micah, Ree, Talon, Yoko, Leelu, Maya, and Teerah".

Micah was the first of the Stellar to speak.

"You know us, but we don't know you." He was polite, but stiff.

"We are Guardians. Your Guardians. We have known you for all of your lives, been with you since your birth and guided you to reach your truest potential. We are together now as warriors of light. We are here

125

to fight this war alongside you." Nafi said.

Micah frowned.

"What is this war? Why are *we* chosen to fight it...and for whom?"

Rala stepped forward.

"This war has been written here on The Earth through the ages as different things. The Apocalypse. The End of Times. The End. In The Passion it is written as Chaya. Life. We are here to fight for the life of the ALL." She said.

Kiru stepped forward and looked intently at The Stellar.

"You were not chosen for this task...you chose this task." He said.

Talon was much taller than the other Stellar and more stealth. His hair was blonde, his skin dark, his features warrior-like, his voice deep and words calculated.

"If we chose this task, why are we just hearing about it now? Why have we not been prepared for it sooner?' He asked.

"Your entire existence in this lifetime and all the lifetimes before now has prepared each of you uniquely for what you will be called to do when the time comes. You each have individual gifts necessary for the execution of our divine purposes here." Kalan, Talon's Guardian said.

Ree had dark curly hair that she pulled into a tight bun on the top of her head. She was taught and muscular. Her skin was naturally tan and her intense, almond shaped eyes made her look as though she could see through walls.

"Out of the hundreds that are asleep upstairs, why are we the only ones down here talking to you?" She asked.

"You do not remember now, but when the time is right, you will. Those asleep upstairs have their own destinies that are at once individual to them and bound by what we speak. We ALL know what to do when the time comes. The soul force that lives inside your human form is not new to your current body. Yours, Ree is as old as time. Your soul force has been longing for the day when you may face what is upon us now." Kiru said.

They all looked at each other sheepishly, not entirely sure what the Guardian's words meant for them. They got the sense however, that whatever was being said was not meant to be argued. It was already a cause set in motion and they would do better to listen and figure out what was required of them than to protest. Yoko was tall and slender. She appeared Asian at first glance, but her ethnicity, like most of the other Stellar present was somewhat ambiguous. She was also the most timid of the seven. It took her some effort to speak, but, standing in the middle of all that was happening around her gave her more courage than she'd ever needed. Her back straightened as she formed her words.

"You say you have been with us all of our lives. Why are we just meeting now?" She asked.

"We have met, Yoko. You just don't yet remember." Ceefi said.

"Who are they?" Leelu, the shortest of the seven, but clearly the most esoteric, with her blue black hair and dark eye makeup, motioned to the sky at the winged beings surrounding them in song.

"They are Seraph. They will go to battle with us when it is time." Kiru said.

"Is there a name for what we are? I mean, I know you said if we don't know, we'll find out and everything, but are we called something specific like they are?" Maya asked, pointing up at the Seraph.

Maya was the youngest of the seven and the most overcome by everything she was seeing. She was suffering from a bit of sensory overload, but she didn't want anyone around her to notice.

"You are The Stellar among woman and mankind. Human form angels. You are the front line of this Great War that has been foretold on The Earth as it is in The Heaven. You are warriors of life itself." Meeuu said.

His vocal gate was as clear, deep and lingering as a gong. As if on cue to Meeuu's words, the Seraph began to sing louder. They were the soundtrack to what was being discussed below them. Each of the Guardians took turns explaining the true nature of The Stellar and the history of Lucifer and what they knew of the war. It could have been days they were in the field-- Stellar asking questions and their respective Guardians answering as they were led.

All the while, the Seraph sang **Om Namo Rah Om.** The Guardians knew the true reason the Seraph were in the sky singing. They were there to put distance between the war and themselves until all The Stellar were awake. The Seraph song was like a divine signal scrambler that formed a cloud around the church and protected them from what was lurking just outside Cathedral walls. Outside of Cathedral it sounded like booming thunder claps. Inside was the beautiful chorus of winged angels.

A dark wind began to swirl on the street in front of Cathedral. Although the old church was set far back from the street, hidden behind ancient and yet vibrant trees wearing year round blooms, the swirling darkness found it easily. The bright white and pink flowers glistened in the moonlight like semi-precious stones. Wherever the dark wind swirled, the flowers dulled and then wilted.

The branches of the trees drooped as the dark swirls became greater in number. Finally, the cool night was thick and opaque with them. Then the crows started cawing, followed by the sound of heavy wings approaching. The bare street in front of the hidden church grew into thick darkness, like smoke before a fire-- from the ugly presence forming there.

19 TRANSFORMATION

"Every genuine boy is a rebel and an anarch. If he were allowed to develop according to his own instincts, his own inclinations, society would undergo such a radical transformation as to make the adult revolutionary cower and cringe." ~John Andrew Holmes

K aiwon had just finished feeding Kaitu and set her in her crib when she noticed Yamin in the doorway of their room looking at her. He stood very still with a strange look on his face. She wanted to ask him what was wrong, but she wasn't sure she really wanted to know. She could tell Yamin was changing and she could tell that he could tell.

"You're still here. I knew for certain I scared you away." She said.

Yamin snapped out of his brooding trance and countered Kai's sass with his own.

"You can't scare away a warrior. You gotta come harder than that." He said.

Kai looked at him funny.

"What?" He asked.

"Is that any way for an Elder to speak to somebody?"

Yamin frowned.

"Did I say something wrong?"

Kai's sass melted into caution.

"No. Not necessarily, I've just never heard you talk so... regular before. I'm used to all the "thou arts" and "thou shalts" and "it is so". Now you're speaking about warriors and "come hards" like you... I dunno. Are you feeling okay?"

Kai had completely forgotten that she knew Yamin's last Earthbound identity. Yamin blew out a loud, lingering sigh and then was quiet. He was pondering the many boiling thoughts in his head.

"Kaiwon... Kai. What if I told you something was happening to me that is completely impossible, but still...is happening anyway. What if I told you that I'm changing? That I'm supposed to change. I still have no idea why, but a part of me that is dead, literally dead, is coming back slowly--without my really wanting it to. What would you say to that?"

Kai thought about Yamin's words carefully. If she were having this conversation with him at home, under different circumstances, she would probably look at him like he was some kind of crazy and walk away without giving it or him another thought. She considered that so many impossible things had happened to her already. The fact that she was even standing where she was—in a waterfall apartment in Eden-- was way more than what anyone, even she, would consider possible. If she tried to make sense of it based on what she was used to experiencing, she was good and crazy. She looked at Yamin with understanding in her eyes.

"I would say...that everything is possible. I'm living proof of that. What's bothering you Yamin?" She said.

Yamin sighed again, but this time it was a sigh of relief. He looked at Kai and wanted nothing more than to hold her in his arms, smell her hair and feel his arms wrapped around her. He knew his efforts would be futile, so he didn't. He knew he was not a man with the kind of physical body that could hold her, no matter how much he wanted it. **Or could it?** He shook the notion out of his mind and tried to find his train of thought.

"I've been remembering things from my last Earth life. I'm pretty sure of where I was born. I remember my mom and...I have a younger brother. I think his name is Jessie. My mom...her name is Carla. My dad...died when I was three. I helped raise my brother. My mom re-married to John... and I have sister too—her name is Carmen. I remember the day when my mom told me I was adopted. I was angry, got into trouble." He said.

As he spoke, excitement grew in his voice like a series of eureka moments happening for him at once. Kai was as breathless and as excited for Yamin as he was.

"Are you supposed to remember all that past life stuff? Isn't that against some Elder rule, passed down to you from your Elder Tanzin, as it is written in the Great Book of The Passion, as thus was dictated by The Creator?" Kai had exaggerated her body to look and sound like Tanzin and laughed. "It's bad enough you know your old name. Did you tell anybody besides me what you remember?" Her voice went from giddy to somber in less than a beat.

"No. I wouldn't even know how to start that conversation with Tanzin. I mean, I tried to tell him about some other stuff that's been happening, but he gave me that same "you must seek within yourself for the answer" that he always gives. Yamin too, exaggerated his body to imitate Tanzin.

Kai started to laugh and then settled on a reluctant smile.

"At least I know we understand each other." She said.

Yamin looked Kai square in the eye.

"I think... the rules are changing, Kai. At least for me. I haven't the slightest idea why, but I know something is happening. Something...really, really impossible." He said.

Kai got lost in her thoughts. She was looking at Yamin like he was an interesting sculpture in a packed museum. She felt like in order to truly see him, she had to get past all the circumstantial things around her and walk on her tippy toes to see over the tops of people's heads. As she looked at him with some effort, she noticed that his once non-descript features were becoming more clear. She could make out his strong jaw and his cheekbones. She could place his perfectly designed nose and his full lips that looked like softly bronzed clouds. She noticed he had hair and it was a dark, thick pile of curls on his head. His teeth were so straight and white. He really was gorgeous. Kai couldn't help but be startled. Yamin literally transformed before her eyes. Only, Yamin wasn't Yamin anymore. He was Lani Jones. Kai took a step back.

Lani took a step forward.

"What's the matter? Did I say something to scare you?" He said.

Kai was speechless. Breathless. She thought that maybe it was the Eden apple she ate earlier, but right now, she wasn't so sure. Lani smiled when he spoke and this captivated Kai for some reason. She could also see his chest bulging a bit, pressing against the robes he wore. She could see his strong hands uncovered when he raised his arms. He spoke now with his hands, as the Lani she knew had. Her eyes crept back up to his.

"I can...see you." Kai said. She spoke so softly, she could barely hear herself.

"What's that?" Lani asked.

"I can see you." She said.

"Of course you can see me. I'm standing right in front of you." He said.

"No. I can seeeeeee you. Like when I knew you before. You look like Lani, the man, not Yamin the Elder, the non-descript person." She said.

It took a minute for Kai's words to sink in. He took his time raising his arms so he could see his hands. Once he did, for the first time in a really, really long time, he noticed their shape and size. He noticed his fingers and nails and the veins that stuck out a bit on his hands, as a beacon of his natural physical strength. He made his hands into fists and then opened and closed them again and again. Kai walked over to him quietly, not sure if what she was about to do was what she should do. Before she could talk herself out of it, she was so close to him, she could feel his chest heaving in and out against hers. The two breathed together in silence. Kai, eyes closed, raised her hands slowly, and touched Lani's face. His skin was smooth as silk. She moved her hands along his jaw and allowed her elegant fingers to brush over his mouth as if guided by an unseen force. There was electricity between them. The skin on her hand meeting the skin on his face felt like magic. Their hearts raced at the same time. He, with some hesitation, put his arms around her and held her as tightly as he could. She let her head rest on his chest and sighed. This was the most comfortable Kai had felt in a really long time. Lani interrupted the silence. He spoke slowly. He was listening to the sound of his own voice with his human ears.

"You know what?" He asked, peeling Kai from his chest and pulling her gently in front of him. He took her hands into his hands, kissed them softly. Kai quivered as a jolt of electricity pulsed through her.

"What?" She asked, rousing from her comfortable head position. She was a bit annoyed by the question.

"I'm starving! I've got to eat something, like right now. I feel like I haven't eaten in a thousand years." He said playfully.

Kai laughed.

"Okay. But for the record, none of this is any of my doing."

Lani turned to Kai. His face went from playful to serious with the furrow of his brows.

"Sure it is." He said matter-of factly.

He let his words linger in the air like smoke after a fire. Then he turned and b-lined it for the crystal table that held the crystal bowl of Eden fruit. Kai stood in the same spot where Lani left her. His words were still ringing in her ears. She wasn't sure what he meant, but whatever it was she didn't like it at all. Nor did she like the implication that she could make him human. That was simply ridiculous, she thought. After a few moments of watching him work through the bowl of vegetables and fruit at the table, she resigned herself to lie down and rest. She didn't know if he noticed when she left. At the moment, she didn't care.

Cinqo's face formed a tight scowl. He was hidden to them, but present none the less. He whisked himself into the breeze he formed, unable to decipher why he felt anything at all. Practically in a huff, he adjusted from breeze back to his more solid form. Quickly he honed in on his destination. He walked casually toward Meoshe and Tanzin who were seated by a large fruit tree adjacent to the river called Tosher. The two were deep in counsel. Tanzin turned as Cinqo drew closer. Without being asked, Cinqo spoke.

"Yamin's transformation is complete. He is in his full human form. Again." He said.

"Is that so?" Meoshe sounded pleasantly surprised.

"It is." Cinqo looked agitated by Meoshe's tone.

Meoshe, noticing Cinqo's demeanor looked over to Tanzin with concern, but did not respond. Tanzin rose from where he was seated and began walking. He motioned for Cinqo to follow him. The two walked a bit before Tanzin said anything.

"The Vessel is supposed to affect us while she is here. It is part of a great plan that Kwa-yin alone knows the outcome." Tanzin said.

Cinqo looked at Tanzin, but did not speak.

"We are not privy to know how or when the effect will take place in us. Our only charge to accept *all* and allow it to be." Tanzin continued.

Cinqo looked as if he wanted to say something, but his thoughts were clouded to him. Strangely, Tanzin could no longer read Cinqo's thoughts, so he could not intercept them. Without another word Cinqo became his breeze form and was gone. Tanzin walked back to Meoshe. She didn't need to say aloud that she shared his trepidation about Cinqo. She knew as Tanzin did that Cinqo was turning. Into what they could not be sure. The two were very clear however, that whatever was happening on The Earth, so it must in The Heaven.

20 A CATHEDRAL...

"Put three grains of sand inside a vast cathedral, and the cathedral will be more closely packed with sand than space is with stars." ~James Hopwood Jeans

Cinqo found himself on The Earth, blocks away from Cathedral. He allowed his form to breathe so he could feel the cool Earth air through his less subtle body. He was pondering and brooding at the same time. Of all the charges he took on as Angelic, he had never been affected as he was with Kai. He could not understand what was happening to him. He sensed something. He wasn't sure if it was in him or he was about to walk up on it. He felt a darkness hovering above him as he walked. Instinct, though slow to find him, drew him to his breeze form and he was gone. What he had not seen was the darkness coming toward him from every angle. They were making their way to devour him with one dark gulp.

Meanwhile, Lucifer sat at the top of Cathedral's dome, legs straddling the massive cross that adorned the top. He looked down among all of the dark beings as they collected in front of the church. He was riveted by the display. He alone had accomplished this enormity. He alone had accomplished this evil.

"Some Creator you are." He said loudly to the sky. "Some Creator you are to allow me to accomplish **this** madness. I am mere steps away from beating you at your own game" He said.

He was talking to the sky in part, but to himself mostly. Lucifer's importance grew in him leaps and bounds. He knew he was only days, hours, minutes, and seconds from fulfilling his dream. He was going to rule over The Heaven and The Earth and then overturn The Seat of Light. More importantly than that, he was going to let Kwa-yin have all he believed she was due. He didn't really care about the souls. He cared about winning. He cared about divide and conquer. He cared about revenge. He let out a grave laugh that rang throughout The Earth like the final gong from that old television talent show. The sound made babies scream in pain. People all over the world held their ears with their hands to escape it, but there was no escaping. At least, it seemed that way at the time.

Cinqo heard the laugh and knew what it meant for those who convened inside Cathedral. In his breeze form he approached the church from the back and made himself inside. The Stellar were still asleep. These beings, the front line of a mysterious battle, were in transition from who they were as unknowing 'humans' to who they were designed to be in their true Stellar warrior form. In their sleep they were evolving quickly. Each of their encoded messages was unfolding as they slumbered. In their dreams, their destinies were being told to them. Essentially, in their sleep, they were awakening. Cinqo knew that when they rose, the battle would be underway. He also knew his divine place at this moment was not where he was. It was with his charge, far from where he stood now. In spite of the divine call that was ringing in his very essence, he could not make himself go to it. He was overcome with rapture. This, to him, was more like a rupture happening at his core.

Despite what he knew was about to happen in this church, he could not place his mind anywhere but where it was at the moment. All he kept thinking was that he would rather be here, in this place, where many like him were about to end their service to The Entwine, than to go where he was created to be. He could not be there. He could not see her. He could not face her and the man-Elder that the SHE chose over him to be the father of her son. Even with all he knew, and all the lifetimes that he had known what he knew, his thoughts were overcome by unfamiliar feelings. He kept thinking. *How could Kwa-yin choose a man Kaiwon barely took interest in when he was alive on The Earth?*

How could she choose that man, over the one who had protected her since her arrival? Cinqo was incensed by this revelation. He was… angry. His anger stirred the core of his being as he paced the alter of the church, not noticing the little old priest at the doorway a foot or two away from him.

"An Angelic troubled. This is a sight I am sure I have never seen in all my lives." Devascus said.

Cinqo spun around toward the priest; his eyes were ablaze where no eyes would have been noticed before. Devascus spoke with intention and a bit of bellow in his voice.

"You are not supposed to be here son. You are supposed to be up there." Devascus motioned to the sky and paused. "With her." He said.

"I know this Devascus, but she does not want me. She is with *him*."

Devascus shook his head and sighed.

"As difficult as this may be for you to hear in this moment child, it is so, none the less. She is not intended to want you. She is intended for another. It is written so for a purpose."

"Why…how…do I even feel this way?" Cinqo was pleading.

"The Earth realm is going through a powerful transformation presently. Every thought has wings tonight, and every fear wears legs. Feelings are powerful energy. In their purest form, they can seem consuming. Especially for you, because you are not used to having them." Devascus said.

Before Cinqo's eyes, a bright light started to pierce through the old priest's pores and pour outward until he was transformed into another, even greater light. Not even a blink later, Devascus was no longer the old priest. Cinqo bowed before Kwa-yin. She spoke only two words to him. Her voice penetrated through his anger, to his very essence and sounded like a succession of thunder claps. The church shivered as she spoke them.

"Go Back." She said.

Cinqo looked up at her, defiance screaming in his skull to do no such thing. Kwa-yin raised her arms of light over him and he was gone. And then, so was She.

At that moment, a warm light filled the room where the Stellar slept. Even though it was dark outside the church, the sun had risen inside. From a distance the familiar sound of creaking wood began to get louder as the little old priest made his way to the alter. Inside, the sound of the Seraph's chant began again. **Om Namo Rah Om** filled the great room. This time, the chant was fierce rather than melodic. The Seraph, too, were preparing for battle. One by one, the Stellar rose from their slumber. As each one stepped out of their beds, a renewed glimmer shown in each eye, and the beds disappeared. The Stellar were ready for what was to take place. Micah rose last from his sleep and walked knowingly toward the front of the church. He walked until he reached the broad, old wood and stained glass double doors. He stood in front of the heavy doors for a moment with no fear. In one swift movement, he opened the doors with both hands.

Light filled the street in front of the church. The wilted blooms of the tuckered trees were revived. As the light occupied the street, the thick darkness that had formed there was instantly transparent. Lucifer's cackle was silenced, if only for a second. All the dark swirls were revealed as Purveyors. The heavy wings in the air above stopped flapping, as the Reapers of Firewah took foot on the street. The crows stopped cawing and all was quiet. The only sound that could still be heard was the Seraph's battle cry. **Om Namo Rah Om. Om Namo Rah Om. Om Namo Rah Om. Om Namo Rah Om**. The Great War was moments away.

21 CLOUDS

"At the entrance, my bare feet on the dirt floor, Here, gust of heat; at my back, white clouds. I stare and stare. It seems I was called for this: To glorify things just because they are."
~Czeslaw Milosz

Cinqo woke on his back in the blank white room he was familiar seeing in The Heaven. He was alone at first glance, but he knew instinctively that he was not. He did not bother moving to rise. He was perfectly content where he was, being watched and not moving. Anything, he thought, was better than being where he was supposed to be.

Clouds began to form in The Eden of The Heaven. The Sun and the Moon moved further away from each other. The day and the night which lived harmoniously there, since the beginning of all time, started to separate from each other. For the first time ever in The Eden, rain fell. Rain too fell upon The Earth realm. The rain was like tears falling in clumps from the sky, washing over both the light and the darkness posturing for war, both indoors and out. No soul, alive or dead found cover from the rain.

Lucifer mocked the sky. He was screaming at it, so he could be sure She heard him.

"Is the great Kwa-yin sad? What a shame! Don't cry for these pathetic souls, Kwa-yin, mother of the evolution... blah...blah...blah..." He grimaced and then coughed like he tasted something horrible and needed to spit it out. "They are all pathetic, after all. Soon, sweet Kwa-yin, you'll be sitting beside me in hell, in your rightful place as my somewhat beloved concubine. My trophy wife... of all things...evil." Lucifer laughed his horrible laugh and began again. "Not to worry, though, you won't have to move down. I'll just move my things up!" He delighted in his rhetoric and laughed and laughed...

The Seraph battle cry grew louder still. ***Om Namo Rah Om. Om Namo Rah Om. Om Namo Rah Om.*** Beams of light crashed through the stained glass of the church. They looked like bright white lasers, glistening as they bounced off the masses of dark spirits who positioned themselves like a wall. Those who were hit became flames of cackling screams. Those who were not, did not wait for permission from their leader. They moved forward, red eyes focused like infrared beams into the light that flooded the mouth of the church, ready to perform their own God's will.

22 RAIN

"A crown is merely a hat that lets the rain in."

~Frederick The Great

The rain came through the crystal dwelling that Kaiwon, Kaitu and Lani shared. Of course they wondered what it meant, and the three walked through the waterfall to look at the sky. For the first time since either of them had been there, the bright, colorful Eden was dark. There were no stars they could see anywhere, no constellations, no colors. The moon and the sun were covered by thick gray clouds. It seemed, it felt, as if the Eden had stopped breathing. It was like the grass and trees and even the air was holding its breath. For what, they did not know. From the darkness, moving toward them they saw a light. It started small, like a spec in the distance and grew as it drew closer to the three. They noticed, wherever the light shone, the rain did not fall. The light was flickering like a candle and soon they became aware of who it was. Both Kaiwon and Lani put their faces to the still grass as Kwa-yin approached.

"Rise my love." She said.

Her bell like voice sang with melancholy. Kaiwon was not sure what to say, but she wanted to know why Kwa-yin was crying. Kwa-yin answered her thoughts, leaving it unnecessary for Kai to speak them aloud.

"The Earth and this place are in disorder. I cry for the souls to be lost and for the souls to be found this day. I cry for the anger and the hate and the death. I cry for the cleansing that must come after my precious souls leave their Earth bodies and have no place in The Entwine. I cry for the many moons and suns that have risen and set. I cry for those who have unknowingly worked against their own truth. I cry for the unspoken truth. I cry for the end and the beginning." She said. Then she turned to Kai and placed her hand of light to Kia's womb. "Soon a soul force unlike any other will be born to you. You, my child, are the key to The Great War's end. The child you hold in your arms is the door. The child yet unborn is completion. Lucifer's reign over the anger will soon end." She said.

Kwa-yin turned to Lani, whose head was still bowed in reverence.

"Soon you will perform your part in our divine plan. Though, it must happen as it must." Kwa-yin took her hand of light to Lani's chin so he could look into her face of warm light. "Child, you have been good to follow your heart. You have been as brave here in The Heaven as you have been on The Earth. The body you sacrificed to save others has been returned to you. We have written all of this in the stars together before and before and before... Life must evolve. The Entwine of our Mirth must evolve. The Heaven and The Earth must evolve. And so they shall. Osho Lovianhal Oshharu Mairahu Nura Osho Osho Lovian Osho. I speak this and this is so." Kwa-yin said.

As her last words rang through the air, she was gone. Kai turned to face Lani, adjusting Kaitu in her arms as she did. They both felt overwhelmingly connected, open. Kai closed her eyes and let the feeling flow through her. Light poured from her forehead, in a long, thick, pink-orange stream. The light connected itself to Lani's forehead. Then it zigzagged and spiraled until the three were engulfed by it, intertwined in a cocoon of light that kept spiraling outward. The cocoon kept growing until it lit up the entirety of The Eden, The Heaven and The Earth. It grew brighter and brighter and brighter until from all sides, tiny dust sized specks of light fell. And then, everything went dark.

The light dust became sparks and the sparks became like fireworks that sprayed all over The Eden. Everywhere the streaks of light hit was lit by the light and roused from its dark sleep. The grass and trees and plants and air began to breathe again and the thick gray clouds began to move from the sky. When the light lassos of the cocoon unraveled, Kai, Kaitu and Lani opened their eyes to see that the Eden they knew was returned. And yet, it felt different. There was a sense that there was something more, something new. They breathed in this feeling and fell asleep beneath stars. Kai woke up next to Lani on the grass in front of their waterfall. The baby was sleeping soundly on Lani's chest. Kai rolled over to face them. Lani was awake staring at sky holding Kaitu tightly, lovingly. Kai smiled and watched for a while and then sat up.

"We should put her inside." Kai said.

Lani nodded, but didn't speak. He felt nervous. He was anxious enough to not look Kai in her face. He raised himself up, and the three walked through the waterfall to their dwelling. Kai watched as Lani put the baby in her crib. She wanted to talk to him, to hear his thoughts, but she wasn't sure what to say. Lani turned to face her. He stepped as close to her as was physically possible and put his arms around her. The two stood together and breathed. Both of their hearts were beating so fast. He put his hands on either side of her face and caressed both cheeks simultaneously. He kissed her forehead and spoke gently.

"Do you know that light actually comes out of the middle of your head?" He asked, teasingly.

"I've never actually seen it, but I've gotten that impression a few times, yes." She said, blushing.

He laughed.

"Do you have any idea what we're supposed to do now?"

She looked deeply into his eyes.

"Yes."

After a few moments of silence, holding each other nervously, breathing and stalling, Kai and Lani held hands and walked through the waterfall and over the river Asher to the other side. The two felt a pressing desire to wash themselves in the river. Without much thinking, hand in hand, they walked together to the bank of the river and slid in its crystal clear waters, allowing their feet to be tickled by the golden sand beneath them. When their feet hit the water, their robes slid away like paper. They continued walking until the water covered them completely. Kai dunked her whole head under the water and began to glow. Lani then dunked his head and he glowed as well. When this was done, they swam together to a shallow place close to the river bank.

Lani pulled Kaiwon close to him and allowed his breath and hers to come to sync with the flowing of the water. He ran his strong hands through her hair and she moved her hands along his head. The two embraced and breathed until Lani moved forward to kiss her. When their lips met, an energy rushed from the center of the universe and poured through them equally. Their lips parted and returned. Their tongues touched and tangled in a dance that only they shared the rhythm. The passion between them escalated. As their dance continued, Kai wrapped her legs around Lani's waist. Lani, for his part, entered her. He pressed his body as gently and deeply into to her as he could. They both moaned as the extraordinary love and pleasure between them took over their dance. The pleasure they felt together, neither had ever experienced before. Kai's head tilted backward. Her pink-orange light streamed from the star on her forehead and lit the Eden sky like a beacon. The beauty of their love making exploded between them until they were both consumed by the love and the light. And it was done.

In the distance, they could hear a song lingering in the air like a whisper.

Om Namo Rah Om. Om Namo Rah Om. Om Namo Rah Om.

A divine seed had been planted in The Eden realm. What they did not know, at that exact moment, by the bank of the river Asher where the two embraced in its crystalline waters; a new tree, unlike any that thrived in The Eden before, was germinating beneath Eden's fertile soil.

23 LIGHT

"Faith is the strength by which the shattered world shall emerge into the light." ~Helen Keller

The streams of light from the fireworks that revived The Eden did not stop in The Heaven. The light looked like tiny lines falling from the sky. They fell everywhere and on everyone but Cathedral. When the light beams hit the people in their homes, something transformed in them. Their anger dissipated and in its wake something else blossomed. They felt warm and renewed. They felt a sense of wholeness and purpose. There was a sense of relief in them that was just as consuming as their anger once was. Man, woman and child. Mutes, Slides, and Sliders—all at once began to leave their homes. Although their fear and anger kept them hidden for weeks from their immediate world, on this night, they walked into the streets and dirt roads and fields outside of the places they lived. They stood in the open air and watched as the light showers fell and allowed the essence of that light to penetrate them.

Even outside Cathedral, the street began to fill with people. Poor, rich, young, old, beggar, drug fiend, thief, miser and every condition in between. They all filed together as a warmth and radiance formed around them. Instinctively they reached out to hold the hand that was nearest them. A song lingered in the air. It was gentle at first like mist remaining after a summer rain. The sound grew until even the thunder claps became this ethereal sound. Soon the song itself became them in the most poetic sense. It compounded their heartbeats. It became their chorus, like a divine conductor had raised his baton to lead the greatest of great concert choirs in the performance of their lives.

Om Namo Rah Om. Om Namo Rah Om. Om Namo Rah Om.

The sound of this song filled the air with a warmth that mixed with the rain of light and settled upon the people until it overcame them. In a scene unlike any that has happened before or will again, the people stood hand in hand with each other in the street and began to sing the song of the Seraph.

Lucifer's wiry legs were still wrapped around the cross of the church dome. Even from where he was perched upon Cathedral, he could not see the light falling from the sky. He was so arrogant and oblivious; he couldn't hear the masses of people around the church singing with the Seraph. He was so caught up in his veil of self-importance and what he thought was **supposed** to happen in Cathedral, he couldn't see what was actually happening just below him.

24 HUMAN, ONLY

"I long, as does every human being, to be at home wherever I find myself." ~Maya Angelou

Cinqo noticed that the rain stopped falling. He also noticed that he felt different. He was moved to sit up, but when he tried he could not. His body was stuck in one spot. He tried to transmute into his breeze form, but could not. It was then he realized he was naked. He felt the blood coursing through his body and he could hear his heart beating in his skull. He was confused and then a part of him was not. Tanzin's voice broke Cinqo's train of thought.

"The will of your soul has been considered."

"I do not know what this means Tanzin." He said.

"Your defiance of your purpose has made way for your sincerest desire." Tanzin said, matter-of-factly.

Cinqo still didn't understand. He also wasn't sure how to explain that to Tanzin. His thoughts were a jumble and a mess.

"In short, you are now human. Again." Tanzin said flatly

"That's impossible."

"No thing is impossible. You have witnessed great miracles in your time as Angelic. You know the truths of possibility more than others." Tanzin said.

"I do not remember. It has been too long. I would not know even where to begin. As man." Cinqo said.

When the words left his lips, a scowl formed. As an Angelic, Cinqo thought himself far better than a mere human man. He *was* better in many ways. He had already done his time in the human part of The Entwine. Certainly, he did not want to go back to that.

Tanzin let out a knowing laugh.

"You will begin as we all begin. At the beginning…again."

The frown on Cinqo's face deepened.

"I go back to The Earth a mute soul?" The thought of such a thing made Cinqo's stomach turn.

"Not entirely. You will go back to The Earth as you are now. You will keep the knowledge you have gained of your experience. You will do as you will on The Earth as a man of powerful understanding. You alone will choose to continue in human form or continue your work here. Your power is in your choice." Tanzin said.

"I am being punished then."

"You can look at it that way if you so choose son." Tanzin paused. "Or you can look at it as a way to make peace with what ails you about your work. You chose not to be with your charge. Until her work on The Earth plane is complete, and Angelic must be her guardian. To replace you, leaves an imbalance. You know as well as I do how grave an imbalance in The Entwine becomes. " He said.

"I cannot help what I feel. I cannot help what I have felt since she has been here. I did not mean for this to happen." Cinqo was pleading.

"Yet, it is your truth. Your truth will always be honored." Tanzin said. His voice was far gentler.

Cinqo was moved to an aching silence by Tanzin's words. His chest heaved in and out manically. He pondered, but did not speak. His scowl softened.

"In three days' time, Earth time of course, you will return to The Earth as you are now. I have been instructed to tell you that your destiny from this point has not been written. You will make your own way. How your destiny unfolds is entirely up to you." Tanzin said.

"Will she counsel with me? May I at least attempt to explain?" Cinqo said.

"There is no explanation necessary, dear one. She only wishes you to be happy. But it is always and only your choice." He said.

Before the last words could ring in Cinqo's ears, Tanzin was gone. Cinqo was left alone in the room Kai was first brought. He was bound where he lay looking at the same nothingness she had. His mind wandered to The Eden's bright colors and greenery. He missed it so terribly; he thought his newly beating heart would explode in his chest. For the first time in a very long time, Cinqo, the once Angelic, guide and Guardian to The Sialovehal--The Vessel Kaiwon, was overcome with grief and a sadness he thought he might never recover.

25 SOUL TRAVELING

"You don't have a soul. You are a soul. You have a body."
~C.S. Lewis

K ai lay next to Lani on their crystal bed with her eyes closed, but she did not feel like she was asleep. Her very essence felt restless. She tried to relax but could not. She decided to get up and walk around the Eden. She sat up and turned to put her feet on the moss rug beside her bed, but her feet did not touch. She stretched her legs in the duskily lit room to feel the floor, but the floor was nowhere to be found. She thought maybe the cloud mattress had risen while they slept and quickly became aware that it was not the mattress, but she who had risen above her bed. In fact, when she looked down, she noticed that her body was still lying next to Lani with her eyes closed and she could see Kaitu asleep in her crystal crib.

What is this? An out of body experience? It was. The only trick, she was thinking, was to figure out how to move about. The air was not a floor and she wasn't sure how to walk on it. She decided to start with a swim movement, the breast stroke of all things. This worked for her to get into the main room, but her 'spirit arms' were tired—she wasn't sure how. She decided to just decide where she wanted to go and see what happened. She took a mental breath and found herself outside of the waterfall that was the doorway to their dwelling.

Wow. This is really cool. I can literally be two places at one time.

She also wondered why she never knew she could do this before. Maybe her last meeting with Kwa-yin had something to do with it. She thought to test her new 'powers', but she didn't know where to begin. Her instinct suggested that she close her eyes and let her mind guide her to where she should be at the moment. As soon as she did this and well before she could open eyes again, she heard the screams. They were so close and so familiar, like a million people yelling at her at once. She didn't want open her eyes because she wasn't sure what she had gotten herself into. The screams were so chilling. Then she heard the song. She still couldn't make out what the voices were singing, but she would never forget that song as long as she lived. It was the saddest thing she had ever heard and instantly she too was sad. She felt like she was being pulled toward them. Wherever she was, the heat started to consume her. She smelled the sulfur and wanted to choke from it. She cracked her eyes and the heat hit her soul force like a forest fire. Then, she saw them. All of them. There were so many it was overwhelming. Souls on top of souls, stuck in what looked like black sand. There were mountains of these souls, screaming at the top of their lungs. Even this close, she couldn't make out what they were saying. She realized where she was. Firewah.

Firewah was the exact opposite of Eden. The sky looked like it was made of blood. It was thick and dull red like, if you touched it, blood would remain on your hands. There was nothing but miles of soot-like black sand. And miles and miles of souls that looked dirty and blurry, like TV static. The souls were everywhere. It was like somebody tossed them around like seeds. Wherever they landed, that's where they were stuck. Some were stuck to the side of massive soot mountains. Some were stuck within soot plains. Some were stuck in the blood red sky. Those souls just hung there, gasping for air in the heat that felt like they put their collective heads in an erupting volcano.

Despite what Kai was seeing, the only emotion she could muster was a deep sense of emptiness. She was sad, of course, for the millions of souls, just hanging or haphazardly stuck where they were. But this place, she thought, did not feel as sad as it did empty, despite how full it was with people. She looked at them and wondered why they did not simply pull themselves out. She couldn't figure out why the ones with arms sticking out didn't help the ones with legs sticking out and why the ones with their heads sticking out didn't direct the others on how to get themselves out. To Kai, they weren't so far buried that they couldn't get out. But there they all were, scattered about all over the place. All they did was scream this horrible scream. The screaming was constant. It sounded like they were yelling at each other or blaming each other. Finally she made out the words of their song.

Namo Rah Rah Rah. Namo Rah Rah Rah.

It was so eerie and sad, it plagued her. She wasn't sure if she should move or which way was the exit if she did. Her instincts began to scatter. The energy in Firewah was chaotic. It seemed to her, the antithesis of how universal law works. It was, put simply, scattered soul force and soul force scattered about. Kai had to concentrate extra hard to become clear enough to figure out what made her find her way to Firewah from The Eden. She closed her eyes and felt something pull at her. The screaming grew faint and when she opened her eyes again, she was in an envelope of light with Kwa-yin.

"The souls you have seen have been herded like sheep, but not against their will. They chose their place in The Entwine because Oshharu Mairahu Nura Osho." She said. Her bell-like voice rang through The Eden and lay on the air like mist.

"Fear lights a man's way to darkness", Kai said.

"It is so. To Osho Lovianhal, my daughter, you must remember that Osho Lovian Osho."

"To light the love in ALL, you must remember that light brings love to light." Kai said.

It surprised her that she knew what Kwa-yin was saying. It surprised her further she knew that she knew Tuahstai. She knew it was her first tongue. She tried to remember all of it. Her beginnings, because she had this knowing that she knew who she was and why she came, but all of it didn't come to her. She looked up at Kwa-yin.

Kwa-yin smiled.

"You are Sialovehal. But you are much more to our cause here. You are The Key, my daughter. When the time comes, you will open the door that frees them ALL." She said and then was gone.

Kai blinked and realized she was still spirit walking. She closed her eyes. When she opened them this time, she was back in her physical body, lying next to Lani. He was awake.

"You were in Firewah." He said.

"How did you know I went anywhere, I was right next to you."

"First, I can smell it all over you. Second, I may be just a man now, but please don't forget that I am still an Elder. I knew you were gone the moment you left." He said, puffing his chest out.

Kai was exhausted. She looked at Lani, who was obviously concerned for her, but she couldn't make herself say anything. She just shook her head.

"What's that about?" Lani frowned

"What's what about?"

"The head shaking. You don't want to tell me about your journey to hell?"

Kai hesitated. She didn't know how to tell him without reliving the whole ordeal. It was so horrible.

"It's not that..." Kai shook her head again. "...my journey to hell... was hell. Plus, I'm confused. She said that I'm the "key" and I'll open the "door" that frees all these stuck souls. Ugh. I'd rather not think about it if I don't have to. Do I have to?"

Lani put his arms around her and tried to ignore the sulfur smell that lingered around her.

"What do you want to do then?" He asked.

"What do you mean?"

"Well, if you don't want to go back to Firewah and free all of those souls, you know you don't have to. You can stay here with me and Kaitu forever and we can live in The Eden and eat all the fruit and vegetables we can stand and sit by all the trees and rivers and look down on The Earth and be glad we aren't there with all the drama." He said. He was matter-of-fact as though he gave the idea plenty of thought.

Kai cringed.

"Isn't that what *you* did all day as an Elder? No thanks."

Lani laughed.

"Clearly, Elders don't eat or raise children, but our work is very important and not at all what you think." He said.

Kai laughed out loud.

"Yeah, right. I even asked Tanzin, and he couldn't tell me what you guys do all day. Sounds like a racket if ever there was one. Just add a "thou art" and an "it is so" in front of something and it's vital."

Lani laughed, but then his face turned serious.

"I think I've been properly acquainted with you now Kai. I can't say I know everything about you, but I know enough to know that you are afraid of nothing. You follow your heart and don't give a care about what anyone else thinks. You do as your soul force guides you to, even if you don't think you're doing it at the time. You weren't brought here because you're pretty or because you're some killer warrior. You were brought here because you have something the world down there needs desperately. It's something only Sialovehal still have. From what I know, balancing The Entwine over all these eons has watered us all down. The Sialovehal left because just their presence in this realm overwhelmed the balance, so only one can come back at a time. Each time, The Entwine gets closer to its true potential, but each time, after a time, the anger takes over again, because he's still here."

"So why bother? Clearly, human kind can't be fixed, and nobody wants to deal with *him*, so why keep trying? What is the benefit of trying to save a people who can't be saved? Or don't want to be saved. Or don't know they can save themselves? Their anger is their choice, is it not?" There was an echo in Kai's voice that sounded other-worldly.

Lani look surprised. Then she snapped out of it. Just like that.

"What?" She asked. "Why are you looking at me like that?"

"You did something very 'Star People' with your voice. Are you starting to remember?"

"Remember what? What do you mean about my voice? I didn't even say anything. I was listening to you." She said.

Lani sighed.

"Alright."

"Finish what you were saying." She said.

"I don't even remember what I was saying anymore Kai." He was exhausted too.

"Come on now, don't be like that. You were telling me how we're this close to fixing what's wrong with The Entwine." She said.

"I know this is a lot for you. It would be a lot for anyone. The fact that I'm human enough to interact with you as a real couple is/was a lot for me too. Remember, this body was dead. It's not dead now. It's just like it was, but better, I think. There are lots of things happening to us and around us that we can't, maybe won't make much sense out of. If I know anything at all, I know that *you* are not here for no reason. The fact that you have that little baby, is not for no reason. There is something big unfolding. So many miracles happening to us and between us. But there are also those we can't see right now who are fighting for us. For *you*. For *her."* He pointed in the direction of Kaitu's room. "We all have a part to play. I don't know what my role in any of this truly is. But I know that I'm here, because you're here. She's here, because you're here. No matter what you think, you have the biggest part of all in this. The only thing you're missing is your own memory. Your own understanding. I don't know for sure, but I feel like, all you have to do is be yourself, as you always have, and everything will work out fine."

Kai kissed Lani on his cheek and caressed his face.

"What if myself is telling me that I don't want this? If I don't remember, is it my fault?" She was holding back tears.

Lani looked at Kai and put his hands in her hair. He wasn't sure what she was getting at, but he knew instinctively she had stopped talking about Firewah and was on to something else.

"I don't know about faults. We do what we are born to do. You've lived your life this far according to what you were called to do. Just keep doing that."

"And you? You're human now and so what will you do? I do what I'm supposed to do—whatever that is—and what will you do? What happens afterward? We go back to Earth like nothing happened? You're dead remember? Or you were. We roll by your old hood and your family like heeeey ya'all, remember me? Here, meet my new kid. Yeah, I know, I was dead but, when I was an Elder up in Heaven, the craziest thing happened..."

Lani was stunned. He looked at Kai and his head pulled back in shock. Her words cut through him like a hot steak knife through butter. He didn't know how to feel. She wasn't being mean. He knew that wasn't her intent. She was making a really good point.

How would they go on with their lives? Were they meant to? Was

this a beginning for them or an end? After she fulfilled her purpose with The Entwine, was there a life for them after this?

Lani began to ponder everything between them. He loved Kai, he knew he did. **Did he?** His love for Kai had never entered the equation. At least, it never entered the conversation with regard to their 'star-determined' union. It was as if everybody decided for both Kai and he that they were supposed to be together and the two of them really didn't have much choice in the matter. One minute he's an Elder, literally a soul force without a human body, and the next he's a man betrothed, 'Eden-style', to a woman he hardly knew, even on The Earth.

Hmmm. Lani let his thoughts travel. He remembered Kai vaguely as a pretty girl who was generally aloof. Like she didn't trust anyone. He remembered their brief exchanges. He remembered she was kind, compassionate, and sweet--she couldn't hide that if she wanted to. But also guarded and brusque. He also remembered how determined she was about her career. She was very plainly obsessed about making something of herself. It was a tick in her. He remembered seeing the sadness in her eyes and wondering how it got there. He never remembered having the inclination to ask her out. He certainly didn't remember liking her as more than an acquaintance. Then he remembered that The Stellar were designed specifically to not be attracted to each other. It was that way to keep certain more evolved soul forces from procreating together and thus creating an imbalance in The Entwine. But they were different. Kai was Sialovehal. She didn't have to follow the rules of The Entwine, because she and The Stai were templates for it. Which means, they just honestly weren't attracted to each when they interacted on The Earth. Of course, Kai was much different now than he remembered her. But that didn't keep him from feeling manipulated.

Kai laid her head down with the intention of attempting sleep. Lani didn't interrupt. It began to settle on him that he really, honestly, had no idea what his role was supposed to be in all of this.

Was he just meant to give Kai a son and then he was done?

The questions kept mounting. Then, a new thought crept in. He remembered Kai's boyfriend was this big time football player named Henry Ball. Henny Ball is what he was called. "Really Big Jerk" is what he actually was. Why Kai chose him, Lani did not know. He asked her once, very casually. She shrugged, said Henny wasn't her type, but was what was expected of her to get where she wanted to go. Thinking about it now, what she said was prophetic. He certainly didn't think that at the time. He remembered one time he saw her at a fundraising event. He mentioned that he saw her and Henny in some magazine posing on the red carpet for some premier. She shrugged and said something like, "How did we look?" Lani remembered being so annoyed with her, all he could think to do was shrug back and walk away. He always wanted to apologize for being rude to her, but he never got the chance. He died shortly after that, so they didn't see each other again.

He wanted to look at Kai now, but he didn't. He let his thoughts go where they wanted. He thought about his old girlfriend. Marina. He smiled at the memory. Marina had a great heart and was about something. He wondered if she ever got that tennis camp she was working on off the ground.

All at once, Lani's mind began to buzz. Kai's words started to ring through him until all he could do to keep his head on, was to literally put his palms on either side of his skull. He couldn't help but think about the practicality of being a man again and being a man with a family. He was to be a father soon, wasn't he? It was a strange dichotomy to him that all of this was happening and it was happening all too fast. He remembered Tanzin's words to The Stellar, Kindred and Comforter when they gathered together before The Great War.

"Time is of little consequence where you stand, but it is of grave importance where you must return...."

He pondered the concept of time and love and how he felt when he first met Kai and how he felt as he began to transform from his energy form to his human form. He had to wonder what would happen to them once they made it back to The Earth and all of this was over.

What would he do? Would he go back to the community center? Would his family lose their minds to find out that the man they buried was actually alive and well? Would his family still be alive with all that was happening on The Earth?

His questions kept compounding and the more questions he had, more questions formed. His head became so clouded with questions; he wasn't even holding his head anymore. He was sitting straight up completely zoned out.

Kai sensed something was wrong and turned over to look at him. He was staring straight in front of him, but wasn't moving. He was barely breathing. She snapped her fingers in front of his face, but he wouldn't snap out of it. She clapped, she yelled, she even shook him. He just stared, his thoughts compiling like sand in an hour glass. The only thing she did manage to do with all her efforts was wake Kaitu. Kia got up to feed her. She didn't bother looking back to see what Lani was doing, beyond what she saw, something in Kai already knew there was much more to it.

26 BATTLEFIELD

"We are young, heartache to heartache we stand. No promises, no demands. Love is a battlefield. We are strong, no one can tell us we're wrong, Searchin' our hearts for so long, both of us knowing…Love is a battlefield."

~ Pat Benatar

Lucifer was still perched upon his temporary Cathedral throne laughing and cackling at the bodies flying in and out of the church. He couldn't tell who was winning from where he sat and it dawned on him that he didn't care. The fact that he got Kwa-yin's Guardians to fight his Minions was, in his mind, entertainment beyond measure. He didn't even need to see it. He had it all planned out in his head. They would fight. He would win. He would be the ruler of The Heaven and The Earth and then take over The Seat of Light and all would be as he wanted. His Minions were fighters. Kwa-yin's lot were lovers. Peace keepers. Surely, this was an unequal battle they fought below. Surely.

He knew that part of Kwa-yin's plan was unending peace. One does not gain peace through fighting. Only more fighting comes from fighting. How else did she think he won over so many of her precious souls? For a minute, Lucifer was in his thoughts. He was, after all, paranoid of everything.

Why would Kwa-yin submit to battle, when fighting-- war of all things-- was the antithesis of her plan? Had he done such good work herding souls that she had no choice but to submit to his will?

A part of him wanted to believe in his cleverness above all else. But another part, one may infer; the part of him that was once Elder, Keeper and even Sialovehal, was whispering something else to him. The whisper was barely perceptible, but it was there. This teeny tiny voice barely heard over his hideous laugh and his loud thoughts whispered: **You fool.**

Inside Cathedral was the culmination of every battle between 'good' and 'evil' ever read in any book or told to any child or seen on any screen. Cathedral had been transformed into a massive battlefield with trees and trenches and places to hide. It wasn't just hand to hand combat, nor was it just head on kill or be killed. This was truly a spirit war. Stellar were contorting themselves to avoid blows with heavy handed Demons and using mudras to stop Purveyors from turning to black wind. There were big muscle bound male types of brute strength—Moyo-- but the lot of them stood outside Cathedral, like club bouncers. There were heavy winged demons called Reepers fighting Seraph in the sky. There were light streams flying through the air, coming from the alter of the church (which was still there, despite the rest of the church being transformed). Every once in a while, streams of light would fly about hitting Purveyors, Reepers and Moyo at will, but no one knew where the light streams came from.

Micah and the now not so shy Yoko turned out to be the strategists of the seven lead Stellar. Ree was hyper-intuitive, so her work was translating a more spiritual perspective than the physicality of what was going on. The others did as these three instructed. What became odd to Micah was that there was little progress one way or the other since they began fighting. For every Purveyor or Moyo that was killed, a Guardian or Stellar was also lost. For every Reeper that fell from the sky, so too fell a Seraph. Micah noticed this, but did not speak it.

The Seraph's battle cry continued.

   Om Namo Rah Om.

The song rang through the air as heavy Reeper wings met with deceivingly delicate Seraph wings. In the sky of the transformed church, the breeze of Guardians met with the black wind of Purveyors somewhere in the middle. On the ground, it was Stellar and whichever evil was standing at the time. The scene was chaos. A fly on the wall would have had a hard time figuring out what to make of it.   The Great War between The Light and Darkness continued. It gained no ground toward an ending, but lost none either.

Lucifer was too busy trying to figure out the subtext of Kwa-yin's part in this, to strategize with his Minions. He thought them stupid anyway. Around Cathedral, where the people had gathered, singing the Seraph song, something was happening. Lucifer was seated in such a way that if he really looked, he could see and hear them as they began to close in around the church. He did not. In one accord, all the people, of every age, race, size, color and creed began to form a ring around the battle ground like their job was to hold it in. The song of the people became louder. Meanwhile, the Seraph's song began to fade as one by one, they fell... upward, through the sky, inside the church.

27 OLD WAY OUT

"Old ways will always remain unless some one invents a new way and then lives and dies for it." ~Elbert Hubbard

Like backward rain, the spirit energy of the Stellar, Seraph, and Guardians 'fell upward' from the battle happening in Cathedral. They looked like glimmering dandelion seeds floating through the sky of The Eden and toward higher realms. Tanzin and the other Elders were struck by the display; it was both awesome and horrifying. There were thousands of them. The Elders couldn't see what was happening below anymore, so they didn't know how The Great War was progressing. Some of the Neo Elders expressed concern. Even Meoshe, as Keeper of the Passion, could not articulate what was happening. Kwa-yin had stopped writing in the stars after The Conception in the River Asher.

"Liaph kaahuru beharu shama. Liaph nom baai. What was written before remains. What is now, must be." She told Meoshe.

This was the first time any of The Elders were completely in the dark about their purpose or what was supposed to happen next. Everything had always been written out for them. They had only to look out into the omniverse to know their place in it. After the rain, everything changed. Now, they were forced to stay in the moment. This was disconcerting because it meant they were no better than mere Earthbound souls. Yasufa was a Neo Elder of Stellar stock. He still had plenty of fight in him.

"Let us make our way to the site of the war, in case our assistance is needed." He said.

"Certainly not. It is not our place to be present on The Earth. Our place is here." Tanzin said. He began to say "it is written". Out of habit.

But he caught himself, because he knew that it was not.

"I am certain there is a divine reason The She left this part of our story blank. We must fill in those blanks." Yasufa said.

"What shall we do upon The Earth that would be different than what the Stellar or the Guardian or Seraph are doing **and** designed to do?" Tanzin asked uncomfortably.

Tanzin was out of sorts. He was behaving like something in him was falling loose. He was of Kindred stock. He was an intellectual, not a fighter. The very thought of joining the war below, as an Elder, caused him to turn up his nose.

"Must we not do all that we are equipped to do?" Yasufa asked.

Some of the other Neo Elders agreed. Most of them were former Stellar. The Elders who were Comforter and Kindred did not agree. Since The Fall, it had not been the nature or design of The Elders to pull rank on each other. They all worked together in accord, rather, in accordance with what was written. The fact that nothing was being blatantly expressed for them now, caused a rift between The Elders. It did not, at this point, dawn on them that their rift was also a part of Kwa-yin's plan. In order to build up an evolution, a breakdown of the old way must take place. The Elders found a new sense of individual power without specific rules holding them together, so they broke themselves into groups. Former Stellar, Kindred, and Comforter clung to each other. Each chose their sides and each group counseled within. Meoshe was the only of the group who stayed to herself. She felt Kwa-yin's presence and did as her instincts told her. She stayed still.

At the same time, on The Earth, the Comforters had all found their way to an old Hospital. Their individual lights glimmered and then dimmed as they were seated in a great hall. The building where they waited patiently, had been sitting forever without being touched or cared for. It was once occupied for medical miracles, but now it was practically a ruin.

As each person filed in, the auditorium grew to fit the lot. Comforters, by design are the compassionate ones. Their job in The Entwine is to recharge The Stellar. Under normal everyday experience, Comforters and Stellar find each other instinctively and become great friends. It is the nature of The Stellar to give of themselves to the point of exhaustion. Comforters replenish their soul force.

This especially large groups of healers, sitting in the old hospital, didn't yet know that not far from them, a war was underway. Soon, they too would be called to fulfill their destiny therein.

At the same time, in an old forgotten library, some blocks away, a very large group of Kindred was forming in the same way the Comforters were. They were also being prepared for their part in The Great War.

High in the sky... further than The Heaven... further than where The Eden sits... Kwa-yin was looking down upon The Earth from higher realms watching the plan for The ALL unfold. Around her were the glimmering energies of those who transitioned from the battle below. A beam of bright silver light streamed toward them from The Seat of Light. It stopped next to Kwa-yin, until The Vessel was prepared for his arrival.

28 REPLAYED MEMORIES

"We all have our time machines. Some take us back, they're called memories. Some take us forward, they're called dreams." ~Jeremy Irons

Kai finished eating and feeding Kaitu simultaneously. The baby was asleep in her arms, but she hesitated putting her in her crib. She sat with her, watching the little life that got ever bigger, it seemed with every second. She thought about all she had been through in such a short amount of time. How she got to this point in her life was a blur. It didn't matter to her anymore that for so long she felt like soiled laundry. She barely remembered the faces of her "parents" or "Aunt Myra.". She felt like a new person in new skin. It was nice. She kissed Kaitu's chubby fingers and she couldn't keep her mind off of the man who helped create her. The idea that any person would not want to witness their child grow up, caused her to frown deeply. Intellectually, she understood what Cinqo told her about why Henny left, but she still couldn't wrap her heart around it. Henny was an ass. Although, the way they broke up, couldn't be misinterpreted as anything other than divine-- if she really thought about it. It was clean and to the point. It happened the day she found out she was pregnant.

Henny was out of town for an away game. When he picked up the phone, it was business as usual.

"Hey baby, what's crack-a-latin?' Henny asked.

Kai hated his 'fake ignorance'. She rolled her eyes.

"You." She said, in all insincerity.

"You see my game?"

"I didn't. Something came up. Did you win?" Kai was clearly

distracted.

"You know we did babyyyyy! Sorry you missed the greatest catch of my career. I practically caught that ball from the end zone. Winning touchdown. Guaranteed boost in my endorsement roster. Yee-ah!"

"Wow. That is soooo great," Kai said. She wasn't really listening. Her mission consumed her. "...Listen... Henny... when you get back, we really have to talk."

"What's up?"

"I'm not sure we should have this conversation over the phone. I know you're busy celebrating your victory." She said.

"Man, I hate it when you do that shit! Why you bring up shit and not finish! I hate that shit, man. You know I hate that shit!" He was yelling at Kai. Very loudly.

Without question, Henry Braxton Ball, Jr. did not get the name Henny in a void. He liked his liquor and he liked his women. Kai knew he had a bunch of both everywhere he went. She resolved that it didn't bother her because she was too busy handling her career to spend so much time caring about what he did when he was away. As long as he kept that crap to himself, wore protection and made sure she knew she was number one, she was fine with his indiscretions. She did not like the way he talked to her when he drank, but, she reasoned, it went with the territory.

"Look Henny, I'm sorry. I know you're excited about your win and I'm not trying to pour downers all over everything right now. If you recall, you've asked me repeatedly not to tell you important things over the phone. Remember? You said it messes with your game. The only reason I brought it up was so you would know to put aside some time for me when you get home. Just a few minutes, okay?"

Click.

Kai shook her head as she looked at her phone. She started to call him back but thought better of it. She went about instead, figuring out what she was going to do with her career and a baby. When Henny got home a few days later, he acted like nothing was wrong. He greeted her with the same hangover smelling kiss and big hug he always gave her. He acted convincingly like he wanted to know all that went on when he was away. Kai cut to the chase.

"Henry, honey… I know we've talked about marriage a few times over the last few months and I'm thinking maybe it's time to revisit that discussion."

"Right now?"

"What's wrong with right now? Now is as good a time as any, don't you think?"

"No. I don't think…do we got any aspirin, my head is pounding."

Kai was quiet, but her facial expression spoke volumes. Henny noticed Kai's very unhappy expression. He grabbed her hand and pulled her over to the couch he constantly reminded her was flown in from across the world. They sat down.

"You know baby, a man's got to feel a sense of urgency when it comes to marriage. You know we got some problems we need to work out before we start seriously thinking about being married."

Kai's face stiffened further. She had heard Henny say the exact same thing at least a dozen times before. One minute he would ask her what she thought about marrying him. The next minute he was talking about urgency. She thought this ebb and flow had something to do with one of his side women. She hadn't cared much until now. She wondered if he knew how much like a broken record he sounded. She also re-acknowledged to herself that she wasn't really interested in marrying Henny. He was an ass, she kept telling herself. However, Kai didn't entirely like the prospect of raising her baby by herself. She had hoped

Henny would calm down a bit if he had a family to consider. Her thought was to reason with him, but her patience had long since waned.

"Henny, I'm not really trying to dig into this same spiel today, I mean—fuck it. I'm pregnant."

Henny looked at Kai blankly, like nothing she said registered in his brain yet.

"I'm sorry bay, you said what?"

Kai rolled her eyes. She could almost smell his brain moving. For a minute, she just looked at him like she was trying to remember why they ever got together. They were so different. She looked him up and down him like she was inspecting him before an auction. He was tall, 6'6". His body was massive and well-formed-- it was a testament to how much time he spent in the gym. His face was beautiful. Clear, golden skin, bright and unusual colored eyes. His lips were full like pillows. He got so many endorsements because he was so pretty. Not because he was a good person.

She admired what she saw as she looked at him. And then she thought about all the nasty things that piled out of his mouth like a sieve. As talented as he was, as good looking as he was, none of that mattered because he was a jerk. A really, really big one. The weird part for Kai was when they were next to each other, she felt utterly comfortable. Being in the same room with him was like being with the other half of her very soul. She never understood how she could feel the way she did with him, and really not like him at all at the same time. She wanted to believe that at his core, he really was kind and generous and decent. She wanted to believe that like her, his ugly childhood made him cautious, so the man that often showed up as him, was just his armor. She hoped that the more time they spent together, the more of the real Henry Ball, Jr., she would meet. So far, it hadn't worked out that way.

She was starting to believe Henny was really just rotten to his heart muscle. It crossed her mind that she just wanted somebody in her life to make her feel more than she had always felt about herself. She realized, with her tears threatening her cheeks, that with Henny she actually felt worse. The last bits of her admiration for him, landed in the pit of her stomach. Now she was just angry.

"You heard what I said. But. Just in case I wasn't clear—I'M PREG-NANT." She said, pronouncing every syllable. It pissed Henny off.

"I'm not stupid or deaf. So don't talk to me like I'm stupid and def."

Kai wanted to scream so badly, but she just sat there looking at him. She didn't want her face to show what was really on her mind. She did think he was stupid and def. She thought him a fool. A waste of human potential.

I came here to procreate with him? Is this how The Entwine keeps balance? With beautiful fools? This cannot be so. Wait. What?

Kai did remember thinking that at the time. She also remembered being so caught up and confused about everything that she didn't do any further exploring about it. She was far too invested in the human dysfunctional experience she was having to step out of it. Most of her human experience had been dysfunctional anyway. She just sat there looking at Henny, beginning to feel powerless. She picked him and she knew he was going to flake on her and their baby. She knew it like she thought she knew her name. She knew it like she felt her heart falling out of her neck, into her hands, and crumbling before her as she watched. Henny interrupted her thoughts.

"So, what you gonna do?" He asked as plainly as he could. His blank look had morphed into a deer in headlights expression.

"What do you mean, what am I gonna do? You mean, what are we gonna do? You mean, sure baby, we talked about having kids, and now we have one on the way, maybe we should talk about getting married?"

As the words left her mouth, she wished she could pull them back. The conversation was already everything she didn't want. She didn't want to beg this man to make sense in the most important decision of their collective lives. It would have been better if she hadn't said anything. Henny interrupted her thoughts again.

"So you trying to trap me now? I'm not moving fast enough for you so you get pregnant so I can marry your ass?" He said.

He sounded serious enough, so Kai just about jumped to her feet. Her forehead itched and burned. She felt a fire rising from her feet and spreading throughout her insides. She felt a rush of power wave over her. Everything inside of her began to pulse and then escalate. The hairs on Henny's arms rose. He was noticeably nervous. He couldn't see what was happening inside of Kai, but he certainly felt it. As if on cue, before the light from her forehead poured out all over Henny and the room, she saw that twinkling face in her peripheral. It spread out and formed a breeze around her until she was able to close her eyes to find her center. All of this happened in as much time as it takes to blink. Henny had only the moment, but Kai, even then, was working from a different torrent of time than he was. She found her place in the conversation immediately, but she wasn't exactly herself.

"Oshharu Mairahu Nura Osho. Osho Lovian Osho. You do not know who you are. I'm looking at a man who wastes away. Your purpose here is so powerful and you don't even know. I look upon you and see a soul force that is so full of holes; you try to fill them with drink and sex. You are afraid of life. You are afraid of being whole. You are afraid of your duty to grow and evolve. To look at your face, I can see why I chose you. But to look at your heart, I see why you cower before me. You should. You are not yet worthy. My people call you deimosho. Dim light. I assure you, our daughter will not be. She will be the greatest thing you ever do on this life plane. You will know." She said.

There was an echo to her voice that kept the whole room hostage until she finished. 'Regular' Kai had no idea she said all of that. She also didn't have any idea why Henny was looking at her so funny. He actually looked scared. Kai sighed.

"Alright. I guess the real question in this equation is what are you gonna do?" She said.

Henny looked at Kai with equal parts awe and gall. He stood from the couch, pulled Kai close to him and kissed her nervously on the cheek. He gave her a big hug, like he was apologizing for being so stupid. She hugged him back, as if to accept his apology. When he let her go, he turned around and walked out the same door he entered a few minutes before. Kai moved out of their house that night. She hadn't heard from him since. Of course, she'd seen him in the papers and heard his infamous egomaniacal rants on TV after games, but during her entire pregnancy, he never attempted to check on her, nor did he come to see their daughter born. He did have his assistant send flowers once the news broke the story of Taylor's arrival. He did put a chunk of money in a trust fund for her, Kai found out later. She refused to so much as breath near the bank where that money was. She called it blood money. She thought Henny did it so Kai would leave him alone. He didn't know that she had every intention of leaving him alone anyway.

Kai frowned thinking about everything as it came to her in waves. Looking at Taylor now—whom she started calling Kaitu—she started to get some perspective. She felt badly for Henny now. He left because he was actually scared. If his voice started echoing and he spoke some language she had never heard him speak before, she would have left the way he did too. She hadn't done it on purpose. She didn't even know it happened at all. She supposed the glimmering face she saw was there to keep her from killing people with the light from her head. Like Cinqo did with that Purveyor.

Her feelings about Henny softened considerably. She didn't know, so how could he? Then she thought about her surrogates. She remembered the way she felt; only a few days ago when she first heard Kaitu speak Tuahstai. A 6 month old breast feeding baby, speaking full sentences of a language Kai didn't quite know. It was disconcerting, to say the least. Finally, definitively, she saw things through the lens of the people she felt abandoned her. Finally, she understood what Oshharu Mairahu Nura Osho means. She understood why she couldn't remember her true self. "Fear Lights a Man's Way to Darkness." She spent her whole life afraid she was not worthy of love. She let her experiences convince her it was true. She was so focused on her own lens and pain; it didn't dawn on her to look in the direction of what was looking at her.

Once it settled in her spirit that the people who wronged her were not actually monsters, just afraid of what they couldn't understand; she let go. She lifted her most sour memories to the highest part of her consciousness and forgave it all. She thanked every soul who came into her life for their powerful contribution to her human incarnation. She knew instinctively that without them all, she would not have been able to understand. She would not have been able to do her true work. She pulled Kaitu closer to her breast and rocked her. Tears welled her eyes, fell off her cheeks and hit the golden sand beneath her feet. She couldn't know that where every tear landed upon the golden sand, a seed of a new plant germinated beneath.

When Lani finally snapped out of his trance, he walked in the main room to find Kai rocking Kaitu in her arms, crying inaudibly. She was not sobbing. She was rocking her daughter and humming softly, her tears like glistening tributaries upon her flushed cheeks. She didn't notice him standing there and he took his time watching her. She was exquisite to him. He had never noticed before how she glowed from the inside. Warmth emanated from her every pore. She looked like a quiet Queen sitting on her crystal throne, holding her child in her arms, as the baby slept in peace.

He also noticed that he was beginning to feel different. Again. The thoughts that a moment before jumbled his head like road blocks everywhere, began to lift themselves. The road blocks were replaced with a familiar sense of order in his mind. His instinct had him raise his arms. The strong veins in his hands had started to fade and the loudness of his heart in his ears became still. All the emotion that had filled him had begun to thin out like he had sprung a leak somewhere in his human body and what was left was only the Neo Elder essence of Yamin. Kai looked up from where she sat. She noticed the difference in Lani right away, but was not surprised. She got up from her seat to put Kaitu in her crib. Before she reached the bedroom, she turned to Lani and spoke gently through her tears.

"I knew this would happen." She said.

"Even I did not know this would happen, how could you?" He said.

"I wish I could tell you that but I can't. I just knew that you would serve your purpose in all of this and go back to what you were doing before. I kept hearing in my head, nothing is what it seems." Kai said, brushing away tears with her free hand.

"I pray you don't think that I planned it this way, Kaiwon. I pray you don't think this was my intention." Lani said, pleading.

"Of course it is." Kai said flatly.

Lani turned his head. Suddenly, Kai found herself gasping for air. She held Kaitu ever tighter. She felt as though the wind had been knocked out of her and in that instant her stomach felt full like something heavy had been placed on her and she could not move. The glow coming from Kai before had grown into gentle rays of light shooting from her skin, flowing through Kaitu as well. Kai looked up at Lani. At first she looked shocked and then she settled into peace. Lani could not move, he could only watch from where he stood. Once the heaviness was gone, all that remained for Kai was a feeling of indescribable love. She felt both powerful and humbled. She knew, in that moment, something magnificent was unfolding in her womb.

As the last ounce of Lani, the man, was turning back into Yamin, the

Elder, he felt such sorrow and joy at the same time. As a man on The Earth, he had never had his own children. As an Elder, he knew his child was growing in the woman he looked upon. The joy he felt was for knowing that a part of him would live on and would grow up to be a great man, was comforting. He felt proud. He raised his slumping body straighter.

The sorrow he felt came from knowing he could not be a part of the raising up of his boy. He wanted to watch and guide him as he grew up to be that man. He couldn't do any of that as Elder. He got a strange sense that someone would, but it would not be him. Not as he was. For this, he was sad.

He walked toward Kai and planted himself in front of her. She stood straighter, tears streaming down her cheeks, holding Kaitu close to her heart like a shield. With his last ounce of humanness, he placed his hand on her stomach. He could feel his son's essence coursing through his own. He put his massive arms around Kaiwon and Kaitu and held them as tightly as his transmuting physical body would allow. He did this until he could no longer feel them-- which meant-- his transformation back to Yamin was complete.

When this was done, his sorrow was gone. Kaiwon and Kaitu walked to the other room to lie down. He stood in a corner of the room watching them. He was unsure what his next move was, but he knew, in that moment, his place was exactly where he was.

29 SHOWING

"It is said that the present is pregnant with the future."
~Voltaire

Kai started showing quickly. Strangely enough, Kai's baby bump glowed from the inside out, like she was carrying a lamp in her belly. Under normal circumstances, one could argue that having a lamp on at all times inside one's body would be annoying. It was, at first, but Kai learned to accept it. Yamin stayed very close to them at all times. He loved seeing that bump of light shining through her stomach. They had not seen nor heard from Cinqo in so long, they assumed that Yamin was her Guardian now. Yamin also assumed that Kai would stay in Eden until she delivered. As the child grew inside her womb, Kai's heritage began to unfold as well. She didn't remember everything about being Sialovehal or Star People, but started to know when she zoned in and out and could remember what happened when she did. It felt a bit like walking around as two people at once, but she wasn't sure how to be just one or the other.

She also had more lucid dreams and traveled much more outside of her body. She was still very unsure of what her task was beyond birthing her son. She didn't remember most of her birthing experience with Kaitu, so she wondered often what giving birth to a lamp in Eden would be like. She thought of Tanzin often. She wondered where he was and why she had heard nothing from him or Meoshe, nor seen any of the Elders for a long while. The only beings she saw in The Eden were Kaitu and Yamin. She wondered what was happening on The Earth and why everything was so quiet.

Then, she thought of Cinqo. She remembered the conversation she had with Tanzin about him. When she asked who the key was that led her out of Aunt Myra's house, she thought that key was Cinqo. Tanzin told her it wasn't. This concept of The Key was nagging at her for some reason. She thought about it all the time. She thought about it more than the sex she persistently wanted to have with Lani, but couldn't because he turned back into Yamin. Her hormones were making her feel so passionate, that pleasuring herself had become a job more than a release. She put her mind someplace more constructive. She let this business of "the key" be a distraction from the closeness she wanted with her lover.

She never spoke of it to him. She didn't think talking about it would make any difference. So much of her experiences interacting with human people ended in sadness and rejection for her. How could it not? She looked like them, but she was nothing like them. There was something about her that was beyond what even Yamin, in all of his understanding, could grasp. She wasn't yet clear about the specifics, but she knew the circumstances of her being here was much more than anyone knew or could tell her.

Tanzin told her, "You are the key, Kaiwon." Kwa-yin told her a few times that she was the key to freedom in Firewah. She understood the idea of 'The Key' as a metaphor, but it didn't make sense in practical terms. How could she be the key that lead herself out of Aunt Myra's house? She thought maybe it all just vivid "Star People" symbolism she wasn't grasping yet.

Is the golden key just a metaphor or something more?

Tanzin said that if she does not yet know who she is, she will. His words echoed in her skull. They begged her to ask the question she had long forgotten to ask.

Who am I? Who am I *really*?

Kai's eyes became so heavy until she couldn't keep them open one more second. It wasn't because she was suddenly tired; it was more like her open eyes were hindering her actual sight. Her body knew how to cure this. She fought the idea of closing her eyes for several moments until her body won her over. Her eyes closed. Within seconds she was transported through time.

Ages buzzed past her like simultaneous movies on either side of her. She was moving so fast she could not see the contents on either screen. When the screens stopped, she was by water. Most specifically, the shore of an ocean. She was watching a man and a golden key pull fish from a boat. She squinted to see the face of the man next to the key, but she couldn't make herself close enough. She sighed and when her eyes felt heavy, she closed them and began traveling again.

When she stopped this time, she was in a desert. There were people in ancient clothes handling the bustle of their lives. Kai caught a glimpse of a golden key standing next to a man who was seated on a throne. People were bowing to him and giving him gifts of spices, precious stones and food. He nodded to those who bowed before him. But he did no more than that. He knew he was above them, more than they could ever be. Kai was turned off by this in a way that bubbled in her stomach and made her frown deeply. She focused her attention on the key standing next to the man. She knew there was a person attached to the key, but she could not see the person, only the key's glowing gold shape. Her attention switched back to the man. There was something familiar about him, but nothing she could acknowledge.

Her eyes felt heavy again and she closed them. The screens on either side of her buzzed and she was traveling. When she stopped, she was in another time. The key was on the throne and a man familiar to her was its servant. Her inner eyes refused to focus on the key this time. Instead, they begged her to stay focused on the man. Something in her knew who the key was already, but she couldn't articulate it yet. Something in her also needed to be very clear about who the man was. She focused her attention on him as much as she could.

Why is this man so familiar? Who is he?

She closed her eyes and she traveled to a place that looked exactly like The Eden. It was different somehow, but not enough for it to be unrecognizable. The grass and the trees were breathing in accord with the flow of life. She saw the key in a group 12 Elders. There was one leader. He was familiar to her also. He was the same as all the other men the key was with in her other visions. Then she saw a battle. The 12 Elders were fighting many others in The Eden. The Eden was scorched and the 12 Elders fell from the sky. The key was one of those who landed in the mud of the Earth.

Kai traveled again. When she stopped, she wasn't on Earth. She was some place she didn't recognize. The sun and the moon were up at the same time, while night and day co-existed amicably, just like Eden. This place was bigger than Eden. There were people just like her, with stars on their foreheads and wings. They all had these gorgeous, slick, glistening wings of every color. Every color she saw, was the most beautiful color she'd ever seen. Every being she saw was the most beautiful she'd ever seen. She heard them speak and understood them. They could see her and bowed to her. Instinctively, she bowed back. "Osho Lovianhal", she said. "Lovianhal Quairu" They said back.

Quairu? Why don't I know that word? Then she entered a crystal castle floating upon twinkling turquoise colored clouds. She knew where she was going. She was going to see him. But he wasn't there. She looked all around his room, to no avail. She remembered they all left together. Her mother was with them. They left to do missionary work on a struggling planet. But only she returned. She remembered, her father didn't come home because he went mad. Her mother had to stay until the work they started was complete.

Her eyes became heavy and she traveled again. When she stopped, she was on Earth in a more modern time. She saw a man approach a beautiful woman in the park. He was talking to her, but he wasn't who he said he was. He was inside someone else's body. Kai couldn't see who was actually in that shell, but she knew the man talking to the woman wasn't good. The woman knew it too.

The woman looked in the direction of where Kai was standing. Kai thought she was an invisible spectator, but the woman was looking right at her, just as The Stai had. No one else noticed her presence at all. Kai looked lovingly at the woman. She noticed how elegant she was and beautiful. She looked other-worldly. The woman turned again to look in Kai's direction. This time, it was clear she was smiling directly at Kai. She was very familiar. Kai knew she knew her, but couldn't remember from where or how. The woman and her suitor started walking. Kai followed them. She was almost too close, because she wanted to hear what they were saying. There were bell-like whispers in Kai's ear. She trailed back because she felt heavy. She decided she no longer wanted to go where she was being led. She was afraid of what she might see. But those whispers in her ear continued. ***Oshharu Mairahu Nura Osho,*** they said. She had to continue. She could not let her fear, drag her back into darkness. She remembered Osho Lovian Osho. Light brings Love to Light...

The woman used a small, but ornate key to open the doors to an immaculate house. She invited the imposter in. Kai admitted, the body that the imposter was hiding in was spectacular. He reminded her of Henny with his height and well-formed body. His skin was bronze and his hair was a thick ocean of raven curls, like hers.

She motioned for the imposter to sit with her. When he sat, he put his substantial hand on her leg. She welcomed his touch. Kai shivered. The scene looked wrong. Kai wanted to call out to the woman to stop. She wanted her to know that the man she was with wasn't who he claimed to be. It dawned on her in that moment that the woman already knew. It was in her face. She was doing all of this on purpose. There was determination there. There was something about the woman that gave Kai's heart a pause. There was a light about her that she couldn't hide beneath her skin. Maybe it was the dullness of the man who was petting all over her. Every time the man touched her, his dullness would give way to a blush. Like he was colorless and touching her gave him color. The woman led him to her bedroom.

Once there, he became overwhelmed by her. He kissed her. When he did, he filled with light himself. It choked him. He pulled himself back from her in surprise. He looked afraid, like she wasn't what he expected. His face and body were full of color now. He and the body he was borrowing merged into one. All of the dullness that was once there was full of vibrant life. Kai watched as the man allowed himself to feel whatever the woman aroused in him. There was passion between them that was both beautiful and weirdly unnatural. She watched them make love over and again, both with an abandon that could not be duplicated. For all the time the two were together, the imposter was full of life and color. He gave to the woman every ounce of energy that he had. When it was all spent on her, he lay like a log on her intricately detailed bed. The beautiful woman got up and walked toward the door. As she walked, Kai could see a glimmer of something through the woman's skin. A tiny, golden key was glowing. Light beams flowed through it, through her. The woman looked in Kai's direction again, but Kai turned her head. When she looked back, The woman was gone.

Kai stood staring at the man that lay nearly lifeless on the bed. The body he was wearing crumbled to dust before her eyes. She looked at him in horror. A wind blew through the room, scattering the dust. What was left was the form of another being. It didn't look like anything Kai had ever seen. Everything about him was lanky and pointy and cold. Kai looked at him closer. He looked so familiar. He reminded her of all the other men she'd seen in her time travels. Then she smelled it. The sulfur. It was all around her. It was coming from him. Kai gasped. **Oh My God.** She thought.

Kai closed her eyes and she traveled to a tiny hospital room. The woman she saw before was giving birth. In the space where a baby should emerge, out came a golden key. The woman whispered something to the key, kissed it and then appeared to die. A blinding light, in the shape of a star came from the top of the key. The light overcame the hospital and when it stopped, the woman was gone. The doctors handed the key to a nurse who appeared out of thin air at the door. The nurse walked the key to a set of parents waiting to see their newborn.

The pair looked like Kai's parents, only much younger. The nurse handed the key to the couple. She spoke with the new parents briefly and then pulled out a birth certificate. She carefully wrote a name on the flimsy parchment. When this was done, the nurse smiled and was gone.

Kai felt dizzy. She watched the new parents coddling over their new baby and she felt like she wanted to throw up. What was she seeing? **What does all this actually mean?** Kai closed her eyes and when she opened them again, she was back in her bed in The Eden. She felt sick in every place of her body. She smelled the sulfur and the hospital room and the sea and the sand and the perfume of the woman she saw make love to the devil. Kai was overcome with every emotion she didn't know was available to her. The key. The key. The key. The key. No matter what she tried to think, all she kept hearing in her head was: The Key. **I am The Key.**

30 STANDING

"I would rather die standing than live on my knees!"
~Emiliano Zapata

Yamin was growing anxious. He stayed tirelessly with Kai, Kaitu and his unborn son, because he had no idea where the other Elders went. The Eden was very different and he noticed Kai was very different as well. She barely spoke to him now. He could tell a burden was laying on her and he felt badly that she didn't trust him enough to help her through it. It seemed Kai was on auto pilot. She was persistently zoned in her thoughts. She barely looked up from her feet to see where she was walking. He didn't want to pry. He didn't feel he earned the right to. He felt, as Kai probably did, that he had abandoned her. Regret lingered in him. He didn't know how he did it—change from Elder to man and then back to Elder. He certainly didn't know how to get himself back to being man again. Every so often, he thought he heard his heart beating or that he could feel Kai's skin when he was standing next to her. A strong part of him was conflicted. It was almost as if, at his whim, he could be human if he wanted, or he could stay Elder if it suited him. Was the choice actually his? He did not know. He did know, as the light in Kai's belly grew, so did his longing to be with her as man *and* confidante, not just as the latter.

Kai was having a hard time processing her visions. She wanted to talk about it with Yamin, but she wasn't sure where to begin or how to tell him what she saw. She knew her story was even more complicated than it had become. She was kind of sorry that she had ever asked the question when she wasn't fully invested in having it answered. The funniest part was the more she found out about herself, a lot of what she learned still made no sense. The stuff that did make sense was like believing in goblins and unicorns—and then telling people about it in all seriousness. She decided that her life was simpler with only part of the story. She realized she was much happier when she thought of herself as discarded laundry, rather than what she actually was. The good news, she supposed, was that at least she knew who her biological parents were. The bad news was that one of her parents is the devil. But she never figured out her mother. She also didn't know the correlation between what she saw in TuStai with the winged people and the crystal castle and what happened when she was conceived. It was all so weird.

The sickness she felt was constant. It consumed her. She tried to shake off the feeling of disgust, if only for her unborn child's sake, but she was unsuccessful most days. The thought of eating made her sicker. She thought maybe if she shriveled up in a ball and died, none of what she knew would matter. She couldn't reconcile what she knew and what she had left to learn. She wanted to forget, but she'd come too far. As much as she didn't want to eat, she had to because the growing body inside of her needed to be fed and would not be denied. Though her own skin dulled with every passing day, her womb glowed ever brighter. Kai sensed that her unborn son was much stronger than she was now.

She stepped outside of the crystal dwelling to watch Yamin play with Kaitu. He was an Elder, so he didn't play in the silly traditional ways that daddies play with their kids, but he did his best and Kaitu loved him deeply. He spent a lot of time her and started calling her Little Kai instead of Kaitu. When she went wandering while Kai slept, Yamin was right behind her. He watched her play and even when he wasn't visible to her, she knew he was there and talked to him. Kaitu was speaking Tuahstai a mile a minute now and Yamin was always there to talk with her. She was a clever, precocious child. Yamin beamed whenever he was with her.

Kai watched them and couldn't stop herself from smiling. She wondered, briefly, what Yamin would say if she told him what she really was. She was sure he didn't truly know the legacy of Star People and Sialovehal. He only knew the glammed up fairytale version Elders tell each other. Kai shut out this train of thought and walked back through the waterfall to get some sleep.

Yamin noticed Kaiwon's coming and going, and was curious. He collected Little Kai in his way and the two walked through the waterfall. He beamed when he saw her. He couldn't stop smiling. But then, he was a little sad for her. She was at once both dulling and brightening. He literally could see that his son growing inside her womb was what made her glow. He also saw pain in her face and eyes and he noticed how this pulled at her natural light. This perplexed him. He wanted to know what was troubling her so. But he couldn't bring himself to ask her. This feeling that she needed him made him long to be with her even more.

A big part of him missed lying next to her, holding her, caressing her. He missed kissing her sweet lips, which tasted like the Eden apples she so loved. His inner conflict grew. The three of them had become a family and he could not imagine not being with them. Kai looked up at him gloomily. She smiled gently. Once again, he started to ask, but he couldn't bring himself to. As he turned to leave the dwelling, Kai called his name. At least, he thought she did. When he turned to her, she was already occupied with Little Kai and didn't look up at him at all.

Yamin moved to sit by the river Asher, outside the waterfall dwelling. He closed his eyes, allowing all that he experienced of The Eden to wash over him. He remembered the smells, the sounds of the trees and grass breathing in one accord with his own. He opened his eyes slowly to the sight of Kwa-yin's breathtaking light. She floated above him, but close enough that if he reached out to her, he could touch the drape of her light laden robes. He took in her light for a moment. Then bowed to acknowledge her.

"Osho Lovianhal Quairu." He said.

She nodded.

"Osho Lovian Osho. You may stand if you wish." She said. Her bell-like voice was music for him.

For whatever reason, he stayed seated, but raised his head to hear whatever Kwa-yin had to say to him. Kwa-yin nodded. She knew his thoughts.

"Your conflict is easily resolved. You may be with them if you will to be." She said.

"I am not sure that is possible. I feel as though my time as man is past." He said, lowering his head.

"If that is the true desire of your heart, so it shall be." She said.

"I do not understand. I have no power to be human *or* Elder. I can only be who I am." He said.

"That is so."

"So how can I be with her... with them... like this?" He asked.

"You will fulfill the destiny you choose." She said.

Kwa-yin's words lay on him like the weight of a skyscraper on his throat.

"I can be man. Her man. I can be father to my children in human form if I choose?"

"That has always been so. It was you who conceived the child that will be born to you both soon. The desire in your being was great enough in this place to make it so. When your desire to be Elder outweighed your desire to be man, that too came to be. Your truth will always be honored." She said.

"But... how... I mean, when it's time to return to The Earth, how can I be the man I was? I died. I was dead and buried. I can't go back alive and well. That would be crazy." He said. He was starting to sound more human by the second.

"The how is not important. Only the what. Discover the desire of your heart and the universe shall do what is left. Kaiwon needs you more than she will tell you. She asked and has been shown who she is. Now she suffers because she must make peace with her knowledge."

"Is it her knowing that makes her sad?" He asked.

"No. Knowing cannot bring suffering. Not accepting what is brings suffering." She said.

"What has she been shown that is so hard for her to accept?"

"She came to bring her father home. But he is not well. He has not been well for many, many aeon. He is the reason The Entwine is out of balance. Only his true daughter can return him home. She needs you. You are *her* balance. Without you, she can't do what she's here to do. Osho Lovian Osho. Love her." Kwa-yin said.

Her blinding light flickered and she was gone. Her words clung to the Eden air like bright dust in the remnants of her light. Yamin was already on his feet, pacing by the river Asher. All kinds of thoughts coursed through him. When the reality hit him that he alone decided whether to be man or Elder, his stomach turned.

What am I doing?

The pull in him was about what was possible and impossible. It was about what was important to him and unimportant. The draw of the two faces he saw every day that were both independent of him and designed for him, circled through his head until he became dizzy. The dizziness consumed him. The words **Balance** and **Love** lingered in his mind. His Elder body fell limp by the river Asher and everything about Yamin went dark.

A breeze that made the trees giggle as it passed rolled him into the water. The river began to rumble until it reached a cool boil. From every corner, beams of light shot through the water until its crystal clearness became opaque with a cornucopia of colors. When the rumbling stopped, the water was clear again. A man's body rose to the surface and floated there. A few moments later, Kai walked through the waterfall to the bank of the river. She stopped because she thought she saw a man floating on the water. He wasn't really floating. He was lying on top of the water like it was a slab of glass. She rubbed her eyes to make sure she wasn't imagining him. He just lay there, flat on his back, naked and unfamiliar to her. Instead of turning her head from him, Kai stood looking. She actually allowed herself to enjoy what she saw until she could figure out what to do. Surprisingly, the sadness that had consumed her for so long started to fade. Everything about this man was breathtaking. His face was strong, like a warrior's. His body was glorious. He was so beautiful, she imagined the water designed him itself and then propped him up on it to be shown off. Kai walked closer to the floating river man. When she did, his unconscious body drew closer to her.

When he was close enough for her to touch, she pulled him out of the river. For her to do this, with little effort, was a testament of her evolving physical strength. She had placed him on the river bank and golden robes appeared on him as though they were there all along. Her son adjusted in her belly and then he glowed brighter than usual. The river man began to twitch slightly. Kai's heart skipped. She wasn't sure if he was breathing. She felt like a school girl when she touched his face softly and then put her hand on his chest. A rush of energy flowed through her body to his. He breathed in deeply and his body shot up into a seated position. Kai jumped backward. He opened his eyes slowly. When they focused, he saw her. He did not speak. He wanted to jump up and hug her, but he didn't. He felt groggy and discombobulated, so he just looked at Kai, longing in his eyes.

"Are you okay?" She asked.

He wanted to say something. Tears welled in his eyes, as all the emotion he felt in the moment washed over him.

"Do you know where you are? Do you know *who* you are?" Kai asked.

He didn't answer.

What was really strange was that Kai had never seen this man before, but he did not feel like a stranger. She felt like she's known him forever. She wondered where Yamin was. Normally he was not far from where she or Little Kai happened to be. She came out to the river to look for him. She found this man instead. Her mind quickly pondered the idea that she was actually looking at Yamin. A new Yamin. But she acknowledged the thought as nonsense.

"Do you know your name?" She asked.

Yamin wanted to speak, but he couldn't.

"Do you have a tongue? I know you have a mouth. It's quite nice actually. Whoever left you here has a wonderful sense of humor. Depending on how you look at it." Kai said exasperated.

Yamin smiled. He was starting to enjoy this game. He was laughing with is mouth closed.

"Wonderful. At least your ears work." She said. She didn't mean to sound sassy.

"At least I know, no matter how much I may change, you won't ever do so." Yamin said.

Kai looked at him both surprised that he spoke and surprised that she found something familiar in his words. She didn't recognize the voice or the face, but still there was something familiar about him.

"Do you know me?" She asked.

He didn't answer.

Kai looked at him bizarrely. She wished Yamin would come back. She was feeling confused. She knew Yamin could not be with her the way she wanted, but she was used to having him around. He was as much her family as Little Kai and the one in her belly. Kai knew Kaitu loved Yamin as her father.

190

It was interesting to Kai that she felt similarly for the stranger in front of her, as she did for Yamin. It was a longing and deep love. It was a love she had never felt for a man in her life. Whatever was going on in her was weird and she knew it was weird. But nothing she found in The Eden surprised her anymore. Yamin did not know why he did not tell Kai who he was. He wasn't sure if it was instinct or some sick sense of humor brewing in him. He supposed he just wanted to know if she would know him without his telling her.

"I can offer you a place to sleep. If you're hungry, Eden is not short on food. I'm sure when Yamin returns he can help you figure out who or what you are and why you came to be here. Forgive my rushing you up. I have a little one inside. You can follow me if you want...or you can stay here if you want. It's up to you." She said.

She tried to help the stranger up, but he politely refused her. He silently raised himself up from the river bank and hobbled a bit behind Kai through the waterfall. She noticed that the stranger did not hesitate going through the water as she had the first time she saw it. In fact, he seemed completely comfortable with where he was. Like he'd been there many times before. Kai was mystified. He walked over to the crystal table and helped himself to the fruit on it. He sat comfortably at the table and ate until he was full. She kept looking at him. In fact, she couldn't take her eyes off of him. At the same time, she kept wondering where Yamin was. And yet, she wasn't. There was a strange mix of thoughts swimming around in her head. She noticed that the closer she inched toward the river man, the brighter her stomach glowed.

31 COMFORTERS, KINDRED...

HOSPITAL, LIBRARY

"A scholar who cherishes the love of comfort is not fit to be deemed a scholar." ~Lao Tzu

Out from behind the curtain of a small wooden stage, a little old man hobbled toward his audience in a doctor's smock. His hair was starch white. He was plump and jolly, wearing glasses that sat a bit too tightly upon his flush cheeks. He walked with a wooden stick that had ancient carvings all over it. It was fat on the end that his fingers grasped, to hold him up.

The Comforters were seated in the auditorium that started out the size of a normal lecture hall, but ended up larger than anyone could imagine, to house them all. The old hospital was transforming before their eyes. They all sat; eerily quiet, watching what was unfolding around them, and waiting for the little old man to tell them why they were there. In the meantime, the room glowed on its own. It had to. The old hospital had no electricity. It was sitting for ages without a single visitor. Now this auditorium in this ancient hospital was full with people of all complexions, sizes and ages, surrounded by a warm light of unknown origin.

Before they were called to The Heaven and heard Tanzin speak, they all lived very normal lives. There was nothing they could say was extraordinary about them. They were just regular people. Or so they thought. What they knew now about themselves, individually, is that they are natural healers. They knew nothing about The Entwine or their place in it. They did not consider themselves the "highest form of human". They had no idea what that could even mean for them. They didn't even realize that each of them had at least one friend who was

Stellar. Or that they naturally would be drawn to that person to replenish their energy. They didn't know any of this before. They wondered how this knowing would change the way they interacted with their world.

Would they do the same things? Would knowing they are designed for more, make them more comfortable with being and doing more in the world?

The little old man hobbled to the center of the stage. He cleared his throat. Without the benefit of a microphone or a sound system, everyone in the room could all hear him as though the walls were made of speakers.

"I... am known by many names, but for as long as I can remember in this life cycle, I have been called Devascus." He said. His voice was the perfect blend of balmy and crackly.

The hundreds, maybe thousands of Comforters that congregated in the old hospital auditorium listened carefully as Devascus gave them general information about who the Comforters were as a whole and that they would learn most about themselves and their grand design individually while they slept that night.

Within moments, Devascus greeted a young nurse named Ono who led them all downstairs to their meal, where they were served by a league of nurses who sang them a beautiful song while they ate in silence.

Several blocks over, at the exact moment the Comforters were making their way to their beds, out from behind rows upon rows of empty book cases--once filled with masterpieces of every century-- hobbled a little man with white hair and an intricately carved walking stick. The hundreds, maybe thousands of Kindred, who made up the audience in the tiny old and forgotten library, were greeted in the same way and given similar instruction. For the Kindred, Devascus relayed to them their intellectual purpose in the grand design of The Entwine. Each soul listened completely to what was being shared with them. They too were led downstairs to their meal by a young librarian named Suno. They were served by a brood of librarians who sung them a song, while they ate silently. Then they went off to their beds, which were transformed for them in the library, so they could receive their individual instruction. They could not know how soon their time would come to serve their purpose in The Great War, already underway.

32 LUCIFER'S BRAND

"Every day people are straying away from church and going back to God." ~ Lenny Bruce

From nowhere, the battle inside Cathedral came to a screeching halt. Silence floated to the surface of the building. Lucifer's cackle ceased. The quiet filled him instantly with rage. He sensed something wrong below. He attempted to move from his perch, but could not. His wiry legs were stuck to the cross he straddled on Cathedral's dome. With all his might, he could not pull himself from the cross. The more he tried, the more attached the cross became to his lanky body. Fear rushed him. And then pain. It felt like the cross was trying to enter his body. It felt like it was eating him from the outside in. Not knowing how to pry himself loose, he stopped moving. When he stopped moved, the cross stopped moving. But then, a blinding light appeared in front of him, threatening to swallow him whole.

The light was so bright; Lucifer couldn't keep his eyes open. When he tried to squint, to catch the tiniest glimpse, his eyes burned. It was so agonizing, the pain made him let out a horrid squeal of anguish that took over all of his wretched soul. Somewhere deep, he knew he was not worthy of her splendor. He failed her in so many ways; he'd forgotten most of them. For whatever reason, he thought of his wings. Then the pictures of a former life spilled into his awareness.

He remembered that his wings were always the glory of TuStai. No one but he wore black wings. They were glossy and raven colored. Their span filled the largest room. He loved that. But then he left. He was on a mission. He had important work to do... he remembered that. Then his head hurt. An intense pain shot through the middle of his face. It felt like someone stabbing him with daggers. He screamed louder. Kwa-yin's light began to penetrate even his closed eyes. This burned. Through his pain, he wanted to say something to her. He wanted to remember all of it. But he knew he was not worthy to hear her voice. He failed her. She couldn't go back because he was here. The loudest claps of thunder smacked the sides of his face with words he was not ready to hear.

"Your time here is nearing its end." She said.

And that was all. Her light was gone. Lucifer heard every syllable of every word as clearly as if he said them himself. The thunder claps echoed through the sky for hours after they were spoken to him. Lucifer was filled with a fear unlike any he had known before. He was afraid, because until now, he didn't even think that he was from somewhere else. He felt like he misplaced something along the way to get where he was. To feel Kwa-yin's presence, reminded him of something long lost to him. His every molecule was shaking uncontrollably. For the first time since his feet hit Earth's soil, Lucifer was unsure of his fate. And more profoundly, he was unsure of who he was. And then, like someone pushed a button and the tape began to play, the sounds of battle could be heard again. It started slowly like the tape was adjusting itself and when ready, it played at full speed, overturning the deafening silence with the sounds of cackles, screams and things being broken...

At the same time, the cross released itself from Lucifer. Along the front of his body, burned into layers of his dark clothes and 'spirit skin' was the form of a five point star. He looked at the cross in horror. He hadn't noticed the gold star that embellished the center of the cross until now. He ran his fingers over his chest. When he did, a searing pain ran through him that made his being shiver in agony. Even when he didn't touch it, at its own will, it tortured him. It acted as a living thing with its own volition. It became his parasite. His fear morphed quickly into anger. This anger morphed quickly into something else. If it was possible for Lucifer's insanity to sink in deeper and become viler, it had. His anger was his affliction. He didn't know how he contracted it, but it was all he had now.

He had not expected her to come to him. He thought her pathetic and friable. The brand on his chest incensed him to no rightful end. As it persistently offended him with pain, he looked to the sky with defiance seething through him. A weaker soul force may have taken a moment to reflect. Maybe take a moment to see what was truly really happening. To see the signs in everything. Not Lucifer. In his contorted mind, he was the most powerful being on The Earth. Once the war below proved successful, he would be the most powerful being in The Heaven too. His arrogance circumvented whatever flashes of good sense he may have had left. His insanity made the revenge he was cooking up for Kwa-yin possible. It also made him scream at the sky.

"That's the best you've got Kwa-yin?! Huh? That's the best you can do? It will take far more than a star on my chest to stop me! I am Lucifer! You hear me Kwa-yin? Do you hear me? I AM LUCIFER!" He was saying these things more for him than for her. "Just wait... I've got something up my sleeve that you will not even believe!" He said.

His rage took over the little Elder voice that was trying to reason with him. He was so angry, he willed himself from Cathedral, and to the place he was most comfortable. His pride and pleasure. The place he's called home for eons. When the heat hit his face and the smell of sulfur crossed his nostrils, the searing pain of the star covering the top half of his body didn't seem to bother him as much. He looked upon the blood red sky of Firewah. Then he looked out upon all the souls he had planted there. He heard the many screams and it was like listening to the symphony of his dreams. The souls were crying for freedom, of course, but in his mind it sounded like they were saying: "Lucifer, the great! Lucifer the king of The Heaven and The Earth!"

The truth was irrelevant to him. It was a trivial thing Kwa-yin had cooked up and he wanted no parts of it. Lies, to him, were what made the world go round. Lies were what made the world bearable to the masses. Lies were what made Lucifer so great, even if it was only in his mind.

His thought about the place on Earth where three small boys and their mothers were being kept. He was going to order them destroyed. He only kept them alive this long to torture Kwa-yin, but Kwa-yin didn't seem tortured much. The more he thought of the children, the more painfully clear it became to him that he hadn't captured the child he needed.

Cliché as it was, he knew the child was the key to his win. It was always written that way. Some sparkling child is born from a virginal mother, to save the world from itself. He laughed to himself. It was always stories like these that made his work so easy. Humans had been taught to feel unworthy. How could they ever measure up to a virgin birth? Then that racket about "original sin". That prose was sheer genius. If you teach people they're already sullied, it's not a stretch for them to stay comfortable that way. All he had to do is put people's desires in their faces. Pressure breaks pipes. Lie to them. Tell them their base desires are everything because someone said they were evil. His work on The Earth was a masterpiece of minimalism. He barely did a thing. He simply stoked the fires of ignorance that had been burning long before he arrived.

Hmmm. He thought. ***Arrived? I arrived?*** He wasn't thinking about his past lives via The Entwine. He was remembering glimmers of something else. He dismissed these glimmers abruptly and went back to his task of revenge. There was no way Kwa-yin would dare come down to Earth to mock him, if her precious 'chosen one' had been captured. She would most certainly gravel at his feet, begging him not to kill the child. Which, of course, he would do anyway. Once he realized this, he knew what he must do. He must find the child and destroy it.

He thought to send another one of his soul thugs to handle this type of work, but he did not trust them to get it right this time. He was devising a plan to capture Kwa-yin's precious chosen child. He knew when he did; the tides would surely turn his way. He was sure this was the answer.

He had no idea he would have to travel where he had been forbidden since The Fall to complete this task. The star branded on his chest sizzled. He laughed through the pain, determined more than ever to ignore that it even existed. It was after all, his own cross to bear.

33 SLOW MOTION

"His breath like silver arrows pierced the air, The naked Earth crouched shuddering at his feet, His finger on all flowing waters sweet Forbidding lay-motion nor sound was there- Nature lay frozen dead-and still and slow, A winding sheet fell o'e" ~Frances Anne Kemble

Everything was going in slow motion. The people of The Earth were still holding hands, but now it felt like they could feel the planet rotating on its axis. It made them dizzy, standing there, hand in hand, singing the Seraph battle song. They were still outside the church, just behind the dark wall that blocked their view of what was going on in front of them. They stood facing the forces inside the church that would determine their fate, but couldn't see anything. It started to get dark where they were standing. The warm glow that covered them had begun to dissipate. "Om Namo Rah Om" started to sound silly in their ears. They decided, one by one, to stop. When all mouths stopped moving and individual silence took over most of them, they looked around and began to see themselves and who they were standing next to.

"Eew Bum! Get your filthy hands off me! You stink! And stop begging for handouts all the time! Get a job!"

An older woman, with grey hair and skin that looked like crumpled note paper, was yelling at a much older panhandler she was standing next to.

"Get your hands off of me, you filthy little monkey! You're an abomination! Go back to where you came from. Don't you know my people were born to be better than your people? That's why you will never be more than property to me."

A white man was looking down over a little black boy when he said this.

He saw how different from him the boy was now. It disgusted him. It wasn't just these two, it was all of them. A Spanish woman released her hand from the hand of an Asian child.

"You're not my child, chino!" She cried.

An Asian man threw down the hand of a Native American girl in a flurry of insults. A religious zealot threw away the hand of a little boy wearing a bright pink tutu. Wherever there were differences, the adults violently flung away the hands of the children next to them, leaving them with only ugliness and insults. Soon, all of the adults had separated themselves from all the children who weren't their own. Then they separated themselves from anyone who didn't look like them. The adults began to scurry around, shouting obscenities at each other, forgetting all about the unconditional love they just experienced together.

It was not anger that consumed them now, for the anger had been dissipated with Kwa-yin's tears. What they suffered from now was habit. They had been so used to being, living, talking and thinking a certain way, that when left with themselves again, they simply reverted back to what they knew. The adults were frantic. They walked about trying to find comfort in people who looked more like them or spoke in the same way. When the light enraptured them, they were so intermixed, so blended, that now they were frustrated to get their homogeneousness back. Pandemonium happened. The adults were screaming at one another to get away from them or to stop bumping them. The screaming and obscenities continued, but in its wake, something miraculous happened. The children were unmoved. The warm glow still filled them. They quietly stepped forward into the darkness, one by one, leaving the scurrying adults behind them in chaos. The children closed in together, raised their arms, held the hands closest to them and again sang *Om Namo Rah Om.* The adults were so busy arguing, they didn't even notice.

34 LUCIFER'S QUEST

"In all our quest of greatness, like wanton boys, whose pastime is their care, we follow after bubbles, blown in the air." ~ John Webster

Lucifer sat in Firewah, enjoying the sights and sounds of his own, private pandemonium. All the screams and cries were music to his ears. He was like a mad conductor, raising his arms and flicking his hands like he was managing the screams into their song. His red eyes flickered, and he leaned back against one of his lost soul mountains. Of course he didn't care that doing this meant there was a face being smothered against his back. He leaned back further and laughed.

"Now. For my quest." He began aloud. "Where would Kwa-yin hide the most precious from me? Surely it wouldn't be among the common fools I just left. Hmmm. She would have found a special place that she thinks I cannot find..."

He pursed his lips as he continued to conduct his screaming choir and then... it hit him!

"NO! She would not keep the child on The Earth. She would keep him close to *her*!"

His sneaky smile foiled into a mucky frown.

"I have two choices. I can lure the child and its mother down here or I can make my way up there. I will certainly be outnumbered in The Heaven..." he continued. "But if I bring my minions, they will know I'm there for sure."

He fiddled his long pointy fingers along his face, working things out in his head. He realized just how much he adored an audience. It charged his mind. He turned in such a way so that as he was thinking and speaking aloud, he was also addressing all the souls screaming at him in scattered defiance.

"Kwa-yin must be expecting that I'll lure the child here. She can't expect that I would dare go up there alone and remove the child personally. Ha! How wrong she is. But I must be cleverer than her this time."

Then his sneaky smile returned to his dull face. He knew exactly what he would do and he knew time was a premium.

35 THE WAR UNWINNABLE

"There is no glory in battle worth the blood it costs."

~ Dwight D. Eisenhower

The battle between the "Light Bearers" and the "Dark Forces" was still going on, but each side was growing tired. The warriors themselves were dwindling, but no side was winning and no side was losing. Micah determined that it was time to speak up on his hunch. He summoned the lead Guardian and Stellar for a brief counsel.

"Are you noticing that we aren't making any headway in this war?" He asked, getting right to the point.

"Yes. Our fallen, have matched their fallen exactly." Yoko said.

"Nafi, do you know what this means?" Micah asked.

"I do not. But as it appears, numbers are important here. Our numbers at this point are exact to theirs. It seems that we are not meant to win or lose this war." Nafi said.

"Why would we be called to fight a war we cannot win or lose?" Ree asked, adjusting her bun.

"Maybe this is not really a war in the truest sense. Maybe... it's more of a distraction for something bigger, like a Trojan horse." Yoko said.

"Don't be silly child. Kwa-yin would not waste warriors for no reason." Said Yoko's Guardian, Reeir.

"I didn't say it was for no reason", Yoko said. "I think maybe we're here for a different reason than we think."

The rest of the group rumbled to themselves.

"What moved you to speak those words child?" Asked Rala, Ree's Guardian. She was looking at Yoko.

Yoko stiffened.

"It was in my dream." She said quietly.

"Speak up child. This is no time to be a wilting flower." Said Meeuu, Teerah's Guardian.

Yoko cleared her throat and began again.

"Before this battle began, I dreamed about a mirror. At one moment I saw myself in it. And at another I saw light falling from the sky, inside the mirror. When I turned from the mirror, behind me was a field like the one from when we all met. When I turned back to the mirror I saw a blood red sky and mountains of ash and soot. I saw souls sticking out from every granule of black sand. When I turned around, I saw rain washing over the soot mountains. When I turned back to the mirror, I saw a woman made of light standing next to a golden key. The key was holding something in its womb that was also made of light. It filled the blood red sky, causing it to open. Then a little girl directed the souls to form a cloud that evaporated before my eyes." She said.

"Are you sure you are not mistaken? Are you sure you saw what you are saying?" Meeuu asked more for effect than reassurance.

Yoko decidedly kept from bristling under Meeuu's gaze.

"I am sure. It was clear to me as though I was there. I didn't understand what it meant until now. We are here, to clear the way." She said.

The idea seemed frivolous. They looked around the battle field and watched as fire and mania replaced evil soldiers and cool breezes caught and lifted the light soldiers upward through the sky of the church. The Guardians were not used to having the desire to question Kwa-yin. The Stellar were quite used to questioning everything because everything at this point was new to them. At the same time, all 14 of them collectively had the prodigious feeling that their best course of action at this point was to call in their troops and stop their fight. From their kneel, all 14 stood in unison. They lifted their arms and hands in separate mudras and a wall of light rushed around them in the middle of the battle field. Inside the wall was what was left of their soldiers— The Stellar, Guardians and Seraph.

The dark soldiers looked around and saw nothing but a giant, bright orb in the middle of the massive battle grounds. The sky of the church was empty and quiet except where for the heavy flapping of the Reepers black wings. The dark breezes stopped swirling, as Purveyors found their legs on the ground. The Seraph song was replaced with silence. Every blood red, evil eye was on the light orb. In unison, the dark warriors looked to the ground, not knowing what they were to do next. This was not what they expected. Their dark chests heaved in and out. They breathed in the same time with the orb. Lucifer did not come to them.

The light of the orb grew ever brighter and brighter and brighter. Rays filled the battlefield until the field was transformed back into the old church. The dark soldiers could only watch as all this happened. They were exhausted from fighting for no purpose beyond the fight. One by one, each dark soldier fell to their knees. They did not look up to the sky of the church. They kept their heads bowed to the tiles of the church floor. At the front of Cathedral, a muffled squeaking sound came toward them from a long corridor behind the alter. An old voice broke the thunderous silence.

"Would you like to see the truth?" Devascus' weather-beaten throat thundered his words from his diminishing body. His question filled the air and then hung there like a bright lamp in the dark.

36 THE FAMILIAL STRANGER

"A single event can awaken within us a stranger totally unknown to us. To live is to be slowly born. ~Antoine de Saint-Exupery

Kai was still trying to figure out her strange attraction to the river man. She still had no clue that he was Yamin, transformed. She fawned over him like a school girl, but her attraction was so much deeper than she could make sense of. She really felt like she knew him and it was throwing her off. She was carrying Yamin/Lani's baby. That notion also threw her off. Yamin was an Elder, so he couldn't be with her to raise their kids. **Would the universe then send her someone who would? Out with the old, in with the new? Just like that?** This idea didn't sit right with her. It felt frivolous to her. **Why put in all that time and energy, just to switch it around?** She rolled her eyes at the river man. The more she looked at him, the less appealing he became. Her thoughts kept finding their way back to Yamin. He just disappeared. She didn't know why she felt like she owed him some sort of loyalty, but she did. She frowned. She contended that no matter how she was feeling, before she did anything, she needed to speak with him. She needed him to know that she really wanted him. That they would find a way together. That's what she wanted to say. It pained her that Yamin wasn't there so she could say it to him.

Yamin felt like a fraud sitting across the room from Kai and not saying anything to her. She honestly didn't know who he was. He looked that different. He wanted her to be able to tell, without him needing to say, "Look here woman! It's me Yamin! I'm your river man!" The entire concept sat horribly in his psyche. He wasn't being romantic about it; he just needed a sense of confirmation from her. That she wanted him and him a alone, no matter what package he came in. He wanted her to know *him*. He was sure he was being irrational, but after undergoing his third body change in so many days, he didn't want to have to talk about it and answer questions there was no way for him to answer. If she just *knew,* he felt like his transition would go smoother. He would feel like he had an ally.

So, he sat across the room and watched her. When he felt her eyes on him, he looked away, finding something in the room to focus on besides her. When she looked away, he was looking at her again. What he really wanted to do was go to her, hug and kiss her until his new lips and arms were sore. He wanted to tell her that he was here for her. That whoever she was, was exactly what he wanted. That divine mind got it right with them and he would never willingly leave her in any form he found himself. It wasn't pride that kept him in his seat. It was his quiet fear that he wasn't enough for her.

She's Sialovehal. What happens if she has to go back? Kwa-yin said Kai came for her father. Does Kai know that? Is it her role to return him personally to TuStai?

The more he sat there stealing glances at Kai, while she was on the other side of the room stealing glances at him, the pettier his fears seemed. He knew he could spend all of his time with her on the sidelines watching or he could be living this moment with her right now.

What am I waiting for?

After a long while, Yamin resolved to go to her and at least make small talk. He hadn't the slightest idea why he hadn't spoken to her already. The longer it took for him to speak, the more he didn't know what he would say to explain why he hadn't spoken already. The whole thing made him feel crazy. He knew he was being silly, but he couldn't make himself do anything worthwhile. He thought going over to Kai was the easiest thing in the world to do, and yet he could not bring himself to do it. And then his time ran out. Kai let out a weak wail, as her body shot up from her chair. She held her stomach and then fell to the ground.

Yamin ran to her and scooped her lifeless body his arms.

"Kai! Kai! No! No, no, no, no. No. You can't Kai! You can't!" He was shaking her, but she didn't move. Her body was limp. Her skin, cool to his touch. "Kai!"

He touched her stomach. The light was gone. Yamin was confused. She is supposed to have his son.

How could this be happening?

Yamin rocked Kai, tears welling his eyes and then he saw little Kai's lifeless body on the ground across the room. He screamed from a place he didn't know lived in him. He didn't understand. He came back to them this way, so he could be with them. Did he do this? Did his fear of Kai cause this? He shook his head in sorrow and let his tears fall to the golden sand. He lifted Kai from the floor and placed her in their cloud covered bed. Then he collected little Kai and placed her body next to her mother's. He kneeled by the bed, and wept. He promised himself silently that he would never let his time run out again. There was a glimmer of hope in his heart that somehow, some way... this too was a part of a greater plan unfolding before his very eyes.

37 RETURN FROM THE FALL

"Hello Boys, I'm Baaaack!" ~Russell Casse (Independence Day, 1996)

Lucifer was in his lair practicing his low-spirited meditative process, preparing for his most brilliant plan yet. He, the greatest Elder who ever dwelled in The Heaven, and he who had been ousted from his manifest destiny, was preparing his own way back to where his greatness began so long ago. He could hardly focus on his task because he was too busy reveling in his own importance! He imagined the face of Kwa-yin and how surprised she would be to see him in The Heaven.

"Ahhhh!" He thought aloud. "The malevolent bliss to finally accomplish my life's work. To be ruler of all The Heaven and The Earth! To walk freely as master of all created things!" Lucifer was almost giddy. Almost.

He began to think of the ways Kwa-yin had foiled his many plans throughout the ages. All the war mongers he helped to rise to power and were defeated. All the manic social experiments gone to pot. Every grand thing he had ever cooked up in his head, somehow, someway, was cooled by Kwa-yin. His chest seared with pain, but he refused to look at the source. Lucifer shivered with disgust. His mouth formed a deep scowl that stayed upon his face until he could force other of his thoughts to peek through. The little Elder voice that found his ears every now and again, sharing reason, wisdom and telling him frankly that nothing was what it seemed; was replaced with Lucifer's unending fear and anger. He was manic with it. He had no idea he was crazy. He had no idea how he ended up here. There was another soul force inside of him, begging to be heard. He called it his Elder voice, but Lucifer knew that voice was older than time. It was there all along, before anything that ever was. It was from someplace else, like he was. His instinct told him he was here for some other task. That he was stricken by madness and lost his way. He let these thoughts roll around in his head, but none of them took root where they needed to. He knew he was great at one time, but something in him transformed. He didn't remember how, all he knew was what he faced now.

His thoughts went back to their current mission. He had to destroy that child Kwa-yin was protecting. He was determined to shut Kwa-yin down. He was determined to live his destiny. He was determined to be more creator than The Creator. Lucifer closed his eyes and focused on his destination. He called to his mind his long forgotten memories of The Heaven. He focused on being there. It was difficult, because he was so out of practice. But after some time, he felt his will move him from the heat of Firewah, upward. Like a breeze he felt refreshed as he kept moving. The more intent on his destination he was, the faster he moved. And then he stopped. When his eyes opened, he saw trees wilting around him. Where he sat, the breathing grass started choking and then turned black.

"Ha! I did it!" He said.

He jumped up from his seat and at first, had a hard time moving. It felt like trying to push himself through steel. He forgot that The Heaven was impossible to move through without truth. But then he remembered how strong his will was when he was an Elder. He closed his eyes, channeled his thoughts and determined he would move freely. The invisible steel that was holding him back let him go. Lucifer took several steps and noticed that everywhere he walked the grass made a choking sound and turned black as the soot in Firewah. This delighted him! He laughed to himself. The foliage around him wilted. With every step he took, beautiful Eden withered.

38 SQUISH, CHOKE

"I wonder where you are tonight/ you're probably on the rampage somewhere/ you have been known to take delight/ in getting' in somebody's hair/and you always had the knack/fade to black" ~Dire Straits

"Maybe you'll love me when I fade to black." ~Jay Z

Cinqo was still in his self-imposed prison feeling sorry for himself, when, weirdly, the whiteness of the walls became transparent. He heard in the distance, sounds of choking. It was more like a **squish-choke, squish-choke, squish-choke**. The walls around him were pulsing to the rhythm of that sound. They thinned out with the squish and went back to opaque with the choke. As the squish-choke got closer, Cinqo felt less trapped. He thought he might try sitting up and realized he could! He lurched onto his feet and moved closer to where the walls were pulsing. That's when Cinqo saw him.

Oh my She! He is here! How is he here?

Cinqo couldn't think of any good reason Lucifer would or even could be back in The Heaven, until an obvious notion hit him in the head like a boulder.

Oh My She! He has come for Kaiwon and Kailu.

He bristled at the thought. In the deepest part of him, he knew what he must do, but another part of him was still bitter. It was as if his entire body wanted to split in half. One half wanted to run to Kaiwon and save her. The other half knew he would face Yamin there, which turned his stomach sour. Cinqo was expecting the Elders to be scurrying about with every **squish-choke** shaking The Eden as Lucifer made his way through her. There was no scurry of Elders. No breezes of Guardians.

There was nothing except him. His instinct was telling him that Lucifer didn't know where to look for the two he came for. He also knew he couldn't get to them more quickly than Lucifer without his Angelic powers. The pull was too strong. He had to help his charge. He raised his head to speak his affirmation to the center of all existence.

"I am so grateful." He began. "I am so grateful for this life of adventure and transformation. I am so grateful for the true nature of my heart which begs to be of service. I am grateful that wherever I am needed most, I will be led. I am further grateful that every one of my needs are met to move me where I'm designed to go. I am grateful for my charge and my duty to protect her. I will fulfill my duty. I am fulfilling my duty right now. I am, as I was designed, since before these Heavens existed, Cinqo, of the Angelic Guardian, brought forth to protect the Sialovehal Quairu Kaiwon of TuStai. And so it is. Oshharu Mairahu Nura Osho set Osho Lovian Osho."

He bowed to The Eden and The Heaven in general and then sat to wait. After a long while, nothing happened. He started to think he had his answer. He started to think he was exactly where he was supposed to be, sitting on the sidelines while his charge met her end. Something in him wouldn't let that be. He decided to go before Lucifer anyway. He stood and pushed his naked body through the paper thin membrane of The Heaven. On the other side, he was wearing his Angelic robes. He smiled while transitioning to his breeze form.

He breezed over Lucifer's head. Lucifer looked up, to see what was buzzing above him, but did not lose his stride. He didn't know where to look, so he was allowing his will and desire to direct him. It always worked for him when he was Elder; he knew it was working now.

Cinqo transitioned out of his breeze form once he reached the waterfall dwelling. He walked through the waterfall expecting to see Kai and Kaitu with Yamin having family time, instead he found some strange man weeping at the feet of the lifeless bodies of his charges. He spun through the dwelling in his breeze form, transitioned back to Angelic, and in one swift movement lifted the stranger over his head.

"What have you done?!" He yelled.

Yamin physically deflated at the sight of Cinqo.

"I have done nothing. They just fell. Her light went out. I don't know what happened." He was in so much pain, he barely whispered.

It took Cinqo a minute to catch his bearings. The stranger, although he didn't *look* like Elder Yamin, he *wreaked* of him. Cinqo was curious enough to put him down. Yamin slumped himself back on the floor next to the bed where his two loves lay, then placed his hand in Kaiwon's limp hand.

"How did you come to look like this Yamin?" Cinqo asked. He was tip-toing the line between curiosity and astonishment. ***Have I been away that long?*** He thought.

"I don't know." Yamin looked at Cinqo like it was too much effort just to lift his head. "It doesn't matter now does it? I did this for her. I thought I did... and her spirit isn't even..."

He stopped. A thought crossed him abruptly. Then his face brightened literally like someone just slapped him in the face with his own life force. He turned to Cinqo.

"Her spirit isn't here, but her body is. She's traveling!" He said.

Yamin jumped to his feet and looked around the room. He didn't see her, but hoped he would. To Cinqo, he just looked crazy. Cinqo shook his head.

"Your words make no sense Elder. Kaiwon is Sialovehal, she has evolved visions. She does not Soul Travel. If she could, she wouldn't have needed to be born on The Earth plane." Cinqo said.

Yamin looked at Cinqo soberly.

214

"You haven't been here to know what she can do. She leaves her body and travels. I've seen her do it." He said.

Cinqo thought quickly back to Kai's apartment, when she first said she saw Firewah. She said she smelled sulfur in her hair, but he thought she was remembering from a sensorial perspective. It didn't dawn on him that she was actually traveling. At the time he was so focused on which side she would choose, he misread what was actually happening to her. While this unfoldment was vital, he had more pressing concerns at the moment.

"Lucifer is here for them." Cinqo said.

"He is here? How?"

"I do not know, but he is coming this way." Cinqo said.

"This place is built on truth, how can he even move here?"

"It is written that before The Fall, his will was stronger than this place." He paused for emphasis. "Not unlike your... not unlike Kaiwon."

"What are you saying?"

Yamin wasn't sure why his face was getting hot, but it sounded to him like Cinqo was saying something important about Kaiwon, disguised around an insult. Cinqo shook his head.

"You do not know, do you?"

Yamin tensed.

"I don't know what? That she was brought here to bring her father home? Kwa-yin told me. What else is there to know?"

"Who her father is."

"What does it matter? Kwa-yin said he went mad and got lost. We already know that more than one Sialovehal on The Earth plane at a time is what causes the imbalance. It explains why everything has been so out of sorts. He probably doesn't even know who he is. So Kai finds her father, returns him to TuStai in whichever way she does that, and everything goes back to almost normal. You don't need to tell me, I already know everything has changed." Yamin said. He sounded like he had it all figured out. Cinqo shook his head knowingly.

"I think it best that she tell you or you somehow figure it out in the next moment. Either way, Lucifer will be here well before then." He said.

Something shifted in Yamin. He felt like Cinqo was toying with him.

"What? What do you know that you're not saying?" Yamin's voice was prickly. His eyes were focused like lasers on Cinqo.

"There is no time." Cinqo said.

He stood silently for a moment. His thoughts started to consume him because he didn't know what to do. Angelic don't panic, they close their eyes and wait. So he did. The colors of Eden rushed his mind into swirls until they manifested a new picture. He nodded. When all the things he needed to see were revealed, he opened his eyes. Matter-of-factly, he turned to Yamin.

"I know what we must do." He said. "Let him come."

39 CINQO'S CALL

"If you want to become whole, let yourself be partial. If you want to become straight, let yourself be crooked. If you want to become full, let yourself be empty. If you want to be reborn, let yourself die. If you want to be given everything, give everything up." ~Lao Tzu

Lucifer was making his way. With each **squish-choke**, he was closer to the waterfall, by the river Asher. He knew, instinctively, what he wanted was behind the waterfall. He slowed down. It was strange to him that he had walked the course of The Eden and was met with no opposition at all. No Elders or Seraph. No Guardians. No Angelic. Nothing. The only sound that could be heard in all of The Eden, besides the sounds of trees wilting at his approach, was the sound of his footsteps. His slow gait turned into a stop. He felt so big walking around in The Eden, but now his fear was creeping back. He looked around and it dawned on him briefly that he was expected. *What if...?* His thoughts began, and then trailed off. *I am here now. The child is here. I must obtain the child.* The **squish-choke** resumed with his steps.

Yamin and Cinqo could hear Lucifer coming from the other side of The Eden. The closer his footsteps, the more Yamin wanted to know what Cinqo knew.

"He will come and you expect that we will defeat him?" Yamin asked.

Yamin was puffed up, but didn't actually know what was expected of him. The Stellar in him was ready for the fight, but a fight would not defeat Lucifer. It would only give him more strength. Cinqo looked at Yamin with pity. He never saw an Elder in such a confused and weakened state. Then he remembered briefly what it felt to be human again, naked and unsure of his future. Unsure of his purpose. He remembered what it felt like to lose grasp of his true self. He turned to Yamin with a stronger sense of compassion than he had known before. He knew his words would save Yamin's life.

"Fear has no place here brother. If we are to be victorious for *our* charge, we must channel our love for her. That is the only way. Otherwise, Lucifer will take them both and he will destroy them. Do you understand what I am saying to you?"

Yamin's eyes were sad. In one sense he hoped his hunch was correct, that, Kaiwon and Kaitu were actually traveling outside of their bodies. But in another sense, he couldn't shake Cinqo's words about not knowing who Kai really was. He needed to know what Cinqo meant. And he needed to know how he was supposed to protect his family. The feeling of powerlessness crept up on him. His options were limited, if he had any at all. Cinqo nodded and moved closer to Yamin knowingly. Before placing his hands over Yamin's eyes, he whispered the truth he knew his Eden brother needed to hear.

"She is The Key. Her mother is of Light, while her father... found his darkness. She is the only truth of his lies." After he said this, Yamin's eyes went dark.

Cinqo laid Yamin's lifeless body next to Kaiwon and Kaitu's. He looked down at them and saw the divine family Kwa-yin had haphazardly thrown together. In his mind, he tried to place himself where Yamin was, but couldn't. He realized his place was exactly where he stood, protecting her, not lifeless next to her. For a moment, he thought again about being a man. He couldn't help but wonder what a kiss was like from her. He bent down and placed his 'lips' on Kaiwon's. He let his Angelic form hover very closely over hers. He tried to breathe in her scent and let it ring around in him. He was no longer man, so his efforts were fruitless. Before he could raise himself up, a deep bawl filled the cavernous, waterfall dwelling.

"Well, well, well. Paint me pathetic. I must say, this is a sight I've never seen before." Lucifer said. The grin on his face said he was utterly tickled.

Cinqo shot up and turned to face Lucifer. He gasped. He forgot how much Lucifer changed. The two were never close, but at one time, he was kind. Cinqo couldn't remember what he looked like before, but now he faced a shell of the man he was once. Cinqo shook out his thoughts. Luckily his tongue was quick.

"Your being here again is also a sight. This..." he nodded toward the lifeless bodies he was standing over. "is nothing... compared to what you have accomplished, just by being present in The Eden again." He said, matter-of-factly.

Lucifer looked down at the three bodies. Then up at Cinqo. He smiled.

"You did this?" He asked.

"I did." Cinqo said.

Lucifer was quiet. He was taking in the scene. What he saw, at face value, was a pregnant woman, a little girl, and a man lying together. They looked dead. Cinqo was standing over them, like a jealous lover. Lucifer looked Cinqo up and down. He recognized the Angelic from somewhere, but it wasn't from his time as Elder. He blew off the thought. He instead tilted his head, adjusted his neck, and laughed his horrible, sinister laugh. His laugh rang through The Heaven and The Eden. It infected all that it touched with darkness. The remaining trees wilted, the grass breathed its last breath and turned black. As his laugh continued to infect everything, Eden itself appeared to die. Clouds filled the sky until all that could be seen of The Eden was darkness. When Lucifer was finished laughing, Cinqo noticed that the crystal dwelling had turned to sand. Nothing was left of the spectacular dwelling except the bed Kaiwon, Kaitu and Yamin were in. Lucifer walked right up to Cinqo's face.

"Where is the boy?"

"I don't know of which boy you mean." Cinqo said. He knew Lucifer wanted Kaitu, but Lucifer didn't know that yet.

"What do you mean; you don't know which boy I mean? Don't play games with me Angelic. Where is the chosen child? I don't know who these three dead ones are, but I know the boy is here. I can sense him." Lucifer said, looking around.

"I assure you, wise one, there are no chosen *boys* here. You were once a brilliant Elder, Sialovehal Lucifer. I am sure you recognize that the child you sense, you already look upon." Cinqo let his words sit in the air like the bait they were.

Lucifer froze his gaze to Cinqo's.

"What did you call me Angelic?"

"Forgive me." Cinqo said. "I said Sialovehal. My tongue slipped. I was referring to the woman there." He motioned toward Kai.

Lucifer's gaze met Kai's face. He knew her. He walked to her, to get a nearer look. His eyes burned. The brand on his chest seared. He knew her. Seeing her face pulled something in him he did not like. It made him sick. The rage in him swelled. Cinqo stepped between Lucifer and Kai before he could escalate. Lucifer was well beyond insane. Cinqo was certain, even his true daughter couldn't return him home. Lucifer adjusted his neck and then returned his gaze to Cinqo like nothing happened. Except, he still was looking around for the chosen child. Cinqo motioned toward Kaitu.

"Her?" Lucifer looked down at the little girl and turned up his nose, repulsed. "Her? Kwa-yin made the chosen child a girl?" Evil spittle sprayed from his mouth as he spoke, searing the golden sand at his feet. "How utterly disgusting. But I am not surprised. No wonder. I assumed the chosen child to be a boy and of course, Kwa-yin picked a sniveling girl. It figures." He said.

Cinqo kept his calm. Staying in the company of a mad man was a delicate dance. He wondered to himself what Lucifer would say if he told him the sniveling girl was his granddaughter. After his reaction to Kai, he kept his clever commentary to himself.

"I usually don't do small talk, you know. I have to ask however. Why did you do it? Why did you kill them? I surely would have liked to do the honor, but if you could replay it for me, maybe I'll feel a better about it." Lucifer said.

"If I cannot have her, neither can he." Cinqo said. He tried to sound sinister, but it came out matter-of-fact.

Lucifer raised his head to the dark Eden sky and laughed again. "You hear that Kwa-yin? One of your own has done my bidding without my even asking. You are finished! You hear me? You are finished!"

His laugher shook the waterfall dwelling enough to turn the crystal bed Kaiwon, Kaitu and Yamin were on, to dust. Lucifer looked at Cinqo and his little Elder voice began its pitch to him again. The voice was telling him it was all too easy. There is no way he, Lucifer, could march back *here* to collect Kwa-yin's chosen child with not one shred of resistance. The last time he was here, it was a full out war. There was no way he gets here only to find the child dead at the hand of a Guardian. Better, an Angelic who was enraptured in a jealous rage. He looked in Kai's direction again. The word Sialovehal lingered in his ears and then dispersed. His little Elder voice was practically screaming inside his head.

Lucifer moved closer to Cinqo. He was standing next to the limp body of Kaiwon, looking at her longingly. Lucifer looked down at the pregnant woman again, and then at the face of the Angelic. Something struck him. He looked at the pregnant girl again. He tilted his head, as though by doing so would clarify his thoughts about her. It was just there, on the tip of his tongue. And then it was gone. He let it go this time. He was content that what the Angelic was saying was true and that was enough to squash the little elder voice and its rumblings.

"You do know you are finished with Kwa-yin." Lucifer said.

Cinqo nodded.

"You have managed to accomplish what none of my minions have been able to do. They are all so stupid. If you were my right hand, you would have all the power you could imagine. You may even have the power to bring your love back." Lucifer coughed, motioning toward Kaiwon.

Cinqo stood facing Lucifer blankly.

"You don't have to answer now, of course. All I ask is that you help me carry these two..." He said.

Lucifer paused, as if he had something disgusting caught in his throat. His sinister smile turned to frown. He lost his train of thought and then found it again.

"...All I ask is that you carry these two back to Firewah with me. I have something special planned for their bodies. If you help me, whenever you want, the right hand of the ruler of all of The Heaven and Earth-- that would be me of course-- is yours." He said.

Cinqo was practically shaking. Lucifer sounded ridiculous, but only because Cinqo knew what he was. What made Lucifer so powerful was that he didn't know what he was. Or Who. Yamin hit the nail on the head. He wondered if the plan for Lucifer was what it had always been. To rescue him. He wondered if Kaiwon was still charged with his return. The TuStai in Lucifer had shriveled and died long ago with his healthy mind. *This is what happens when the human condition infects the Sialovehal. This is what happens when fear lights a man's way to darkness.* There weren't even glimmers of his true self left. Cinqo was clear about what he must do.

"What about him?" Cinqo said, looking at Yamin.

Lucifer waved his hand.

"I don't even know who that is. He is of no use to me. Leave him here." He laughed. "He's in good company with the sand." He laughed again.

Cinqo picked up Kaiwon and Kaitu. Lucifer placed his pointy evil hand on Cinqo's shoulder. It sizzled against Cinqo's life force. His jaw tightened, and then they were gone.

Yamin heard everything that happened. His mind was dark, but his ears were clear. In his sleep he was able to gain enough perspective to figure out what was going on. When he opened his eyes, he was blinded by the light of Kwa-yin floating over him. Kwa-yin was the only light in The Eden now. Sadness had begun to fill the air. He looked up at her with tears brimming his eyes and regret filling every pore of his body. All he could think about is how he should have done something. Even more, he should have said something to her, before... Kwa-yin interrupted his thoughts.

"Look...Up." She said.

He squinted and when his eyes adjusted, he saw them. Kai and Little Kai's subtle bodies were floating next to Kwa-yin. He looked lovingly at Kai and noticed the bright light glowing in her subtle womb. Their son was still with her. He was so relieved, he let his tears fall however they wanted. Kai floated down to him and put her subtle arms around him. She kissed him on his mouth and though her lips were not flesh, the action caused warmth to fill his skin. His sadness was replaced with a bliss so overwhelming, there weren't any words. Little Kai floated down and kissed his cheek. When she did this, he felt so powerful he thought he could take on Lucifer and all of his minions at once. The light in Kai's womb glowed ever brighter and he reached his hand to touch it. He leaned in to kiss Kai's subtle belly and light filled his own body. He floated upward and then was laid gently on the golden sand in the dark cave.

"For now, you will remain here. The Key and The Door must go retrieve their bodies. They will return to you soon." She said.

Her bell-like voice twinkled in the dark Eden air. Then she and Little Kai were gone. Kai lingered, smiling at him. She was glad her instincts about him were right. He *was* the river man. Before she disappeared, she heard Yamin say...

"You are THE Key, Kai, but I am your balance."

Then she was gone. He didn't know if she knew what he meant. Or if she knew that he knew who she really was. He got it out, at least. If his saying so mattered, he would find out later, when she returned to him. Yamin lay peacefully on the golden sand breathing in the fragrance of the light Kwa-yin and his family left behind. Beneath him, a small tree was budding, where Kai's tears had planted seeds months before.

40 THE DEVIL, MISLEAD

"Ever dance with the devil by the pale moon light?" ~The Joker (Batman, 1989)

Lucifer was pacing. He was actually fiddling around his lair trying to find the perfect place to plant the bodies of Kai and Kaitu. It was an odd predicament for him to have actual bodies in Firewah. He hadn't really expected to bring back **physical** bodies. Subtle bodies were always preferable. But he thought, if Kwa-yin cared enough about these bodies to hoard them in The Heaven, maybe there was something important about them. And so, there they all were. He looked at Cinqo and frowned. He thought Kwa-yin a fool for entrusting anyone with something so important to her. He chuckled to himself about Kwa-yin's limitless trust. And then, a more private thought crossed him, about himself once being the closest to her. She trusted and believed in him limitlessly, also. He let the thought pass. He continued pacing. He was jittery, wondering what he should do next. In his hastiness to return to The Heaven, he hadn't bothered to filter through several important details.

First, he didn't know the names attached to the bodies he abducted. As a former Elder, Lucifer knew how important names were to Kwa-yin. She took special care that each soul force had a proper name to help them remember themselves in each cycle through The Entwine. Surely, the soul forces associated with these two bodies had very important names to Kwa-yin especially.

Second, he never bothered to question where the soul forces had gone. As a former Elder, Lucifer knew quite keenly that if Cinqo had killed them in The Eden, their subtle bodies would either still be there, or they would have transitioned to higher realms. This meant that Kwa-yin could return their subtle bodies to their physical bodies at any point. It also meant that Lucifer had not, in fact, stolen anything from The Eden that could not be replaced. In his haste, he overlooked the fact that bodies are simply a protective covering for what truly mattered.

Third, he didn't fully consider why his entrance and exit from The Eden was so easy. When he was ousted from The Heaven, he return was impossible. On more occasion than he could count, he tried. Just thinking of being there caused him such unbearable pain for so long, he eventually stopped trying. But this time, he was successful without much effort. Lucifer's little Elder voice was desperately trying to get his attention. It was trying to point out these things, and more, but Lucifer was too busy reveling in his self-created glory.

The bodies Cinqo held hovered just above his open hands, while Lucifer continued to pace manically. Cinqo was pointedly trying not to look about Firewah. The heat and screams were wholly offensive to him. He kept thinking to himself, **how could anyone bear to live in such conditions?** He missed the natural order, beauty, splendor and peacefulness of his true home. Firewah was so loud and confused. It was exactly the kind of home a mad man would manifest for himself. Cinqo frowned. Lucifer interrupted his thoughts.

"I've asked you three times now, Angelic. What are their names?" He said. He looked impatient.

"Whose names?" Cinqo asked, rousing from his trance.

"Are you toying with me boy?"

"Certainly not. I was taking in the... interesting... sounds of your... minions?" He said. He was trying to find something kind to say about the horrors around him. He wasn't sure what Lucifer would like to hear.

"They..." Lucifer began and then paused to form his stark white hands in a manner that added theatrical emphasis to the rest of what he wanted to say. "They... are not my minions, angel man. These..." He continued the theatrical hand gestures "These...are *my* souls! Aren't they wonderful?! Their screams and cries are music to my ears. Yours?"

He looked at Cinqo and waited for him to give the appropriate response. Cinqo was quick with it.

"It is like nothing I have ever heard before. Nor will I ever again." He said.

"Damn right!" Lucifer said.

From Cinqo's matter of fact tone, Lucifer couldn't tell if his words were complimentary. It didn't matter. Lucifer continued.

"Do you know where you are Angelic? You are in Firewah! Hell! The great down under! The place where mere angels, like yourself, have always wanted to be. The place where all of my glorious wretchedness takes form. Yes, right here, where you now stand. Heaven is okay. It's peaceful and quiet and pretty—if you like that sort of thing. But it is no paradise. Thiiiiissss…" he hissed. "Thiiiiissss, Angel booooy, is true paradise. No ruuuules. No laaaaws. Just meeee! They don't say 'As in Hell, so it is on Earth' for no reason!" He said, laughing and squealing with delight.

Cinqo blocked himself from falling out in laughter himself. He was well aware of the saying 'As Above, So Below', first made famous by Hermes Trismegistus. He was fairly certain it was he who whispered those words into Hermes ears so many thousands of years ago. He was also aware of how the saying evolved through millennia to suit the needs of whoever was saying it. It is a metaphor for mind and body—what the mind thinks, the body lives. He knew Lucifer knew this. He didn't dare shake his head in Lucifer's direction, but he couldn't help the pity he felt for him. *How does one truly forget all he learns from the source of all life force? How does one fall to such depths to such emptiness and ignorance?* Cinqo truly felt sorry for Lucifer. The feeling was fleeting.

He knew he was in Firewah as part of a greater plan than Lucifer's madness could comprehend. He was hoping, rather anxiously, that Kwa-yin would hurry up and manifest it. He was growing tired of Lucifer's silliness. He wanted to get back to his own home, or what was left of it, sooner rather than later.

"You have a plane to catch, Angelic?" Lucifer asked, sensing Cinqo's restlessness.

"No." Cinqo said. His irritability with Firewah and Lucifer was becoming hard to mask.

"Careful, Angelic. Do not forget who you are speaking to." Lucifer said, posturing. Then he moved slowly toward Cinqo. He was looking for something that was out of site at first, but was now showing itself to him.

"Forgive me." Cinqo said. "This place, I mean, your lair is affecting me in a way I am not accustomed."

Lucifer continued moving toward Cinqo. He saw a glimmer of it. He was being deceived somehow. This was a trap. He inched closer to Cinqo and then stopped a few paces from him. His little Elder voice was in the forefront of his thoughts again. It was saying:

This is too perfect. All of this is too easy. Don't be a fool Lucifer! This Angelic is tricking you. Can't you see it in his pathetic face? He didn't kill those two. They probably aren't even dead. He was there waiting for you. And what about their subtle bodies? If they're dead then where are the subtle bodies? You fool! You led The Chosen Child and its mother right into your lair! Now Kwa-yin's can come here and you helped!

"Shut up!" Lucifer screamed aloud to his inside Elder voice.

"As you wish", Cinqo said...

"Not you fool! " Lucifer said.

Lucifer lost his train of thought and was trying to get it back. But it was too late.

Quite unexpectedly, a blinding light filled all of Firewah. The bodies floating just above Cinqo's hands moved on their own above his head. He knew what this meant, so he breezed himself out of the way. Lucifer squealed with pain. The star seared to his chest was scorching him mercilessly from the inside. He was so lost in his own scheming and self-importance, he totally forgot about his brand. His squeals of anguish turned into blatant screams of unimaginable pain. His eyes burned from the indigo colored flames streaming from them, until the blue flames took over his entire body. Lucifer was burning from the inside out. The pain was unbearable.

"Please stop! Stop it please!" He screamed out.

The burning continued. Lucifer was not flesh, so there was nothing to burn off, besides his affliction and the karmic accumulation of his madness. So he kept burning, like a terrible bonfire. His screams could be heard throughout all of the omniverse. Finally, the blue flames formed an orb of blue fire. It crashed itself into the blood red sky of Firewah, to hang there where Lucifer could just barely see, through his burning and pain, what was to happen next.

41 OM NAMO RAH OM

"In the sky, there is no distinction between East and West; people create distinctions out of their own minds and then believe them to be true." ~ Buddha

"It is better to conquer yourself than to win a thousand battles, then the victory is yours. It cannot be taken from you, not by angels or demons, heaven or hell." ~Buddha

The Comforters marched out of the old hospital in a single file. Each of their individual lights sparkled on them like tiny spotlights coming from the night sky. They looked like stars walking the streets toward Cathedral. The children were still gathered around the old church, holding hands, singing the Seraph battle song. When the Comforters arrived from the right side of the old church, they let go of their hands, to let them pass, but didn't stop singing. The adults were still scurrying about in their anger. A few noticed the line of hundreds, maybe thousands of lights walking toward them. They were curious enough to stop bickering and pay attention. Some tried to shush the singing children, but it only made them sing louder. The singing children couldn't hear, see or feel anything but the task they were called to perform. When the adults realized this, they stepped back and watched.

The voices of the children lifted high above Cathedral into The Heavens and down below into Firewah. ***Om Namo Rah Om*** drowned out every sound in all of the omniverse, and a dramatic shift took place.

At the same time, from an old library on the left side of Cathedral, The Kindred walked single file, with their twinkling lights shining on them. The children on their side released their hands to let the Kindred enter the church. The adults could not help but notice the two lines of people, walking together in exact time, perfectly succinct in every way, filing in Cathedral, from the left and right, two by two. It was a magnificent sight. It was the personification of what balance looks like. Thousands of Kindred and Comforters filed into Cathedral until first light. When the last two walked across the threshold, the doors closed. The streets around Cathedral were quiet, except for the voices of the children. They were still hand in hand for miles, singing the Seraph song. ***Om Namo Rah Om.***

42 ORB OF FIRE, KEY OF LIGHT, CHILD OF ALL

"It is not light we need, but fire; it is not the gentle shower, but thunder. We need the storm, the whirlwind, and the earthquake." ~Frederick Douglass

"No Child of God sins to that degree as to make himself incapable of forgiveness." ~ John Bunyan

"All God's Children need traveling shoes."~ Maya Angelou

O*m Namo Rah Om* rang through Firewah for the first time. The voices of the children sounded like carillon in the sky. The lost soul forces of Firewah, that screamed their pain from every crevice of their malevolent world, finally stopped screaming. It happened in waves. One mouth closed which caused another to close and continued until the only sound in Firewah was ***Om Namo Rah Om***. From out of nowhere, rain fell. It was a storm at first, falling in big puddles over everything. Every inch of the black sand, became black mud. The blood red sky became a brilliant blue. Like lapis, it had glittering gold flecks speckled throughout. In place of the soot mountains, were diamond ones. Instead of nebulous arms, legs and heads scattered about, there were whole bodies of clean souls sitting politely next to each other. Firewah was transformed.

Lucifer was still ablaze and screaming from his orb of blue fire, but no one could hear him. He watched in horror as the rain stopped and three lights appeared on the plateau of one of the diamond mountains. The millions of souls in Firewah looked up, awestruck. A moment later, a light as bright as a thousand suns filled the cavernous Firewah with warmth and love. Kwa-yin appeared through the light and smiled.

The song of the children, still playing in the background, became Kwa-yin's melody. When she spoke to all of the souls in Firewah, her voice became the sweetest song they ever heard. Each soul force began to sway. The more they swayed the more open, willing and ready they were.

"Your ancestors greet each other by saying 'Osho Lovianhal'. It means, 'Light the love in ALL'. We bow to each other to acknowledge the light we each possess. We then say 'Osho Lovian Osho', which means 'Light Brings Love to Light'. This greeting is a shortened version of our original mission. The whole phrase is 'Osho Lovianhal bah Oshharu Mairahu Nura Osho. Osho Namoru Namoru Yahmehrai Yasuru Yahmehrah bah Osho Lovian Osho.' It means, 'Light the love in ALL because fear lights a man's way to darkness. Light covers, covers. Stillness rises peace stillness settles... because Light brings love to light.' This is your creation story. This is your true destiny. It is who you are. Light. Your true language is Tuahstai. The Tongue of Stars. This is not your true home. I do not need to tell you that you are here because you chose to be. Your fate has always been your own. If you wish, you may remain here. Or you may go home, with me."

Every soul rose to their feet. Without being asked, they joined in singing the song floating through the air. ***Om Namo Rah Om. Om Namo Rah Om. Om Namo Rah Om.***

Through his silent cries of pain, Lucifer could see and hear everything happening below his orb of fire. If he could have guffawed through the flames, he would have. Kwa-yin said that none of them were from here. Where were they from then? He wanted to laugh, but he couldn't. There were glimmers of memories of another world he once lived, but he couldn't focus. The only things loud and clear in him now were his pain and his Elder voice.

You should go too. Humble yourself. Bow at the feet of Kwa-yin. Tell her 'Osho Lovian Osho', sing the song they're singing and do anything else she wants, to get out of here. She won. The war is over... *It said.*

Though he burned and the pain he experienced was so great he almost couldn't feel anything at all, Lucifer resigned himself to hang where he was. All he was now was a burning ball in his former Firewah. He watched helplessly as all of his life's work turned to mud and washed away with some rain, a speech and a song.

When every soul was standing, Kwa-yin nodded at Cinqo. He walked from the base of Firewah with the bodies of Kaiwon and Kaitu. Each of the singing souls turned and bowed as he passed, like a wave. Once Cinqo stood at the foot of the diamond mountain, Kwa-yin nodded again. The bodies lifted up, until they reached the plateau. One of the three lights lingering next to Kwa-yin entered Kaitu's body. Another of the three lights morphed into a giant golden key. It, and the third light, a light much different than the others, entered Kai's body. Both Kai and Kaitu began to glow with such voracity that beams of every color light sprang from their pores, and then leveled into a gentle pink-orange glow. They stood to face the singing souls of Firewah. Without warning, a stream of light poured from Kaiwon's forehead and flooded their eyes. The light bounced through each soul, which caused a web, which attached them all together.

When this was done, Kai arched her body backward, so the light stream pointed toward the top of Firewah. The light turned golden, and looked like streams of liquid gold, flowing upward from the center of her skull. The miles of Earth, energy, loss and lies that covered Firewah for eons was burst open. From this opening, another, far brighter light streamed down into Firewah intermingling with all the lights already there.

Kaitu raised her tiny hands and slowly began moving them. Her movements were very slow at first, like she was conducting her first symphony. When she found her bearings, her hands moved more quickly. Finally, she found her rhythm. One by one, each soul transformed into a glimmering breeze. Each breeze compounded one to another until they were all, a gorgeous glimmering cloud in the center of Firewah, swirling in front of the diamond mountain.

Kwa-yin nodded. Kaitu raised both of her hands and the glimmering cloud moved slowly upward through the light at the top of Firewah. The souls were still singing *Om Namo Rah Om* as they traveled. They flowed like a backwards waterfall. When they passed Cathedral, the people gathered there began to dance uncontrollably, like their joy couldn't be contained. When the singing soul cloud made its way through The Eden, wilted trees bloomed with life. Blackened grass revived to plush greens, darkened waterfalls and rivers and lakes glittered again like diamonds. The pitch, starless Eden sky was again light and glistening from every corner. All of Eden began to breathe again.

43 STAR FRUIT

"I'd rather be a could-be if I cannot be an are; because a could-be is a maybe who is reaching for a star. I'd rather be a has-been than a might-have-been, by far; for a might-have-been has never been, but a has was once an are."
~Milton Berle

When Yamin woke from his sleep, he found himself in a grand new tree outside of his former waterfall dwelling. He didn't need to climb down from his perch, he simply willed himself to be down and he was. He looked around and sighed. Then he closed his eyes and breathed it all in. He was alive, as a man, in The Eden. He allowed himself to take in the entirety of his experience. The Eden was breathing with him again, as she always had.

Hanging from the tree, was a fruit he had never seen. It didn't look like an apple or a pear or a berry. It was shaped like a five point star, but it was plump and bright pink-orange. He pulled one of the star shaped fruit from its branch, took in its intoxicating smell, then put the fruit to his mouth and took a big bite. He chewed slowly, savoring every flavor. Unlike Eden apples, this fruit had a core, shaped like a heart. Yamin chuckled to himself. He looked up to the Eden sky, as his way of acknowledging the ever clever work of The Creator. He smiled now as he chewed. The fruit was so good to him, he ate a few. He also noticed, he didn't get full. He felt good, but the more of the fruit he ate, the more room his stomach seemed to make. He made a mental note of this and then sat for a while in silence, pondering the mysteries of everything around him. A dull throbbing made its way through his insides. He missed his family. He wanted more than anything to be with them now.

A crystal bin appeared at his feet. Again, he looked above and chuckled.

He picked as many of the fruit as he could fit in the bin and then walked toward the waterfall. He stopped for a minute and looked around. Eden was as beautiful as it once was, but it was not the same. The Eden he knew as Elder died, and a new Eden, a different Eden had been born. He smiled and closed his eyes to breathe in as much of the sweet Eden air as he could fit in his lungs. It was time, he thought. He walked through the waterfall out of instinct. He had no idea what would greet him on the other side.

"You were a fine Neo Elder." A voice behind him said. Yamin turned to see Tanzin and Meoshe smiling at him.

"This is my going away party?" Yamin said, laughing.

"Of course not. We will meet again." Meoshe said, also laughing.

Yamin smiled.

"I know we will." He said. "Osho Lovianhal Elder Tanzin. Osho Lovianhal Passion Keeper Meoshe. Thank you for being a part of my journey." He gave them both a deep, reverent bow.

Both Tanzin and Meoshe returned his bow and said together,

"Osho Lovian Osho, Elder Yamin. Your work has just begun."

Then they were gone. Yamin turned and walked through the waterfall with his heavy bucket of star fruit. There was nothing left of their crystal dwelling. In fact, there was nothing in front of him but a light at the end of a dim tunnel. He walked and walked for what felt like days, thinking only of Kai, Little Kai and his unborn son waiting for him, hopefully, when he got to the end of that tunnel. Finally, at the end, was a big red door with ancient carvings etched all over it. The light he saw guiding him was coming from underneath and around the door. He had to put down his heavy bucket of fruit to turn the knob. When the door opened, the light was gone. Everything was dark.

His hands fumbled in the dark for the bucket. When he found it, he picked it up and walked through what looked like an old church basement. There were old pews and dry rotted robes strewn about. He tripped on the legs of a few chairs as he made his way blindly through what he thought was an old office. He smelled burning sage. It was fresh enough, that he thought maybe a mass was going on above him. A light came on at the far end of the office. It wasn't attached to anything; it was just there, showing him where to go. He came to another red door etched with ancient carvings. He didn't spend much time looking at it, he just walked through it. A few paces later he was staring up at a steep stairwell. He climbed the stairs gladly, but noticed that each plank was a little less ornate and red as he went. Whatever ancient symbols were carved on them, were a lot more worn and less visible, the closer he got to the top of the stairwell. The last three stairs were just plain, old wood planks. He opened the red door at the top of the stairs and walked through.

His chest sank at the sight of another long corridor, but he trudged himself onward. Then he heard voices. He walked slowly at first, and then moved more quickly when he realized how many voices there were. It sounded like a football stadium full of people. He put one piece of the star fruit in either of his hands and then he took off in the direction of the voices, leaving the heavy crystal bucket behind. When he reached the church sanctuary, it was full of beings of every sort. He saw Seraph, Guardians, Comforters, Kindred, and Stellar. They were all talking. Some were hugging. He felt like he had walked in on a convention of Star People. In the center of the sanctuary, in a clear orb of light, were thousands of dark figures kneeling with their heads faced down. They looked like they were waiting for something. Yamin shivered and continued to look around. Of all the beings around him, he strained to see the three he was really looking for.

Then he heard a familiar giggle. A little girl was laughing just a few feet from where he stood. He nearly broke his neck, tripping over pews and people to find the girl who belonged to the giggle. She got to him first. Her little giggle was coupled with her little arms wrapped around his knees that almost knocked him off his feet. He was so happy to see his Little Kai he swept her up and kissed her cheeks until they were red.

"I missed you so much. You hear me? Daddy missed you." He said and hugged her tightly.

"Daddeeeeeeee!" Little Kai said.

Yamin started to choke up because she never called him daddy before. Even when they spoke Tuahstai together when he was Elder, she called him Yamin. But now, to hear the little girl he's grown to love so deeply as his own, recognize him as how he saw himself to her, was an amazing feeling. He felt honored and redeemed. His chest poked out a bit as his kissed his daughter's chubby cheeks.

"Daddeeeeeeee!" Kai said, walking toward them.

Yamin couldn't help smiling from ear to ear as she waddled closer to them. He scooped Little Kai in his arms and ran the ten or so paces to meet Kai. When they were face to face, as close as they could be, he put the little one down and wrapped his arms around the big one as tightly as he could. He kissed her cheeks and her forehead and her chin and when he made his way to her lips he kissed them tenderly, at first. But then they remembered The Eden in each other. They remembered everything they went through to be together now. The kiss they shared was the culmination of their journey. Finally, Yamin peeled his lips away from Kai's. They looked in each other's eyes, smiled and then held each other, quietly.

"Lovian Kaiwon Osho." He said.

"Lovian Yamin Osho." She said.

"I love you too little one." He said, bending down to kiss Kai's baby bump.

He looked up at Kai confused.

"He doesn't glow here?" He asked

"Of course he does, just different now. Which is a great thing. We'll have less explaining to do." Kai said, laughing.

He handed Kai and Little Kai a pink-orange star shaped fruit.

"What is this?" She asked, putting the fruit to her nose. "From Eden?"

Yamin nodded.

"We'll save this for later." She said and kissed him on the mouth. "You weren't too worried were you?"

"I knew you would handle yourself." He said.

Kai moaned loudly and grabbed her belly. Yamin jumped back.

"What's the matter?! Are you okay? Is he okay?"

"I'm fine. He's fine. You're fine. He was kicking *me* so he could say hi to *you*. So I guess that means it's time we go home." Kai said.

"Not so fast, dear ones." Devascus was hobbling toward them. "Kai, you should eat the fruit before you leave." He said.

"Why?" She asked. "It's from Eden, I want to save it."

Devascus coughed. His voice sounded weak

"You need it, Vessel Kaiwon, to save you. None of this is over. It has only just begun. Remember why you came. You must fulfill your purpose. Eat the fruit." He said and disappeared into thin air.

Everything around her started to fizzle in and out. It was an energy earthquake. Some things stayed and some disappeared and then returned. Yamin was there and then he wasn't. She was pregnant and then she wasn't. Cathedral. All of those people were there and then they weren't. Finally, all she could see was Kaitu and their two pieces of pink-orange star fruit. They both took bites of their fruit at the same time, and the earthquake stopped. Then everything went dark. After a long while, Kai saw little slits of light in the distance. She couldn't see what was around her, so she walked toward the light with her arms out in front of her. The closer she got to the light, the brighter it was, until finally it was so bright, it filled her head. Suddenly, Kai's eyes burst open, and she shot up in her bed, awake. It was 2:22 AM.

EPILOGUE: WINGS

"Once you have tasted flight, you will forever walk the earth with your eyes turned skyward, for there you have been, and there you will always long to return."

— Leonardo da Vinci

She grew wings. Long, black, silken wings. Raven black wasn't the color she would have chosen for herself, had she the choice, but there they were. She allowed them to wrap around her like a hug. Then, all by themselves, they flung out to their full span. Their reach awed her. Her heart fluttered. ***Could she fly?***

She decided to give it a try. Without much effort, only wishing it to be so, she felt her naked toes lift from the earth and soon there was only air beneath them. Her eyes were closed. She was afraid to open them. She wasn't sure she wanted to see what was happening to her, around her, about her. She was in the midst of an inner push and pull. A dialogue with herself about what was possible in 'reality' and what was in the moment. She felt the wind brush her cheeks. She heard the sound of wings. A big, golden feeling of power rushed through her being.

The push she felt to fly began to pull at her until she found herself falling. Her eyes squeezed tighter, legs like cinderblocks, gravity pulling downward, downward until she heard and felt the painful thud of her body hitting earth. She began to cry, but never opened her eyes. She just cried. For her fear. She cried for the pain in her legs and arms from her fall. She cried so hard and so much that her tears formed a lake around her and the lake overflowed until a river formed.

She cried and cried until her tears threatened to drown her in them. Her only recourse was to try her wings again, but they were soaked, limp and stuck to her back. There was no way she could fly like that, she thought.

She was so afraid, her body trembled in deep ripples that started at her core and worked its way outward to her skin. **Fly or drown** she told herself repeatedly, franticly. Her panic made her tears unbearable and she was unable to stop her crying, all at the same time. There was no way she could make her wings spread enough to dry out so she could fly to safety. She resolved instead to let herself drown. She simply let go. Her body stopped trembling. Her tears stopped, and she breathed in the quiet that came when she made herself still. She welcomed the silence and soon, her final breath.

But instead of drowning as she wanted to, she began to float. Her eyes remained closed, but she felt herself moving—she thought-- the length of the lake and then the river until she stopped and found herself on dry earth. She crawled to shore. Her wings shook themselves out on their own and then, finally, she opened her eyes and saw paradise. Again. The place she longed for most.

Her raven colored wings splay out in their full glory and she allowed them to glisten in the blinding sunlight. She took off to see the splendor of the place below her. She breathed in the trees, as they did her. She admired the many flowers and colors. The brilliance she saw all around her moved as she did, as though it was flying with her, as though it were a part of her.

And then, midair, she stopped. She came to the end of paradise. There was a distinct line drawn in the earth and sky. Move one more inch toward it and she was beyond return. She would be stuck on a barren land with no trees, no color, no... wings. She knew this without anyone having to tell her. She didn't know what to do. Her thoughts began to crumble again, one piece at a time. As the last piece of rational thought made its way to dust in her head, a bell like voice sang the words: **Oshharu Mairahu Nura Osho**. Then, she woke up.

ABOUT THE AUTHOR:

Even when we can't see it in ourselves, our truth always sees us with the clearest eyes. It is absolute reality. It is light itself. WE are light itself and there is nothing the light we are cannot penetrate...

Envy McKee

Envy McKee is a Star People who writes about Star People as it pertains to helping Earth people figure out their secular spiritual path. She does this by writing soul-stretching speculative fiction, also known as SOUL-Fi. She also does this by occasionally creating independent conscious content for radio, TV, print, film, and the web. Envy is a media professional, speaker, voice-over artist, farmer, and parent. Not necessarily in that order. She lives and works via varying iterations of The Farm at Aphroditia with her awesome daughter, Aubrei.

L.O.V.E.

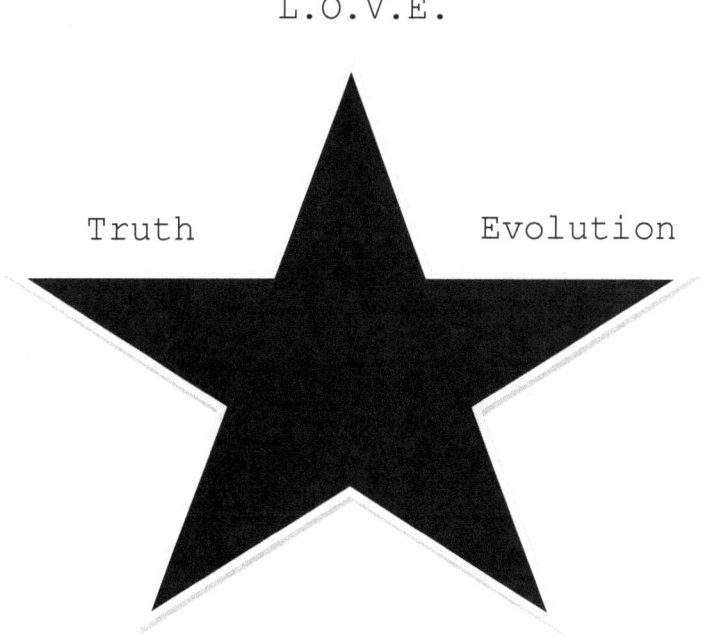

Truth
Evolution

#TheStellarTrilogy

www.ingramcontent.com/pod-product-compliance
Lightning Source LLC
Chambersburg PA
CBHW060628260626
47161CB00008B/2835